THE VOYAGE OF A DRESS

AMY HARTMAN

GOODSPEED BOOKS

TO MY MOTHER

Who inspired me to imagine, to write, and to look at the sky

PREFACE

*T*here was once a time when to a seafaring New Englander the Pacific Ocean was a faraway aqueous frontier reigned by wooden ships that carried adventurers and fortune seekers—those who counted success by barrels of whale oil, and those who counted by souls saved. Life was quick and farewells held no guarantee of a returning. Sextants, explorer's maps, Bibles, and rumors were all they had to chart with; by sailors' tales that told of mermaids, mighty whales that could sink a ship, and of people they did not understand.

This is not a Hawai'ian history book. The characters are imagined, sometimes composites of those who once lived and breathed, drawn together in an attempt to create the most accurate setting possible. The curious reader is encouraged to seek out historical facts from native historians.

This is neither a Bible of fashion history, yet Western clothing was highly sought after in Hawai'i, and the latest in fashion could have found its way to her. By the dawn of the 1800's, Hawai'i was a strategic port for provisions and precious sandalwood, so all of Europe came to court her. With exquisite images from the New York Metropolitan Museum's Costume Institute collection and La Mode fashion engravings in mind, I let imagination play in order to serve the story.

What history books rarely record is how, stitch by little stitch, love

—the gift, the loss, the miracle, the quest, the power of it—is what creates movement and fates and meaning to the fabric of life. It is the story of our past, and a compass for our future.

~

More than one hundred years ago, stories lived within paper pages or on the tongue—told on a porch after dinner, or in the twilight after the lanterns and cigars were lit.

A dog or two might curl up at your feet. Your tea is too hot to drink, or maybe your scotch lies bitterly strong at the surface above cold, hard ice. It rests in your hand; you will bide your time.

You sit back on thick cushions and let yourself be carried away by the sound of her voice.

This might have been one of those tales.

~

PART I

CHAPTER 1

October 1st, 1839
The Old Pine Dome Sea Chest

You could set a watch to it, if that mattered to you. At nearly one o'clock the trade winds begin to move across Honolulu and the clouds slowly dance like white feathers above the knifelike jade mountains.

How the sight of it often lifted my eyes up in wonder, and how hard they fell down to earth the day I felt him near me once again. Then there he was, impossibly, despite each year that I had marked with a smile celebrating the fact that I would never see his face again: Reverend Herman Webster, floating towards me in a carriage, his black cape flying and swirling about him slowly like ink moving through water. I could almost smell his black wool coat, seeped with the sweat and toil of a missionary man, and there upon his sleeve were still the mis-matched buttons I had sewn when I was once his missionary wife.

Sometimes great change comes in on tiptoe. In many ways I was still a girl when we came to the Sandwich Isles; I was at the cusp of womanhood when lingering innocence was taken, mine and theirs—the people we had come to save from eternal despair.

I remember the shape of the wind in their long capes of a million feathers. What I first thought, seen through my New Bedford eyes, was that they were a kind of bird people; magnificent and free. For the rest of my life I will close my eyes and be able to see what I saw in those faraway days: a satin feather helmet, like the scarlet head of a red cardinal, shining as the young king turned his head. A cape thick with tiny yellow feathers floating, lifting, breathing about the shoulders of a princess, whom I had been recruited to save, armed with my mighty needle and thread. In the end, she helped save me.

But when I first arrived to the Kingdom of the Kamehamehas and stood on the dais with them gazing across the sky-mirror waterways and shady breadfruit trees spread out before me—I beheld an unimaginably beautiful land and an unexpectedly majestic people.

But so many things changed before this day as Herman Webster materialized before me on a dusty Honolulu street at one o'clock in the afternoon. I slowly stepped behind two Sandwich Islands women who were exchanging flower lei and alohas, and I thought myself well-hidden behind yards of cheerful cotton calico all ruffled and draped about their abundant flesh. Past sweet perfumed petals and their singsong voices I could just see the profile of that dark-hearted man who had once sought, with the fury of one of his sermons, to kill my Diego.

Herman surveyed the busy street and turned his head my way, as if he too had felt me near. His hair was now dusted with silver, and his gray eyes glinted like mercury glass. Then, like a bullwhip, they lashed out at mine. He bid the driver to pull up the horses. He stepped down, and began walking slowly towards me, stabbing the dirt before him with a bamboo cane; then he waved it at the women between us as if to part the Red Sea. He had never carried a cane before. A missionary ages quickly.

"Catherine," he spat through curling lips. "Still here in these islands. I had no news of ye. I once had a young wife—just a girl—so fine and fair and sweet and lovely. Thou hast taken her place." He looked up and down with disdain at my fine cotton gown, a stylish day dress with jade blue silk stripes.

I unconsciously moved a hand against my stomach, and through my thin and delicate white kid gloves I could feel the lushly gathered fabric at my waist. Clothes can sometimes say as much as words, and my dress eloquently told him I was back to wearing my old nature—a happy, powerful spirit that becomes every free woman. My years were blossoms in my hair; I was wiser than that naïve young wife. Too smart for him, too well-armed.

"Herman. If only that girl you once courted had known that your soul was blacker than the cover of your Bible."

He leaned closer, urgent and wary. "What is thy true name? Dost a legion of Satan now inhabit thee? For it has been told unto me by Brother Ives that thy own bastard child lives right here among us." His tongue clicked in the spit behind his front teeth as he shook his head. "I think of Matthew 8:32," he said, eyeing me for a reaction, and then quoted "...*And the unclean spirits were driven off the cliff into the sea.*"

He pulled out a pocket watch, his crude way of measuring life. "The day is progressing. Tomorrow is the Sabbath, but come Monday I will take the child to the *pali* above the sea and cast it to the sharks. I shall not bother with thee, for thine unclean spirit shall follow it over the cliff and be choked by cold, deep waters."

There was no need to run this time. My fingertips touched the golden sun hanging from my neck as I chose my words. "I thought it not possible, but your hate has multiplied, Reverend. Just as your offspring that run wild across that island you tried so hard to tame."

A shadow of guilt moved across his face, or perhaps it was a cloud brushing past the tropic sun.

"So it was thou that told them. I am surprised they listened to a woman like thee."

"They wouldn't. 'Twas not I. Perhaps you remember a woman with a tattooed face. She had good reason to speak out."

He winced, blinked, and then uttered quietly, "Pray for that child's soul come Monday." He backed away, stopping once to jab the air between us with his cane, and then away he rode in the rumbling conveyance, his stiff body floating supernaturally along despite the rattle and lurch of the wheels over the washboard street.

The Hawai'ian women beside me had witnessed it all. Shaking their frowning faces, they draped a precious ilima lei about my neck. After we shared heartfelt aloha I strode off with purpose, for there was much to do, arrangements to be made, and now not much time.

I had been on a busy schedule of errands that afternoon: 1. Buy more oilcloth to finish wrapping my dresses in for the long ocean voyage, 2. Spend a sinful amount of Captain Jonathan Swift's money on brandy and French champagne, and 3. Call on my old friend Emmaline to remind her that she could surrender my baby back to me, as promised, now that I was engaged to marry to the respectable Captain Swift and would be sailing away back to New England.

Providentially, I spied the Captain's cabin boy and waved him over to me. "Boy!" I said, pulling a Spanish dollar from my purse. "Tell Captain Swift that I will be ready to leave on the morrow."

I took out another dollar. "And, this: tell Mrs. Emmaline Ives that the event we discussed must take place on the wharf at dawn tomorrow at the side of the *Fair Wind*. Hasten along!"

The sunlight was shining like water on the fronds of the cocoa-nut palms, telling me that the afternoon was no longer young. I hurried through my list of errands and breathlessly arrived at my last stop: to call on Miss Helen at the Flower Palace, a haven for opium eaters.

Once you smell the opium flower burning, you never forget it. Sweet and thick, it beckoned me away from the sunshine into a shaded world where the wealthy and the lost adventurers, the respectable ladies and the ragged sailors all found comfort.

I found her there, a silkworm moth of a figure dressed in a flowing gray gown that looked like folded wings. From the edge of her shoulders fell a bright vermilion red Chinese robe lit up by a beam of daylight cutting through the dark, smoky room. I needed to tell her of my abrupt departure, for Miss Helen had been my angel for the past few years employing me as seamstress and giving me the attic room at her house of entertainment for men. There I had been hidden from a certain society who thought me lost, and would otherwise have sought me dead.

She turned towards me. A swirling ghost of smoke vanished and I could see her more clearly; it was not Miss Helen after all, yet it was a face I knew well. I had watched her rosy New Bedford cheeks change to a milky absinthe as our ship swept up and over each wave leaving America in our wake. Then, as Hawai'ian seasons softly passed, her face hardened and her threadbare smile thinly cloaked deep exhaustion. There, standing in the gray shafts of light was my old friend Abigail Adamson.

Sweet Abigail was a Massachusetts country doctor's wife turned missionary who had never pictured herself living on an island in the middle of the Pacific Ocean. Her husband Henry, finally realizing that he could do nothing to keep the hardships of missionary life from killing her, had mercifully tucked her on a ship heading back to New Bedford; he wrapped her in quilts, a dose of his opium and a promise to follow her as soon as he could. Everyone said that she lost her senses with grief over the fate of her daughter, and of course I shared that opinion but I held that it was also caused by the overwhelming strain of being a missionary wife. For this I know.

There, in a house of opium, Abigail stared back at me, caught. We rushed together and embraced as if time meant nothing at all, and began to exchange tales of the peculiar paths we had trodden.

"I thought you back in New Bedford!" I said.

Out of the dark places where she dwelt she reached for my hand as if I were a light; I removed my gloves and took her bare, cold fingers that had the strength of insect wings, trembling like a moth. "The ship was held in Honolulu to wait out a storm," she said, looking around at the smoky web in which she was now caught. "Judge me if you will, darling Kittie, but there was not enough opium to last me the voyage and I let it sail without me. Forgive me, for I am no longer worthy to be your friend."

"Abigail," I said, pushing words through the anguish in my throat. "Will you forgive me for deserting you on the night of my escape? Did you or Henry tell them I was at your window? He still loves you,

Abigail. Send your husband word, and he will come for you! His required service is nearly finished—surely the mission will set him free to take you and your boys back home."

"I left them with Henry, and he could never love this lonely sinner," she sighed, her voice languid. "I have fallen and so have you. In the eyes of the church we have plummeted from Heaven."

She turned away from me and went to hand a porcelain pipe to a customer, and I wondered if she planned on ever speaking to me again.

I yearned to find the Abigail I once knew. So, I stayed. I stayed because I wanted to tell her, *make* her believe that Henry's devotion was big and true enough to trust, even now. Somehow, perhaps a belief in love still beat on in my own heart, steadily, despite everything. Keeping time, remembering, heartbeat by heartbeat. I could set a clock to it, if it really mattered to me.

CHAPTER 2

I tried to catch Abigail's eye, but failed, and then she disappeared into the thick, sweet smoke. So, I sat down on a velvet divan to wait.

It was then that I became aware of two wizened old seamen seated nearby through the lattice of a carved mahogany folding screen. The yellow light from the pipes in their palms seemed to float in the dim light.

"'Twas along the coast of Alta California where they found the dead man," one said, his throat thick with salt and sea and a thousand ports. "His ship was stove upon the rocks—was headed for Monterey until they met with a devil of a storm."

"He was no sailor. A horseless vaquero, they tell. His stallion washed up by Santa Barbara."

My heart began to pound. I was no longer in an opium house: I was standing on a great long stretch of empty beach; Diego was turning in his saddle to say something to me. *Kittie, could you ever love a vaquero?*

"He died but the horses lived," wheezed a sailor. "Swam ashore."

"Upon my life, I heard the sorry man was found alive on one o' the Channel Islands. D'ya know of 'em?"

"Both latitude and longitude!"

They fell into a mumbled argument of compass points and maps as I impatiently leaned forward, straining to hear. If not for their deadened senses they would have heard my frantic breath. Then, to my frustration they began to drift away into a half-awake, half-dead sleep.

I drew in the deepest breath my corset would allow, and then held it—hoping the opium smoke would numb my heart. Abruptly, one sailor coughed so loudly that my shoulders flinched. He cleared his throat. "Half man, half beast when they rescued him. Was found living like a Chumash. But that was not his greatest misfortune."

I had lain his memory to rest between cotton corsets and silk petticoats. In a sudden flash he came alive again—I remembered the way the corner of Diego's mouth would flirt with a smile before he spoke to me. *My mother was Chumash, my father a Spaniard; I am two worlds away from yours, my dove.*

The glow of their pipes hovered, then darted up and sideways as the old seamen gestured with their hands.

"Not dead as you claim, but starving and crippled. They tell that he wore the silver-buttoned breeches of a vaquero, and despite his miserable circumstances he wore a velvet jacket embroidered with gold braid."

My breath was audible. Leaning forward on the edge of the couch I hugged my thick skirt and petticoats, desperate for an anchor. The room was moving, and not because of the opium smoke. It could not be. They were telling yarns, as old men do. Vaqueros were common to California.

"A velvet jacket, ye say? Ye embroider the truth. A more pitiful tale was never told," said the other.

"A beast in silk stockings!" was the answer as the rough voice made an effort to trip his thick tongue over the word 'silk' to make it sound fancy and delicate.

A low laugh scraped like gravel. "Swear upon the Devil's tail. He was found on the beach sitting regally upon a silver saddle!"

The men wheezed with laughter that tumbled into heavy breaths and then they fell into dead silence.

A vapor of smoke was captured by a ray of sunlight against the dark room, making thin, lazy, ornate curls looking like cursive letters of white ink. I stared at it, transfixed, as I twisted my gloves between my hands. The opium had begun to play with my imagination, as if writing a message from my faraway heart. *Face what you have shut away. Open the sea chest.*

I fled. Beyond the den's dark shadows the light was blinding—colors were brighter than fabric unwound from a bolt for the first time. A tear slid off my lower eyelashes as I gasped great draughts of fresh air. I bolted so quickly that I left my gloves lying on the velvet divan and forgot my packages at the door.

CHAPTER 3

*D*own I ran across streets of red lava-dust cast in the yellow light of a farewell sun and past a hedge of sleepy yellow evening primrose just opening their petals to proclaim the end of the day. Around to the back staircase of Miss Helen's house I fled, up four flights to my little room, and slammed the door—my corset-back hard against it—staying there, motionless—shocked—as I tried to catch my breath.

The room was almost empty. All of my trunks had been taken down to the ship except for my old sea trunk that sat faithfully alone against an empty wall. A tiny girl's dress still hung hopefully from a low rafter. By the window that overlooked the wharf a dressmaking worktable sat forlornly, missing its scissors, fabric and not even a stray piece of thread left to keep it company.

Upon it was a note from Captain Swift—as joyous as a hunter, proud of his catch. They would work through the night to make ready. I was to be there by daybreak and wearing a wedding gown, for we were to be married on deck as soon as the *Fair Wind* was under full sail.

I looked over at my trunk as if we were two near-strangers that shared a significant past, suddenly alone in a room and forced to speak to one another. It had always held my most precious things, and now it would need to hold everything else necessary and dear to me. I reached for an ebony ladder-back chair. On its top rung my green parrot held on with her little feet, refusing the bother of leaving her perch. She leaned in to keep her balance as I pulled the chair, wooden legs humming along the bare floor, up to my old pine dome sea chest.

My eyes rested on the humpback lid made so long ago by my father the shipbuilder, he who never dreamed that a brig would one day sail off with his rashly determined daughter, suddenly old enough to marry a missionary man and departing only four weeks later, her course set for the Sandwich Islands.

The tarnished brass plaque above the keyhole bore the name *Mrs. Catherine Webster*. How it once shone so brightly announcing my new name to the world, when the pine it was nailed to was fresh, our clothes were new, our hearts pristine, our ambition boundless. We were seminary graduates given the keys to go out and change the world we were stepping foot into. There were the going-away gatherings, the gifts, the elation of being lauded for our bravery and conviction. And beneath it all, properly clothed in saintliness and virginity, burned a pure, naked light of excitement. There were the wedding rings, the unaccustomed feeling of a partner's hand, the thrill of signing letters with a new last name.

I placed my palm upon the dome of the trunk that was once my closest companion, my only connection to home, where I kept my most important belongings. It was waiting to speak.

I rummaged through my sewing basket and found the key. I weighed the heavy iron in my fingers for a moment, then pushed it into the keyhole. The lock was stiff with rust from the damp sea air. I tried three times to turn the key before it clicked. As I opened the lid, air from another year rushed towards me with the scent of memories; it shoved my unwilling heart awake as if it had been sleeping, not wanting to open her eyes—and, quite cross about it.

I might have never opened it if the Captain had not whisked away all the other trunks, would not have disturbed the contents if not for the yarn told by old the sea-worn opium eaters. I had been too excited to give my trunk much thought, for I was sailing back to New Bedford, family, and friends. How pleased and relieved Emmaline had been when I told her I was leaving, that Captain Jonathan Swift had built a house for me with views all the way to Fairhaven and that I would soon rejoice in a new life as the rightful mother of my little girl with the ample purse of a successful whaling captain's wife.

There are two ways to prepare a trunk. One: you can tear through the task, quickly debating what to throw and what to keep, and then call it done.

The other way to prepare a trunk, if you treasure what is inside, is to unpack each moment of your life one by one, relive each one once more and see what it might tell you, and then carefully wrap that memory back up in oilcloth to protect it from the dampness of a long voyage.

I trimmed the lantern and the whale oil rose up to life in a clean, bright flame equal to the dying sun filtering through the wavy glass of my western window.

I hesitated. My heart was a trunk, locked up tight.

I took in a deep breath and then reached inside. The contents were shrouded in muslin. My fingers slid beneath the sheer white fabric and found something smooth and cool. I pulled out an unworn pink silk lace Parisian chemise. It still had the yellowed tissue paper inside it packed by my Aunt Sallie as she had prepared my trousseau. My heart went out to the tender girl I was so long ago.

The pull was too strong now to stop. There were many articles inside: an ivory comb, letters, tokens, ribbons, hats—but mostly dresses. I pulled out a ripped black silk gown and draped it across the bed. A thread hung, the seam fell open, and a memory fell out... I was rushed back in time to a girl I'd forgotten: a happy executioner of perfect stitches, with wishes sewn inside of each one.

I reached again for the dainty silk chemise and held it up to the window. A last piece of aged paper fell softly away. The fabric blushed apricot in the splendid rays of the sunset.

Each article had a story to tell. I took up the comb, its ivory yellowed and scarred with a darkened crack. It took me by surprise, it took me back.

PART II

PRELUDE

Article One: The Ivory Comb

FALL, 1829

The older woman paused and then held the comb so tightly that a row of whalebone teeth bit into her palm like a perfectly straight line of red stitches. She was staring at her niece as if she had never seen her before.

Life passes us quietly, politely enough, in tiny movements like the chime on the hour or a birthday, marking merely one more year. And then, as if it cannot hold back any longer, a moment comes when the years rush by with terrible force—like the spring and wheel of a clock suddenly slipping, or a large wave crashing after a period of calm. This was that moment.

Just as she had done for almost eighteen years the woman pulled the comb through the razor-straight part in the center of her niece's scalp down through ash blond hair and back again, then again. Eighteen years old. She could no longer pretend. The girl that she had taken as her own had grown up.

She had kept the child close to her, away from the attentions of boys, boys who became men and left West over the Shenandoah river never to return. She had sewn exquisite little dresses for her dolls, hoping to tempt her to linger in that girlish world. She had hidden her anguish when her niece went to female academy for one long year, and on the happy day she came back she brought heartbreaking news.

She wanted to leave with her friends across a new Shenandoah—the great Pacific Ocean where far away on the other side of the world lay the Sandwich Islands.

The woman put down the comb and let out a long-held breath. She didn't know how she would bear it. The light came softly in through the window illuminating the young woman like a Dutch Master's painting. She hardly looked old enough to marry. Her luminous skin was cream velvet, and from her aunt's hands her hair flowed into silken braids, then lifted from the nape of the slender neck to be coiled at the crown of her head. The older woman turned to her dressmaking notions and chose ribbons the color of her niece's rosebud lips. She expertly tied them into bows above two long wheat-colored curls that hung at each temple.

The dress would cause envy in Paris; the waist was set low and tiny, the sleeves set wide at the shoulders. Then those slim shoulders suddenly twitched as if stung by a bee when three sharp raps sounded on the front door.

It would be the handsome young Herman Webster knocking, not the others who had recently come calling, such as the older man with salt-and-pepper hair stained with whaleship stink, who'd asked if her niece could bake a good pie, and how long would it be before she was old enough to be a wife? Transfixed by beauty, he had forgotten all manners, reached his thick hand out to touch her knee and was promptly banished with scissors of words and sent fleeing back home down a street which would be forevermore avoided.

The knocks hammered again. Her niece looked up at her, those young pink lips firm, determined. She wanted so badly for life to start.

"Aunt Sallie, do I look all right?" She looked down and smoothed invisible wrinkles from her well-made skirt.

The older woman was too overcome to answer. The girl was frozen in her chair, so her aunt walked over to the door and then bid him in.

CHAPTER 1

HONOLULU

SPRING, 1830

Article Two: The Pink Silk Lace Parisian chemise

"They ruined my organdy."

Emmaline was holding a sheer cotton night dress up to the fierce sunshine coming in from the window.

We were in the large Honolulu Mission store room, still finding our steady legs after the long voyage. Mine were weak from the dead finality that we were really there; all morning I fought back a windowless feeling. It was not the way I had imagined I'd feel. Now faded was the excitement of finally spying land, the lifting of our exhausted spirits by the sound of waterfalls spilling from steep green slopes down into the sea as our ship drew close where the water was deep, the scent of flowers and earth floating towards us across the water on the sweet breath of the islands.

"These pantalettes were never imagined to be washed in a stream and pounded between rocks," Abigail sighed sweetly. As she bent over to sadly inspect them two thick auburn curls slid forward against her long pale neck towards her large green eyes. She wore a dove gray cotton dress with a crisp, white pelerine that primly covered her chest from collarbone down to the top of her bodice; it had three layers of thin cotton, each one a different length edged in fine lace. Longer than a collar, shorter than a shawl, the pelerine fell modestly just below the top edge of a corselet.

To the world she appeared as peaceful and serene as a harbor on a foggy morning—yet, as her close friend, I knew a different Abigail.

"Here we are to spread the Gospel of Love," I said, "yet the very ones we've come to save have lovingly saved us from doing our six months of laundry, knowing we must be completely spent after escaping that briny prison we have endured."

"Praise God for their help," Emmie said with a frown as she folded a fine cotton petticoat. "Yet, I may have to do without native help if I want to have anything left to wear."

Emmie was like that; stern judgement born of good intentions sometimes lived inside her somewhere beyond the warm world of our friendship. She brushed away a rebellious strand of hair as if it were irritation itself and then her face softened into a smile as if she had just finished a prayer.

She wore her hair like Abigail and I, combed perfectly up off the back of the neck up into a tightly pinned topknot at the crown. The hair at her forehead was parted neatly center front, her brown eyes framed by stylish temple curls that were allowed their freedom.

As I put a stack of clean petticoats back into my trunk my hand whispered against the soft pink silk chemise. Nestled beside it was the beautiful English Wedgwood pitcher and bowl given to me by Herman during our courtship. I held it up by the delicate handle, smiling at the hand-painted blue floral border and equestrienne scene on its cream belly. It had made the journey unbroken.

"About having nothing to wear, have you noticed the mission women here?" Abigail said. "I must confess, they frighten me. The old phrases they use, their old-fashioned, faded clothes—as if they are ghosts from another time."

"They seem clothed in drudgery," I said. "I can help with that. Lifting spirits can help lift souls."

"Ever since Academy we've dreamed of changing the world we would set foot into," Emmie said passionately. "I can't believe we're finally here. The world will be a better place."

"And my Henry will help save them from their heartrending sicknesses," Abigail said, determined to help her husband's medical cause.

"I suppose we all use our gifts no matter how valuable they are," Emmie said, looking over at the wicker sewing basket I pulled out of my trunk. "Even if we have just a widow's penny."

I pushed away the insecure girl I'd left on the other side of two oceans, having decided, as all young women do, to carry myself in speech and manner as the very mature, married missionary that I had recently become.

"Surely my contribution will have more value than that," I said.

"Forgive me, dear Kittie. A penny was precious in Jesus' eyes, and if you can lead a half-naked princess to Christianity with your dressmaking skills we will gain many a lost native soul. Curry her favor and half the job will be done."

She suddenly gasped as she held up another chemise of hers that revealed a small rip up the front. After a prayerful pause, she said "Kittie, will you also share your dressmaking gifts with us?"

"I'll gladly restore your wardrobes as soon as I find my fabrics among those mountains of crates and boxes. I had never imagined our *Fair Wind* so heavy that there would be hardly room for all my goods."

"Your supplies being just as necessary as the Bibles," Emmaline said generously, her smile all sunshine but her eyes still freckled with doubt.

Two dozen ruffled shirts can curry more influence than a sermon, the men from the American Board of Commissioners for Foreign Missions had declared to me, *What greater call can one answer? Rescuing the lost! Everlasting joy!*

They had determined that I, having been brought up at the side of

New Bedford's best dressmaker was the perfect recruit for a special dressmaking mission. My sadness for leaving my Aunt Sallie was softened by her presence floating around me in all the stitches and ruffles made by her dear hand; I fondly remembered everything she had taught me about dressmaking as we had spent many hours together over dress pieces, the perfect placement of hat ribbons, the well-fitted gown.

Aunt Sallie had a way of spinning enchantment into dressmaking. Since I was old enough to remember, I had been deposited daily to her studio by my father or one of my brothers, away from our male household where my mother was only a painting on a wall. As I would make my way up Aunt Sallie's stairs a feeling of magic would grow stronger and stronger the closer I drew to her door. Inside I would find beautiful sunlight or bright golden lanterns glowing and a merry parade of new ribbons and trim, beautiful fabrics, and a rainbow of thread spools. I would run straight to her smile and smell the scent of roses when she hugged me close.

In the two short weeks between my marriage proposal and the sailing, Aunt Sallie's workroom had been as busy as a beehive. She had carefully cut her dressmaker's shears through silk, calico, poplin and linen, and reinforcements were called in to join her: women who helped us sew twenty-two changes of pantalettes and chemises, ten corsets, eight corselets, twelve embroidered aprons, and fifteen dresses—most of which were still carefully packed in three other trunks. And here they all finally sat at their destination in a place as far away from New Bedford as the moon.

Emmaline patted her stack of neatly organized clothing. "That's such a beautiful night dress, Kittie, but I can see you never unfolded it. Beautiful underthings can serve a purpose; Stuart and I began our union as the Song of Solomon would have had it."

"Now that we are finally done with sea-sickness and bruises I will feel more inclined to wear my pretty things," I said, touching my delicate pink silk chemise and feeling a tiny snag in my heart. Aunt Sallie had it sent from Paris, paying as much as she would earn making a dress for her clients. I remembered the teary shine in her eyes as she had given it to me, she who had packed her own trousseau for a beau that had crossed west over the Shenandoah and never returned.

I had already known that Emmie and Abigail's intimate bridal nightwear had not made the voyage still folded chastely in tissue paper. Our rooms, or more accurately cubbyholes inside the belly of the *Fair Wind* had been so stocked that one had to climb over trunks with her head against the ceiling to get to the bed. There was little privacy save for night—dark as the belly of a whale—and once the awful sea-sickness wore off, there was an unspoken fact that we all knew: it was a ship of newlyweds, and below the decks each young couple—who had met and wed only weeks just before our ship cast off—forsook the prayers and hymns of day for the breathless discoveries of night.

In the beginning I had expected a honeymoon of perpetual tenderness and pleasure. Were all marriages a voyage of one tiny heartbreak to the next? My nights at sea were spent at Herman's back. His was muscular, and his body lean, his head full of dark hair that any woman's fingers would desire. Yet before the voyage was over the ceiling above our bunk had become more familiar to me than his body. I had memorized each knothole an arm's reach from my face as I lay smelling the tar, the canvas, the leather trunks, the human beings, the whisper of lilac in my lovely chemise. I wore it once and then wrapped it quickly back up in tissue before my heart could have the chance to notice.

I was frightened, longed for comfort, and did not find it from my new husband. I would listen to the sound of each wave against the hull of the ship, hoping they would not grow louder and rise up like mountains and then drop us as if from the roof of a house. I lay there imagining the vastness of the ocean, fathoms deep beneath our little ship, and the monster leviathan and great sharks teeming below.

I first discovered the darkness in Herman's nature on the day our *Fair Wind* neared the dreaded passing around the Horn. The seas had been the roughest yet, and I had not wished to go up on deck for my husband's sermon, something he was always nervous to deliver having had no church yet of his own but desiring his own pulpit as much as a sinner thirsts for peace of mind. We were all on edge, and even Emmaline's husband, Reverend Stuart Ives, had suggested that we hold our Sabbath down in the fo'c'sle.

Herman had cornered me alone in the little hallway that held cedar steps up to the sails and sky. "Mrs. Webster," he had said. "Up the stairs! Do not make me look a fool."

"You may not command me, and despite our vows I will not obey you," I had replied after recovering from the furious wind of shock that reached down to steal my breath. "If you had expected a child for a wife, and have no sympathy for my feelings, I will leave you." But of course a woman did not have that choice.

He had stiffly laughed at my preposterous words, then reached for my arm and dug his strong fingers painfully into bone.

And then a thunderous shout above was commanding a sail to be tightened, another quickly furled, all hands to look sharp, and then Captain Swift's boots stomped towards us down the wooden stairs. Herman had instantly released me.

"Reverend Webster, you will not have your church service above," he ordered, his square jaw set, his body taut, ready for a battle with the sea. It had not been a morning to use a razor on his face and his cheeks were rough, but his neck scarf was tied neatly and his appearance as orderly as his ship and her sails. For a fleeting moment the ferocious wind brought me his scent of sandalwood and fine brandy.

And so I had sat down for Herman's clumsy sermon in steerage as Emmaline and Reverend Stuart Ives prayed to the right of me and Abigail and her husband Doctor Henry Adamson prayed to the left. A blacksmith and his wife bound for the island of Kaua'i and an older missionary returning to the Sandwich Islands had composed our somber little group as the boots of sailors drummed along the deck above. The ship creaked and lurched violently, whipping the hanging lanterns and baskets of oranges against the ceiling as Herman had preached his sermon on Jonah and the whale; an insensitive choice under the circumstances.

Emmie's Stuart led us in a hymn and we all found comfort in our valiant little group as we sang, but my ears rang with fear, making our voices sound far away.

> *Eternal Father strong to save*
> *Whose arm doth bind the restless wave*
> *Who bids the Mighty ocean deep*
> *Its own appointed limits keep*
> *O hear us when we cry to Thee*
> *For those in peril on the sea*

My anger cooled down verse by verse leading me to the edge of tears. Then a song of my own began to rise up, echoing in my thoughts like a persistent melody. It was the truth, and it mocked me.

> *Go right ahead and lose him then*
> *Like a ribbon or a comb*
> *you're trapped between two oceans*
> *miles and miles away from home.*

Emmaline and Abigail's laughter whisked me back to the sunny afternoon at the Honolulu mission. Back to the life before me, I finished folding the pink silk chemise neatly back over its crisp white paper form and tucked it carefully back into my trunk. I promised myself that I would take it out and wear it once the *Fair Wind*, relieved of her cargo of supplies to the Oahu Mission headquarters, delivered us on to the island of Maui. Perhaps there Herman would be a true husband. Perhaps he had endured sea-sickness and was too proud to admit it. Marriage was said to be fraught with challenges, and Aunt Sallie had always said that unexpected trials encountered in making a dress would only contribute to its success. I had my work cut out for me.

Emmie reached for my hand; she had noticed me deep in thought, and that most of my trousseau was unworn. "Can you imagine it, Kittie?" she said kindly, trying to make me smile. "Did you hear me say we might become so happy here with our loving husbands and grown children around us someday that we peer through our little spectacles at a ship come to take us home—and being so satisfied, we turn it away!"

Our trunks back in order, she headed for the door, so enthusiastic and eager to save at least one heathen before dinnertime. I closed the dome to my pine sea chest, relieved that I had agreed with Herman to sign on for only three years, a thought I had once considered manageable.

Abigail hesitated at the doorstep. "I cannot help but imagine it," she said, her face pale. "Beyond the American Mission buildings lies a wild island where lurks the untamed, the violent, the lost—that's what Henry told me. He says that Satan has made this land his domain; that there are shrines with gruesome idols carved with dark intentions by those doomed souls, lost, without the Light of our Savior to illuminate them."

"Come along Abigail, one would think that you boarded the wrong ship," Emmie told her firmly. "That is why we are here."

I took Abigail's hand and we stood at the threshold of our new world. The sweet scent of flowers greeted us through the open door— a surprisingly tender gesture to come from a land one compass point away from Hell. Nothing had yet matched what I was told to expect. I checked my sleeve buttons; they were fine. I smoothed the pelerine above my chest.

"Don't worry Abigail," I said, making myself sound as brave as Emmaline. "We will strengthen each other, come what may."

Emmaline took Abigail's other arm and together we walked outside, our skirts swinging in the wild island wind.

CHAPTER 2

THREE WEEKS LATER

Article Three: The Fashionable Black Silk Dress

 My shoes struggled through the deep, loose sand on the shore of Maui. Emerging from a towering emerald volcanic mountain range to the east, fingers of sunshine were reaching through the cocoa-nut trees to touch the cool blue sand about me. The surf softly crumbled at the grounded stern of the long-boat that had brought us in from the *Fair Wind*.

From the depths of green the first sounds of the island came—a chorus of gossiping birds welcomed us from strange, pagan, feathered throats. It had echoed against the loosened mainsail as we anchored, and as we were rowed in it fluttered towards us on the surface of the water on the cool flower-scented breath of early morning. Along the edge of the beach stood a great canopy of trees, their branches formed like a great huddle of green parasols; it was hard to tell where one tree ended and another one began.

Moments later I stood with the island under my wet black shoes. The fresh air rushed through my body, mingling with my racing heart as I stood transfixed, looking up in awe across the lush kingdom that lay beneath the mountains that presided over it. I lifted my eyes to see a deep purple-green cleft wearing a pale rainbow hat that revealed more peaks beyond it, and I sensed a queer, fleeting feeling as if I had once dreamt it, or knew it, or it knew me.

"Mrs. Webster," Herman said to me, pulling out his pocket watch. "Hurry along. We are here to make an important impression. Check thine appearance." He gestured to the amber necklace at my neck that had once belonged to my mother. The baguette-shaped gemstones reached outward from a golden center, making the pendant look like a little sun.

"I have worn this since I was a child," I told him as I worked my way through the sand. "If the streets of Heaven are paved with gold, cannot I have a tiny bit around my neck?"

"Thou may never walk those streets with such an impudent mouth," he said then paused, looking at me critically. "I should be reluctant to introduce a fancy woman as my missionary wife." Then he turned to leave me alone there on the shore, quickly outpacing me with his thin long legs in black trousers so unencumbered by thick skirts.

"See if you prefer having no wife to introduce at all," I said to his coattails as he bounded to catch up with the rest. With a bit of effort I tucked the necklace inside the tight neck of my black silk dress.

The backs of black wool coats and stiff corsets moved away from me in zealous procession. I wanted to catch up to Emmie and Abigail but the thick hem of my skirt was heavy with seawater and sand; Herman had dropped me in the shallows as our husbands had carried us from the rowboat to shore. I slowly navigated my way along the beach, winding past a great number of sleeping monk seals, their hides black and shiny in the new sunlight. One stretched like a dog, nuzzled the sand, and sneezed. They were coated with white sand, looking like the back of my sandy wet dress that swept the beach smooth behind me.

A Sandwich Island boy came running towards me along the lacy white edges of water. Near fifteen with rich golden skin and a flashing white smile, he was dressed in a clean ivory cotton shirt and cream-colored sailor's breeches. I struggled to compose Hawai'ian words to greet him but my nervous mind went blank.

He stopped before me. "I am Thaddeus. Welcome to Lahaina," he said. "Your boat came in too far south. I have been charged to collect you."

"I have fallen behind," I said, pausing once again to marvel at the beauty all around me.

"Your arrival has been eagerly anticipated, and is most welcome," he went on in perfect English. "Are there more? Is there a returning teacher in your midst?" His eyes eagerly searched for another boat coming in from the ship.

"No, I'm the last to arrive," I said as he offered me his arm. I leaned on it gratefully as we proceeded north towards the mission houses.

"Have you heard of the teacher Betsey Stockton?" he said. "I was seven years old when she began the first school here and I became her best student. She began training me to be a teacher, but suddenly had to sail back to America." He glanced once more at the *Fair Wind*, disappointed.

"A woman founded the school?" I asked. "A single woman?"

"Yes—her master was president at Princeton; he supported abolition and granted her freedom." He guided me away from the reach of white foam as a wave to our left disappeared into the shiny sand. "She read all the books in his library and was the first missionary here to start a school for common children like me. They had called us *'bands of wild children moving about in their own society, too untamed to teach.'* We quickly proved them wrong. I wish Miss Stockton could find me now, training to pastor my own church. She once answered a letter of mine and told me that she hoped to return someday."

I was overcome with admiration, and I admit some intimidation, to think that a single woman was capable of founding a school. What challenges had she overcome to begin as a negro slave and end up starting the first school on the island? It was a historic achievement no male missionary could claim—in fact I had never heard her success proclaimed at all.

Thaddeus continued to gaze longingly out over the water—no longer at our ship, but at the surf boiling in. As we walked along he kept turning his head back to look at each swell that wrapped its way around the curve of the coast and fell into a cascade of thick cotton lace. I strained to see what sea creature or craft might be vying for his attention, but saw nothing on the deserted waves.

The sun had now risen fully above the peaks of the towering volcanic mountain range. Inland to our right, regal cocoa-nut trees rose high like royal standards, and quiet waterways and ponds sparkled in the morning light. It was untouched by merchants, adventurers, and even missionaries. Native structures, the grandest I had yet seen, stood regally on a small island that presided over a surrounding lake that connected to a network of waterways; a feeling of sacred, stately silence emanated from it.

"We call it Moku'ula," Thaddeus said in a lowered voice as he tore his attention away from the sea and looked at me. "The ali'i, or royals, live there." A shiver of tiny goosebumps tickled the back of my neck that was made long and bare from the back of my collar up to my hairline just below the edge of my black poke bonnet with the jaunty stovepipe-shaped crown.

Through deep thickets of bright flowers edging the pond I caught glimpses of well-appointed houses and the graceful, discreet movement of attendants. "Our most noble queen and her family live there," Thaddeus told me. "This is our kingdom's capital."

We continued along the edge of Mokuhinia pond which was separated from the sea by a narrow length of beach and green, open space. Stretching north grew sugarcane and mulberry next to serene, parakeet-green taro patches that glowed brighter as the sunlight discovered them.

"This is where chiefs and chiefesses live," he said as he guided me past a line of handsome cottages that stood sentry between the sacred area now behind us and where the lush, green forested town of Lahaina began.

"We traditionally called this area Hauola—the dew of life," he told me. The thriving shady breadfruit and cocoa-nut trees made it indeed look like an Eden.

By and by we came to a canal that cut inland from the sea. As we drew closer I heard a crescendo of rough shouts, of cursing, singing, and laughing. Sailors paddled their longboats in, empty and high, past others heavy to the rails with fresh water barrels returning out to the ships from which they had come.

We walked across a bridge that spanned the canal and soon approached the thick vegetation that edged the beach. Filtering through the trees came the unintelligible sound of many voices, then through a hedge of large red blossoms Thaddeus led me to behold a cluster of grass and palm-frond thatched mission buildings. Surrounding us were more islanders than I had ever imagined. Thaddeus melted away into arms reached out to him by a large, smiling woman with a mother's pride in her eyes, and a little girl about five years old with sisterly adoration in hers.

I CAUGHT up to Herman just as our group reached the missionaries that would soon be our daily companions: Reverend Goodwin with his wife Mary, and Doctor Thatcher and his wife Charity.

The Goodwins were First Missionaries which made the Reverend the respected, admired, and unspoken leader of us all. He was tall, and his tanned face was deeply cut with ravines like the slopes of an ancient volcano. His hair was pure white, which would have made him look old if not for his keen eyes and bodily vigor.

"Mrs. Webster," he greeted me, looking down to my sandy hem, up to my stylish bonnet, falling back down the line of black velvet buttons from neck to waist and then rested, heavy as a raven, on my chest. He turned and addressed the men present. "God has answered our prayers. Her sewing skills will no doubt have some influence with the Princess. And, just in time."

I was grateful that I had worn one of my best dresses to meet the princess who I was to win over by needle and thread. It was the latest fashion, with wide bands of silk, black as India ink, trimmed with bows in just the right place at shoulder-edges and elbows, smooth skirt falling down to more bands and bows above the hem; all black to qualify as a missionary, yet stylishly sure to impress a native princess.

Reverend Goodwin's wife Mary embraced me gingerly as if I were a doll too fine to be played with. She had an air of authority gained from her standing as his wife. Her wide, thin lips were framed by a small, serviceable bonnet out from which peeked her severely parted and combed salt-and-pepper hair. She stepped back, looking at me doubtfully and then cast a look of irritation towards her husband before turning back to judge my value.

"She's too pretty to be a missionary," she said flatly.

Her frankness caused all heads to turn in my direction and my hand flew up to feel that the top button of my dress was securely fastened. Then she remembered herself, endured a smile and spoke directly to me.

"Bless your heart, Catherine. I hope you brought practical aprons to put over your pretty dresses. We expect you to help us with our work while carrying out your dressmaking duties."

The Thatchers were British missionaries who had come independently prior to us all. Charity Thatcher took my hands and smiled warmly. She wore a sturdy smile like the curved welt pocket on a well-tailored riding coat, firmly sewn into place, never changing shape, and it blended into a chin that draped down into her neck. "What a blessing, what a blessing, you precious girl," she said, tears in her light brown eyes, her hair a warm shade of hazelnut beneath her faded brown bonnet.

She came close and pushed a gift of fine cotton kerchief into my hand, its edges trimmed with simple cotton hand-worked lace. "I made this for you; the climate here is warm, and the sweat of thy brow will find comfort in it."

Her husband, Doctor Thatcher came to her side and smiled at me kindly. "So good of you to join us here," he said in a rich, English accent like hers. "Welcome, welcome my dear."

Emmie and Abigail drew close to me and we exchanged weighty

private glances of alarm as we studied Mary and Charity. These ladies in their tight narrow sleeves, high Empire waists, and thin skirts looked like they were trapped in an olden time. An uneasy feeling crept over me; I was now caught in a land so far away from home it seemed to run on its own kind of clock. Abigail crossed her arms, her fingertips feeling the fullness of her sleeves. Emmie touched the sash around her long, low waist. I absent-mindedly grasped the thickness of my stylish three-petticoat skirt. There was no turning back now; we were not only miles and oceans away—but perhaps years and a lifetime—removed from everything we had ever known.

Bearing warm smiles and fragrant lei, the islanders surrounded us, placing the flower necklaces upon our shoulders. We all surrendered to the peculiar custom, Herman and Stuart exchanging stiff looks that said, *Imagine a man being adorned with flowers on the streets of New Bedford!*

"A wasteful art," murmured Mary Goodwin. Long dark hairs reached out from inside her nostrils and moved as she sniffed with disapproval. "They spend hours of idle time creating these adornments that last but a day. If only the same amount of time was spent learning the eternal Word of God!"

Mary had only just imparted these words when a girl approached her, stood up on tip-toes, and draped a thick garland of red blossoms around her neck. Protests smothered in petals, Mary managed a Sunday morning smile, making her gesture of thanks as brief as possible.

As we turned to study the inhabitants of the island, Emmie and Abigail's jaws dropped to their bonnet-bows in shock. The pictures we had seen had not prepared us. Some wore articles of clothing, but many did not. They wore intricately patterned garments—not woven, but a kind of cloth made of pounded mulberry bark, and they were adorned with feathers around their necks, wrists, and ankles.

I was secretly thrilled by their appearance. Sweltering in my black dress under the fierce sun, I envied their freedom and the suitability of their clothing to the climate. Aunt Sallie always said that a dress was never completely successful unless it served the wearer comfortably under the particular environmental condition.

A group of young chiefs drew up before us—terrifying, tall, and athletic. Their skin was cut and dyed with gruesome designs of ink: triangles in a chessboard pattern along a bare leg and chest, pictures of birds and animals like rock carvings upon their very faces. Most had shorn their hair close on the sides leaving the crest long and high like cardinals. The women also bore tattoos, and some had bleached white the short-cropped hair that framed their face making them look like owls—their eyes wide, sensuous, and bright with curiosity.

It was the luxuriant cloaks of feathers worn by those carrying an air of significance that stole my breath: we had learned that thousands of birds sacrificed their pride for a single cloak. Almost hidden beneath the cinder black wings and tail of the *Mamo* and *O'o* species grew several bright yellow feathers, and the *'I'iwi* birds gave the gift of red feathers. The birds were captured using the sticky wax of the breadfruit tree, only a few choice feathers plucked, and then released. A most merciful method for a people recently thought to have been cannibals.

We met two queens, and from that day forward I would think of them as the Yellow-feathered Queen and the Scarlet Queen. One was friendly and the latter wary. The former was wrapped in an *O'o* feather cloak of lemon with a fringe of long black tail feathers, and upon her head was a crown of the same yellow feathers painstakingly strung into a thick circular crown. She bore a smile as wide as her girth and had a melodious, deep voice. The other queen wore a guarded expression and her cape of scarlet *'I'iwi* feathers ruffled up in the soft morning air. The thought was held of course that we missionaries suffered their uncivilized ways in order to win their souls, yet I had the feeling that she held her own similar view—tolerating our strange ways to receive education and other advantages for her people.

Both women were as massive and powerful as kings. "Their size is quite large because that is the standard of beauty," Mary Goodwin informed us. "Four hundred pounds is considered quite attractive."

Emmie leaned towards me and whispered, "After always denying myself second helpings of cake at tea, I think we have come to the right place, Kittie," she said. "Soon we will have to sew ourselves larger dresses in this land where beauty is measured by the pound."

I smiled at her, glad to see her in a playful mood like the schoolgirl I once knew. "Look at their manner," I said, feeling secretly thrilled. "So free from our concerns of what should be said and done, as confident as a man, unconstrained from being strictly measured for beauty at all."

WE MISSIONARIES, along with Captain Swift, began walking in procession to be shown a tour of the surrounding area. On the far eastern shore of the sky-blue lake that surrounded Moku'ula stood a lone, unfinished white church, its new steeple rising like a sword between the green cleft of the mountains behind it. We proceeded forward to view it more closely.

Reverend Goodwin's proud eyes glowed from his sun-browned face as he commanded our attention, gesturing towards a coral block foundation that surrounded the steeple. "The Royals have finally given us their blessing: behold the first stone church and first white steeple in the Sandwich Isles, soon to be graced by a bell, a monument to Christianity and civilization rising up against these savage mountains, as green as poison, that loom above this village of Lahiana!"

Doctor Thatcher cleared his throat. His body was tall and imposing, but his spirit was as gentle as a lamb. "A proper hospital will soon be ours as well," he said, his concerned voice tempering the blast of Reverend Goodwin's. "Medical attention is much needed here."

Reverend Goodwin continued on. "Our old native-built sanctuary had upwards of a thousand souls last Sunday, counting all who gathered outside the walls, along with our regular congregation of stray cows attending that reach up to graze upon the roof."

We came to a place where a view of the entire royal lake and waterways spread out before us. I took in a quick, deep breath and exhaled it into words. "An Atlantis of sorts," I mused. "It's beautiful.

Water surrounding water, and then more waterways spreading out in all directions nestled in such lush, green—"

I suddenly felt all eyes upon me. I slowly pulled my gaze to meet their scrutiny.

"Mrs. Webster," Reverend Goodwin said sternly, glancing at Herman as if he were responsible for my contribution. "We do not entertain the secular ideas of Plato here. A *mikanele* should know that."

Herman looked at me horrified. "Thou shalt see what worthy missionaries— mikanele—we will become, Reverend Goodwin," he said, his voice strained, higher than usual.

My face grew unbearably hot in the humid shade of my black hat and I gratefully pulled Charity's gift from my pocket to press it along my forehead.

Goodwin waved his hand over our view of the rich green taro patches, water canals, fish ponds, lake, and the sacred Moku'ula set in the middle like a pearl. "We envision a different use here someday. This Moku'ula—rhymes with the lascivious *hula*, to remember the word, and just as pagan—together with its surrounding lake, Mokuhinia, will someday be an orderly agricultural area. Once the Royals relinquish it, industrious natives will desert their old, frivolous ways and support themselves with American farming techniques and useful pursuits—when they are not studying God's Word."

Doctor Thatcher exhaled a long breath from his nose. "Remember, we are here together on a mission of love, Goodwin," he said. "We have come to heal every sickness and disease, and to tell the good news of Jesus to these priceless souls, not to conquer them."

"Of course," Goodwin replied, threads of tension running beneath his pious demeanor. "While your England has generously approved of Americans being here—and you will experience this, Webster and Ives —we sometimes battle each in our own particular way towards a common purpose. In Christ we are peacefully united now in our war for souls, no longer fighting against each other like our Revolutionary fathers did."

As we approached an opening in the cocoa-nut palms Reverend

Goodwin glared back over his shoulder at the coastline, now visible. Herman, Stuart and I, walking closest to him, followed his glance and saw nothing but the ships that were anchored out in what was called Lahaina Roads.

"We have accomplished much through years of trials," Goodwin said. "See the natives sporting on the waves?"

Herman, eager to curry his favor, squinted earnestly and then finally said "I beg your patience, yet I see none."

"Precisely," said Goodwin with a satisfied smile. "The sport of *he'e nalu*, or wave-sliding, was once carried on right here in front of God's mission buildings; it was first imagined by Satan who then whispered the idea in the impressionable ear of a savage."

"Judge not so harshly, Goodwin," interrupted Dr. Thatcher. "I must say, that when the surf acts impetuous, they place themselves astonishingly on the largest summits to glide rapidly along; and I find that those who spend more time in the water spend less time in my infirmary."

Reverend Goodwin paid him no heed. "We have forbidden them to conduct this wave-sliding especially on the Sabbath when only Jesus should be said to walk upon water. The missionary Williams, once here at our station, had not the dedication to help our cause, and for that among other reasons he was sent home. I last heard that he became a postal clerk in Connecticut."

Herman's face went pale. "A sorrowful disgrace," was all he could utter.

Captain Swift had come up alongside and overheard the conversation. "You may have God on your side, but it might take more than that to pry these Hawai'ians away from their beloved surf-riding."

"Well, Captain, God is not running short on His supply of miracles, I can assure you," Reverend Goodwin answered firmly, sharing pious little smiles with Herman and Stuart. Dr. Thatcher was then pulled away by several islanders with pleading, worried faces.

"I have also achieved the dismantling of a frivolous *papa holua* slide," Goodwin went on.

"Pray tell us what devilment was that?" Stuart asked.

"'Twas a wicked waste of cobbled lava-stone nearly a mile long running up the side of this mountain; too steep to walk on, much less be of use for a carriage. The natives would begin at the top on wooden sleds and fly down it until projected out onto the sea, which at that speed provided them a hard surface. As they slowed down into the water they abandoned their land sleds to slide again, this time on waiting surfing boards and then off again down those hills created by ocean waves bringing them back to finally rest upon the shore. To this double sin they added a third: wagering to bet on who was fastest!"

Herman and Stuart offered Reverend Goodwin grunts of sympathetic outrage. "The papa holua slide was conveniently located there along our hillside, and provided ample stones for the church foundation and garden walls. They protested grievously, but God prevailed," he concluded.

We had just reached the edge of the new church construction where the last of the lava rocks were being set in place. It was there, standing in a grove of trees that lined a slowly moving waterway where I first saw the savage princess whom I had traveled oceans to save, and I lost my breath in surprise.

CHAPTER 3

Sunlight filtered down through the leaves and lit a parrot-green satin Chinese parasol that rested upon her shoulder. Her matching gown made me blink twice. I had seen one like it just last fall in Aunt Sallie's pattern catalog from Paris.

She moved towards me and her ladies-in-waiting followed, their breasts bare but for their flower garlands, and they wore lengths of blue and ivory-striped Chinese satin at their hips wrapped expertly into skirts.

"I am Princess Leilani," she said eagerly, smiling at me and then my dress.

I fingered the blue velvet bow on the side of my black straw bonnet, stunned. I was glad that I had been smart enough to take my hatboxes on the ship, despite the men's protests.

"I am so pleased to make your acquaintance," I said. "What a beautiful gown!"

She was tall, shapely, ample, seventeen. "I had it brought from Europe, do you like it?" she said, moving her Rubenesque figure gracefully side to side, seeking my approval. She then leaned her dark, flowing tresses towards me, her head crowned with a garland strung of thousands of little yellow feathers. "I am taken with your hat," she whispered, "and your strange blue eyes. They almost match the color lining it—it looks is if you wear a blue sky hidden inside your bonnet. My hats from our journey to Great Britain are old and too small. And your dress is beautiful."

"I will make you one just like it if you wish," I promised, wondering why the Mission had been so wrong in their description of a wild, despairing princess pleading for salvation in nothing but grass skirts smoking from Hell's flames.

Followed by her barefoot ladies-in-waiting and the approving looks of the mission men, we strolled along under the breadfruit trees, enjoying the shade after intermissions of warm, humid sunshine. Our talk of the latest styles trailed off and her lighthearted steps slowed, her mood becoming pensive.

"Tell me," she said, taking my arm as we walked. "I hear that another doctor is with your company. Is it true?"

"Yes, Doctor Adamson and his wife Abigail." I said, looking down at her fingers that grasped my forearm so urgently.

"He is desperately needed. So many of my people are dying. I traveled to London with the Royal party when I was a girl and we returned heartbroken—both our king and queen died there of measles after a charitable visit to a hospital. Surely white doctors hold the cure to white diseases."

"Rest assured," I placed my hand over hers, "Doctor Adamson has arrived with the latest in medical knowledge and supplies: mercury, opium, and leeches."

She then turned to me and clasped both of my arms as if I might save her from drowning. Her sudden gesture stopped me short.

"My mother—" her whisper caught in her throat. "Tell me," she began again, "Do the measles and cholera plague your New Bedford?" She looked at me intently, as if only her eyes could finish what she was trying to say. And they did. Her mother had died. Our hearts shared a common sorrow. Everything I had been told to think about her suddenly fell away, and I was no longer a missionary, and we had no longer been born on opposite sides of the world.

Captain Swift walked up alongside us and all was formal again as the Princess invited him to join us. She comfortably exchanged a brush of her nose to his—the customary native salutation.

We had proceeded beyond the view of the other missionaries and he cast a look around us to make sure our exchange was more or less private. "Would you have a taste of rum, ladies?" he offered, producing a glass bottle from his coat. "The day is already warm."

The princess glanced about and her eyes caught on the pretty waves not far away breaking and tumbling in towards us. Like Thaddeus, she studied them with a queer look of longing on her face. I followed her gaze but nothing was beyond, before, or upon them. From right to left they broke in solitude.

"Your majesty, are you searching for something?" I asked her.

"*'Uo* has become lively," was all she said, distracted. "Perfect for He'e nalu."

The Captain pushed his bottle in her direction; she tore her eyes from the wasted waves breaking at the spot she called 'Uo, reached out for his rum and took a deep draught. Then she tipped the bottle towards me.

I shook my head and nervously smoothed my palms along the elaborate tucks in my black skirt, hot to the touch from the sun.

The Captain pressed close to me with a spark in his eye. "I will not tell," he said, his personal attention to me having not lessened since our days on the ship.

"Have some, and then you cannot think worse of me," Princess Leilani urged with an air of expectation as if I had already agreed, for she knew no other reply than obedience.

"I am a missionary, as you both know—would you have me excommunicated on my first day here?" I asked. My throat was dry and my head dizzy, as if my world was now the globe in my father's library spun from Massachusetts to the Sandwich Isles.

The princess looked disappointed, and a veil of shame passed over her face. "Of course. They would have not sent for an unChristian dressmaker."

"Everyone I know in New Bedford is a churchgoer," I said. "I have never met anyone who wasn't."

"Welcome to the wide-open world outside of your familiar society," Captain Swift said.

"I am sure that you are an authority on all that goes on outside of church doors," I replied.

Undeterred, Captain Swift offered his arm to me as Princess Leilani took one more sip of his rum and then drifted away, swept up by a crowd of her maidens and the imposing men that were her guard.

It was customary to take a man's arm, but touching his felt like a sin. His coat sleeve was well-tailored blue wool, his arm as sturdy as a mast. "I might do you a favor if I caused you to be expelled," he said, looking me straight in the eyes. "Are you certain you must go ahead with your Grand Calling, Mrs. Webster? A missionary wife trods miserably to an early grave. Would you not rather choose a more comfortable life near friends and family, holidays with sleighing parties, and summers with your own rose garden as a New Bedford Captain's wife? The *Fair Wind* is will head back to New Bedford by way of Canton. We might reach home by Christmas."

"It may have never entered your rapscallion mind that a woman does not just leave her husband."

But his words had hit a mark. My new life by Herman's side was not unfolding as romantically as I had imagined, and the prospect of three years cast away on this island was like a wet cloak pulling me, wave by wave, deeper into the sea. I squirmed beneath the weight of my fading dreams.

"You resemble a pearl, Mrs. Webster, so luminescent in the morning sunlight. This bevy of golden curls that frame your face—the new fashion, I am sure. So unaware of what life will bring you. Is there not a Bible verse warning not to throw your pearls before the swine?"

"You are cruel to call these poor lost souls swine, Captain."

"I didn't mean them. I was thinking of the Board of Missionaries and the life they're throwing you into—their muddy business of saving the innocent."

"I deserve the privilege of a calling just as any man has. I am not one to spend my life caught up in merely the latest fashions or gossip.

I came here to bring love and hope and learning. Good day, Captain." I broke step with him and began walking in another direction. Yet he relentlessly pursued me, just as he had nearly every day on our voyage over.

"Your odds are not good," he persisted. "Exhaustion is not all of it. Should your husband put down his Bible long enough to turn his attentions to you, you'll have childbirth to survive as well."

"It is dangerous business, no matter where a lady is," I countered. "My mother died birthing me nestled in the safety of civilization, and that is all I will say of personal matters to you."

Emmie, Abigail, and I had already discussed the matter, of course. Together with the older mission women we planned to give each other the care we would need to live through it.

I walked faster, looking for them.

"When the *Fair Wind* reaches America you can be home from your adventure, with tales to tell," his voice called after me as I walked directly towards the reassuring embrace of the Mission grounds.

W E W E R E C A L L E D the Third Company: the third wave of Missionaries to answer the call. Relieved to leave my ruffled feelings outside the grass church, I entered to find the others already gathered together for the official indoctrination.

Reverend Goodwin stood before all as I found my place on a rough wooden pew between Herman and my friends. "Brothers and Sisters, as mikanele here in this forlorn seaside village, thou wilt meet many challenges," he said, his black eyes aimed across heads towards my face. In them a glint of man's pride spoke as he preached, glancing in my direction. "I have forbidden them the entertainments of song, dance, and sport, so that their hearts may open up to God's Word. Our victory lies in the cast-off systems of heathendom."

There was a chorus of enthusiastic 'Amens' but Emmaline, seated next to me, sounded weak and breathless. She had a strange look on her face, and the way she reached out and pressed my hand so fervently made my stomach lurch.

"Although Doctor Thatcher here finds it natural, thou wilt no doubt find it most un-American to fawn over royalty, yet ingratiating ourselves to them is the key to our success," Reverend Goodwin went on in his sermon-voice.

"We must not fail! It is critical that we are placed where we will do the most good, which brings me to relay some sorrowful news that just came in from a ship on your wake. Another one of our missionaries on O'ahu has gone on to his Heavenly reward. It has been decided that Reverend and Mrs. Stuart Ives shall sail back to Honolulu and serve there where most needed."

I tried to swallow but my throat was as dry as sand. Abigail and I embraced Emmie as if we would never let them take her from us. We would be one less in number in this frightening land—and would we be able to be at each other's side when it came time to bear our children?

Before we all bowed in prayer, as was done after any notable news or turn of events, Reverend Goodwin continued his decree. "There is more. Doctor and Mrs. Henry Adamson will be stationed over on the isthmus of this island, where another doctor is sorely needed; having two doctors here is extravagant."

"I was told that one is already stationed there," Abigail's Henry said.

Reverend Goodwin's brown face twitched as he paused for the right words. "We have a challenge peculiar to these isles," he began.

"We lost him to a wild beast," Doctor Thatcher explained sadly. "Both he—and his wife—unfortunately met with the long horns of a feral bullock. These monstrous animals, once a mere handful given as a gift to a king, have multiplied up in the steep, deeply wooded slopes of the volcanoes, impossible to catch. More than once I have stitched entrails back into the stomach of an unlucky person who had met with the tip of their horns."

Abigail's face turned as white as a page in a freshly printed Bible. I drew close to Herman's ear.

"Did you know we were to be split up and sent to other stations?" I said in a demanding whisper.

"Of course," Herman said. "Henry and Abigail will journey around the island once he is sufficiently trained by Doctor Thatcher here."

I was stunned. "You could not bring yourself to tell me I was going to lose my two friends? To keep this knowledge from me was cruel." He just turned his head the other way.

The meeting was beginning to fray. Abigail was crying soft tears into her husband's chest, and he looked stricken.

Emmaline whispered, "I just found out before you came in. Where were you?"

Herman rose up and stood by Reverend Goodwin. "Perhaps a hymn might be helpful," he suggested. At Goodwin's grateful nod, Herman took a tiny silver pitch pipe from his chest pocket and tooted a soft tone. He matched it with a hum and then began to lead us all in song.

There is a fountain filled with blood drawn from Emmanuel's veins;
And sinners plunged beneath that flood lose all their guilty stains.

My fingertips pressed white into the ebony leather cover of my Bible, shut tight. I was as mute as Abigail, but Emmie dabbed the corner of her eyes with a handkerchief and began to fervently sing along.

Lord, I believe Thou hast prepared, unworthy though I be,
For me a blood bought free reward, a golden harp for me!

The blood in my body pounded in my ears, deafening me, and I suddenly longed for a swallow of Captain Jonathan's rum. And for the decks of the *Fair Wind*. Even the thought of an arduous voyage back over the seas we'd just crossed no longer sounded revolting.

AFTER SERMONS, prayers and a meal concluded late in the afternoon we dried our hands from cleaning up dishes set for fifty—Royals, chiefs and chiefesses, three sailing captains and a merchant—and Emmie and I proceeded down to the beach.

Up the seacoast, beyond a thicket of palms jutting out into the sea, I could see the edges of the *Fair Wind*'s mizzenmast. The late afternoon light fell beneath the bow illuminating her carved wooden figurehead. She once had black hair, but as I had observed when we had been lowered down the side of the ship, the paint that was once fresh in New Bedford had splashed her way through oceans of salt and wind and was now bleached gray. Life on this island had also faded Mary Goodwin and Charity Thatcher's hair, early for their age, and I dreaded being left without my friends alone on this island of the spinning clock hands.

"You will not even stay the night here?" I pressed Emmaline.

"I will sleep on the ship in a good American bed, Kittie." she said. "When God calls us o'er a difficult path we must always compare our pain to what Jesus bore as He carried his cross; it makes our hardships nothing. I will miss you so—let's promise that we will never be too busy to write letters."

"The company of Mary and Charity will not be exhilarating," I said.

"Just tread carefully with the Goodwins," Emmie answered in a low, cautious tone of voice. "Stuart says that they have significant influence with the American Mission Board and will be watching you closely. You must help your husband in every way possible, for his lot is yours. If he fails, he will have no occupation here or back at home. You know that a shamed missionary cannot expect to own a pulpit in New England."

I knew that. And I knew that Herman was driven by some dark reason not confided to me. Inside him lived a heavy sense of guilt, carried since boyhood, that had grown into the marrow of his bones and sometimes flickered in his eyes. Only when he preached did the light of peace fall on his countenance, his voice became strong, his shoulders relaxed, and he became the young man that I had agreed to marry. The pulpit was his lifeblood.

I was there alone at dawn to see the *Fair Wind* ready to raise anchor—her full water barrels strapped tight, sailors shouting a song up the ratlines and along the yardarms, canvas sails unfurling. In lilac shadows beneath the bow a lantern softly illuminated the carved figurehead. She looked hopeful now, and I was envious of that painted wooden woman who owned a new day and the promise of freedom. Across the surface of the water and in the quiet lull between a set of small waves came the cry 'Anchor's awash!' and the stuns'ls released to catch the light breeze. Captain Swift strode along the decks barking orders, king of his mighty wooden castle. *I will return to fetch you when you have had enough of this,* he had told me the evening before. Imagine that. A man who wanted you enough to throw customs, rules, and conventions all to Hell.

And so the *Fair Wind* sailed off into a pewter sea, carrying away my best friend and a Captain's proposal. It became a tiny boat at the horizon between the two distant islands as their gray slopes slowly grew emerald in the morning light.

Our first week in the islands left me feeling constantly out of breath and always thirsty from the roaring sunshine. Herman was a stranger by day, leaping from one new thing to see or do to the next. As the nights passed, after Herman had seen every delicate chemise, my best corselets, silk pantalettes—and still had not given me a second glance, I began wearing my more practical cotton underthings. They were beautifully made with scrolls of white silk piping or cotton scallops, designed for beautiful days but not passionate nights.

Sometimes I would pull my corset laces tighter than tight, just to feel held.

CHAPTER 4

Article Four: A Letter from Halfway 'Round the World

September 15th, 1830

My Dear Kitten,

How are you faring, my little niece? I devoured your first letter, which came quickly by way of that schooner your ship hoved to off the coast of Chile —it took only ten weeks to reach me.

After your description of the incessant heat, I thought: Swiss muslin! Of course! I should have thought of it sooner, although it was hard to imagine a land where the sun shines so fiercely. You know of course that every pattern I make is of muslin, and the affordable price of this fabric is sure to please your new missionary friends. I will make you cooler dresses and send them along with more straw bonnets. Since I could not prevent you from leaving us, I have consoled myself that you will be clothed in stitches of love.

I am counting the days until your three-year term is finished and you return home. Your husband will have earned his place at the pulpit of his own church here, and your father will see to it that you have a better house than one of a church-mouse. I have told him I am content in my little place above the shop until my betrothed finally returns from the West. Everyone I know has given up on the hope of him ever returning; after all, it has been, I admit with difficulty, fifteen years. You were too young to remember. I regularly hear well-intentioned comments that it is past time let him go, but the other men who have courted me cannot hold a candle to the memory of my first and only love.

Bon-bon and Button were quite forlorn after you left us and they didn't eat well for days. Their little tails drooped, and their sweet brown eyes looked up at me sadly until I could stand it no more. So, I groomed their white coats, adorned them with pretty bows, and took them for long walks in an effort to cheer us all. The poor creatures finally look like poodles again instead of sad little ghosts. I told them we must be brave and replace every lonely thought with one of love and the hope that in time we will all be together again—this side of Heaven, if we have our way.

Your loving Aunt Sallie

~

Article Five: A Letter, Unsent And Forgotten

October 20th, 1830

Dear Emmie –

I thought of you as I sat upon a velvet chaise aboard a British gun ship, waited upon by a handsome Admiral who served me tea from a lovely painted butterfly-and-gold-edged china cup. If only you had been here. We would have talked about it for weeks.

I confess I took two extra cakes and let the Admiral flirt with me. He reminded me a bit of Captain Swift. You know Herman acts reserved, and I feel like sometimes the pressure to act stiffly pious is just too much in this beautiful place. It moves me. Don't you ever feel it too? The sea, the lush green forests, the riotous flowers, the stark lava shaped so mysteriously since the beginning of this world?

Please don't be envious or upset with me for enjoying luxuries; even Mary

Goodwin approved because they gave us flour and Earl Grey tea. I haven't received one letter from you, and hope very much that your health is sound. Perhaps you are sick? Perhaps you have written to me but the letters have not yet sailed. Perhaps a letter has gone off to the wrong island. Perhaps there is no paper to be spared, or ink to be had. I miss you. Please write.

Kitten

PART III

CHAPTER 1

Article Six: The Dress of Blue-Striped Lawn

FALL, 1832

I had counted off the days until the sum of them were more than two years. They had fallen into an orderly procession, dependable, almost ordinary, until one day came when time stopped —a day that would remain vivid for the rest of my life.

We stood that afternoon on the royal dais before a throng of islanders not far from Moku'ula, and gathered from other islands we missionaries stood together once again, shoulder to shoulder, as if nothing had changed, but on that day everything changed.

Emmaline, Abigail and I looked across a sea of moving dancers, our arms around each other, feeling the hard touch of corsets, stiff as a doll, but with the swaying movement of life inside them—the comfort of female friendship for which we had yearned for too long.

"You look too lean, and your hair has turned to straw from the sun," Emmaline told me. "I have been praying for you. You sounded in your letters as if this place might steal your Bible and capture your soul."

"What are friends for, if not to show sympathy for our weaknesses and struggles?" I answered, and we both shared a smile.

Her beautiful face was slightly thicker around the chin, her hair still ebony. Her corset was laced loosely, for she was with child for the second time. Her dress made me believe that she had forgotten our secret project to improve the appearances of the mission women. Upon our arrival two long years ago we had conspired to put them in beautiful new wardrobes and I was to write with any news of achievement. I had indeed made Mary and Charity dresses, sometimes sewing late by candlelight, but they had kept them safely stored away, saved for some grand occasion which had not yet, and would likely, never arrive.

Abigail's eyes were still soft as a doe, but the corners of her face were tight with a grief that had lived there ever since she had borne a stillborn child. Her boy of ten months squiggled safely in the arms of a sweet, motherly Hawai'ian woman.

The new church had long since been completed and it stood firmly and determined, starkly white against the emerald mountain, its coat of plaster made of sand, water, and ashes from pyres of burned coral reef. Above us, tall royal standards topped with yellow, black, and crimson feathers rippled proudly against the deep blue sky. I breathed in air scented with flowers and cocoa-nut oil as we surveyed the scene.

"I had not guessed there were so many souls yet to save—look at them all," Herman said into his friend Stuart's ear. Herman, his sun-browned face and eyes cool as silver, had been nice enough to me. He spent much of his time up at Lahainaluna, the new boy's school, where he was in charge of the printing press; many nights he worked up there until dawn. He had proudly given Stuart a tour of the new *Hale Pa'i*—printing house—and together they boasted: *this printing house is an impressive achievement—such great works He hath done through us in just three years since we were students together at Williams College.*

Reverend Stuart Ives looked every bit of two years older from his work on O'ahu—his dark, thick ebony hair and sideburns were brushed with threads of silver but his face was still as pale as bleached bones. Emmie said that he worked tirelessly, yet still made time to be a good father and husband. Her words burdened me with the task of having to pray away the envy that they caused.

By Herman's side, as always, was Thaddeus, who had shadowed Herman faithfully ever since the first morning when he helped me up the beach.

His father had sailed away years ago to the Alta California coast with other *kanakas*—Hawai'ian men—and word was that they lived a simple, happy life on the beach in San Diego. They had taken up the Spanish guitar, and there the ancient chants so natural in their voices took on melody and became song, and all who came near relished their music. In from the land, from ranchos deep with cattle, came the hides to be stripped, soaked in water and salt, and dried as stiff as a board. The kanakas then stacked them tight in the hold of ships. The Californios were rich from the hides, and those California Banknotes, as they called them, bought anything a merchant ship could offer. The hides sailed away, but Thaddeus's father didn't. He had made a life there.

Thaddeus was well-educated by Betsey Stockton, the missionary who had started the Lahainaluna school years before the mission men claimed credit for it. Thus qualified, Thaddeus eagerly assisted Herman at the church and at the printing house putting hundreds of tiny metal sorts perfectly back into their alphabetical home in the type case, and he knew the Bible so well he could recite verses with the best of them. One day, when he was ready, he would surely be given his own church.

We stood there beside a governor and several high chiefs near the Royals, who commanded the attention of four or five thousand, young and old. Some young mothers held babes with sailor's eyes; blue, green, hazel. It was the rare gray-eyed ones that arrested me; as unique and light and piercing as Herman's. I carried a stone inside my heart whenever I saw the resemblance, and had finally tearfully confessed my distress to him over the subject months before. He had become furious that I could have even thought up such an idea, and in a rush of remorse, tenderness, and embarrassment, I apologized. I had been a fool to suspect my husband; certainly those gray eyes were borne of some sailor's lust.

Emmie and Abigail were whispering together softly when I was swept back to the present moment by a melodious call, as if from a female bird—there before us was an army of women dressed in leafy skirts, bedecked in flower garlands from head to neck to ankle. They answered their leader in unison, and the effect of their voices was astonishing. They began to dance as they chanted, with swaying hips and musical feet and hands like an artist's brush, and when they paused it was so silent, even surrounded by the great multitude of people, that a pin might have been heard if dropped in the sand.

And, the Princess. She stood boldly in a gown that I had sewn for her of many yards of yellow silk and she wore a mantle of blood-red feathers draped over her left shoulder. She bore herself proudly, one never guessing the scene that had unfolded the day before when she had refused to wear the priceless red feather *pa'u* that was intended to be wrapped traditionally about her waist leaving only garlands of flowers covering her chest. Like a shamed Eve with opened eyes, she held firm to wearing the modest, modern dress. Finally, as a concession, she had donned the long, exquisite feather cloak over one shoulder.

Reverend Goodwin swiftly darted as quick as a blackbird before the dancers, waving his hand high in protest to silence them. The Scarlet Queen frowned, her cape of red feathers ruffling like a bird unpleased, and with one look summoned two vigorous men tattooed from foot to temple. With powerful arms they brought the Reverend back to where we all stood. The strong female leader resumed her singsong chant to the troupe of dancers, and they answered back in unity—the fierce beauty of their voices charging the air with strength. They moved their legs, then their arms in one motion, each body part a word moving in story.

Mary Goodwin's hard mouth was set in firm disapproval. Her square face reflected an iron will, and when she smiled it was awkward, ghoulish, as if the muscles being summoned were not used to the task. Her frugal nose was neatly tailored: straight, unassuming, as if she had asked God for a serviceable one and stopped Him before He could add any style or character. Close to her side was her fourteen-year-old daughter Tabitha, just blooming into a beauty who was trading glances with Thaddeus. Standing guard on Tabitha's other side stood Mrs. Charity Thatcher, her everlasting smile still as sturdy as if it were pinned and stitched, her kind face ever-delighted, as if being offered a hot cup of her favorite Earl Grey tea.

At least three hundred ships were gathered in Lahaina Roads, their masts a floating forest. One ship had captured my attention the preceding afternoon when it sailed in down the Pailolo Channel between our island and Moloka'i, all her sails magnificently billowing, long red and blue pennants streaming from mast-tops, her brass glinting in the sun. It came from Alta, or upper, California, and she was presently anchored offshore until she would continue on to her destination of Hawai'i, the largest and most southeastern island in the Sandwich Islands archipelago. The ship was well-fitted, armed with cannons, and flew an American flag; I had counted at least two dozen gun ports above the waterline on the side of the hull facing shore. It was a monument to mankind's power and modern achievements. Something about her had caused me to stop and stare, as if she carried my fate in her hold.

They had landed just after dawn. With great orchestration they had assembled down on the beach, and from our view there on the dais we all searched for the first sight of them to enter through the trees. The royal guard stood peering in the direction of the beach— their muscled bodies dressed in kapa, leaves and feathers, their eyes as sharp as hawks. They were warriors, and rarely seen by us—kin to the legendary Bird-Catchers.

The Bird-Catchers were feral bird-men who lived on the forested slopes of the volcanoes, and with stealth and cunning caught wild birds in order to add feathers to the King's treasury. I was told that the fingernails of a Bird-Catcher were as long as avian claws, able to nimbly snatch the precious O'o or 'I'iwi bird to pluck a single yellow feather or two before setting it free to grow another.

A movement could be seen through the grove of breadfruit and cocoa-nut trees. The warriors stood still, ready for any command, their fingers twitching as they faced the shore. Then the young king, who had suddenly grown up from boy to man in the past two years, sprang up in front of us from a thick pile of finely woven grass mats. Above his muscled calf swung the bottom of a feather cloak blocking my view; it was thick, with a striking pattern of yellow, black, and red feathers that moved liquid in the island breeze. The two queens turned their feather-lei-crowned heads to face whatever might come next to change their island.

The horses appeared first. They came two by two led in silver bridles by Californio men: snowy white mares, and stallions—chestnuts, and blacks. Then, with a sudden gust of wind, the young king's magnificent cloak pulled back like a curtain and I saw the vaqueros.

They wore the peculiar costume of Alta, or Upper, California: boot heels boasting ornate spurs, trousers split wide around the boot and then pulled tight below the knee with a small velvet kerchief. Above that, silver buttons ran up the side of close-fitting trousers from knee to hip. Around their slim waists were tight-wrapped sashes of Canton silk. Short velvet coats, hemmed at the waist, were tailored to give room for strong shoulders and were richly embroidered at cuff and lapel. Their tanned faces were knife-shaven, save for a mustache, and they wore unusually wide-brimmed hats. Their names were Kossuth, Louzeida, Ramón, and Cruz.

They had come by royal request from the port of Monterey, halfway up the Alta California coast, to train the Hawai'ians to ride, rope, and tame the wild bullocks that terrorized the land. It was generally known that the Spanish soldiers of old settled with the native Chumash there and blended into a culture of horsemen and ranchos, now under Mexican rule, and were frequented by American and European trade ships.

"The Royals here ask if you can truly subdue enormous beasts as you claim," their captain translated from Hawai'ian to Spanish for the vaqueros.

They smiled. The captain then returned their answer to the royal court. "They can capture not only wild bullocks, but the feared grizzly bear!"

This boast was lost on many of us who did not know the animal being referred to. Then an engraving was unrolled depicting a fierce animal with long fangs and a thick coat the color of dark golden cane sugar. It stood on its hind legs, towering over a vaquero on horseback that held a long rope with a wide circular noose suspended in the air above him.

The young Sandwich Island King planned to sail with the vaqueros and their horses on over to the Big Island. "One vaquero stays, and the rest will sail on to Hawai'i," said the Queen of the Yellow Feathers, the one most sympathetic to missionaries. She reclined back upon a thick pile of woven mats as the Queen of the Scarlet Feathers wore a face of wood. Slowly that face nodded, approving of the knowledge and skills that the vaqueros would share.

The strawberry blond hair on the sides of Dr. Adamson's head had thinned. He shook it with worry as he confided to us in his thin, sweet, nasal tone. "Let us hope these vaqueros will help us. We have been busy healing the sick over where we have been stationed, yet disembowelment has recently become almost as common as lives lost to foreign disease and sharks. These giant bulls seem to think they rule the island. Abigail and I had a narrow encounter with one on the journey around yesterday."

"Then you have unfortunately experienced it," said Doctor Thatcher. "Pray let me show you when time permits the new surgical instruments I have just received from England. They are very sharp, and the saws are strong."

Shipmen brought forward waves of wooden boxes: gifts of oranges, leather, lemons, and colorfully woven woolen cloth. Then the four vaqueros moved forward and stood directly before us all.

The vaquero named Cruz was the tallest, his lean, muscular body statuesque. Draping behind his wide shoulders over his forest green short-waisted coat and down to his tightly fitted canvas and buttoned knees was a startlingly blue velvet cloak. He stepped up to the young king and presented a guitarre. His attention traveled from chiefs to queens, to the missionaries all in a straight line, and then stumbled onto me.

He blinked, as if stunned. His eyes fell on my blue-striped ivory waist, so lonely for the weight of a man's hand. They dropped down to my blue-banded hem that hid ankles never kissed. His gaze followed up the marine blue lines of my billowing ivory skirt, the creamy cotton lawn fine enough to hold a glow of sunlight, and I was a lantern lit for the very first time. Up each Egyptian-blue glass button above my corseted heart his eyes traveled, and finally, after his long voyage, they landed on mine.

He was torn away to answer a question, maybe about the guitarre or the oranges or the pelts of leather, and I heard his rich voice: a tobacco-and-molasses tone that started in mid-range and then fell deeply, as if he had slid his thumb down the thickest string on the neck of his guitarre.

My fingertips brushed my ivory skirt, feeling the almost imperceptible fine woven edges of its blue stripes. I had never worn the dress. I usually wore my plainest ones, and forsaking style I had lately kept the curls at my face combed straight, pinning my hair perfectly flat. I was tired of feeling as if I were a fish in a glass bowl, enduring attention from strange men, and having Mary think I was not a good missionary. But something inside me that morning had suddenly wanted to fold away my mended brown and black calicos and dig deep into my pine sea chest. I had unwrapped the pretty dress, put it on, and discovered a delight and joy that had long been missing in my life.

Two years as a dutiful wife in name only—save for a frugal handful of disappointing attempts—730 days crossed off my calendar, eight seasons of hard work and needle-pricked fingers and lonely nights would make any woman wear her most practical dresses.

And my favorite blonde straw bonnet was finally set free from its hatbox. It had a cornflower blue ribbon around the stovepipe crown, bows by my chin, and long streaming ends.

I turned the brim to keep my face hidden from others so I could study the vaquero in private. He moved away from them all to take a thick fur cloak out of a trunk, but he looked straight my way again. There was no mistaking it; he was staring right at me. Transfixed.

I could not look away. For so long, everything around me had been as gray as Herman's eyes and as black and white as his Bible. And like the rainbow of thread spools in Aunt Sallie's studio, the vaquero Cruz was every color in my heart.

CHAPTER 2

Article Seven:
A Bundle of Indigo Cotton Scraps Saved To Make a Quilt

The next morning, Emmie, Abigail, and I helped Mary and Charity put on breakfast for fifty-six—really just a preface for a long sermon held for the benefit of the captain in from Monterey, several Nantucket whalermen, sailors from a British East Indiaman, traveling merchants, and a handful of devoted islanders. It was early afternoon before I left the neatly stacked towers of dry dishes, took off my damp apron to find my skirt damp too, and so returned to the grass-thatched hale that Herman and I called home. I had changed out of my dress and was in clean pantalettes and petticoats when little Pua called softly at the bamboo-thatched door.

On the very day we had landed on Maui, Thaddeus' mother had asked me if I would take his little sister Pua under my wing to teach her how she might learn things that would help her navigate the world that was washing up onto their shores. She was a slender wisp of a girl, now seven years old.

Compassion had led us over two oceans, required our sacrifice and loss of everything and everyone we held dear in our selfless quest said to save sad, agonized souls—and yet I had never seen Pua's little face without a smile. The warmest, most innocent smile you had ever seen. When I was new to the islands this would confuse me, and on days when nothing in my new world seemed to make sense and my old world felt lost, I confess her smile had vexed me.

Looking forward to another precious day spent with the Ives and Adamsons I stepped into my good indigo dress and turned around so that Pua could help me with the long row of little buttons up the back. We both knew there were exactly twenty-seven, because that is how I had first taught her to count in English two years past.

Pua had made a song of it, and her affection for the melody had kept her habit of counting each one. The buttons were dark blue and covered with the same glossy silk as the two-inch bands that circled from hem to knee, and a single band at my waist. The rest of the fabric was sturdy cotton, the same hue as the faraway deep blue sea.

"Down on our beach the boys are learning to ride the new horses," Pua told me, on button eighteen. "The vaquero Cruz is teaching them to sit their horses in the soft sand. I am worried that my brother will be found on the back of a horse instead of working up in the church-yard." She fastened another button. "Twenty."

"I should think that any minister would do well to be a good rider," I told her. "Horses are becoming more and more common here."

A large set of waves came crashing in, audible from where our grass hale sat on a little hill close to the Mission buildings. "My, how ill-tempered Neptune is this morning," I continued. "He must have had too much to drink last night."

"Twenty-two," Pua said, unamused. She was always distant and quiet whenever I taught her Roman myths, along with beginning Latin. "Then Neptune had not been good at wave-sliding," she said. "But he is a strange story. We have our own name for the God of the sea."

Pua would have been punished for speaking that way in front of the other missionaries, as so would I for teaching myths, but she had always been comfortable with me.

She climbed a step stool to reach the middle of my back. "Twenty-four. I just passed Reverend Goodwin, Reverend Ives, and your husband making their way down to the shore. Twenty-six."

She finished the last button behind my neck. "The Princess is also sporting in the surf, Mrs. Webster."

I took a sudden breath as deep as my corset let me and rushed out the door, Pua running after me with my blue straw bonnet.

My shoes dug to a stop in the loose sand. Transfixed, I squinted at an eerie sight. There, like shadows in the light the wave riders moved like spirits over the surface of the water. Blue and gray translucent figures danced in the sun as it shone through the waves that rose and curled up behind them.

Then I spied Princess Leilani standing elated and powerful by the edge of the water, surveying the sea. She had thrown her dress down on the sand and with a small wrap of cotton about her hips she was not much more naked than any lady trying on a dress at Aunt Sallie's studio, yet she was far from missionary approval. The water rushed up over her bare calves and splashed up on legs she had always kept hidden beneath petticoats. Indigo tattoos of lizard scales curled from her ankles, her knees, and up to her mighty thighs. Another lizard pattern rose up from the back of her waist emerging from the edges of her small tightly wrapped red cotton skirt and it continued on up her spine to the middle of her shoulder blades. She held a large board made of *wiliwili* wood, perhaps eighteen feet long, and stained into the wood were black interlocking triangles looking like the scales of a water snake.

She left the side of an older man who was chanting a heathen prayer, reverence and delight upon his wrinkled face. He was her *kahu* —attendant and guardian, who, I had learned, always prayed for her safety as she rode the waves. It was not merely sport to her, but something sacred. The old Hawai'ian words in his singsong voice, so ragged with age, were difficult to understand. He continued even as

Leilani was a faraway shadow out on the smooth water kneeling upon her surfing board as if before an altar.

Then her surf sliding board lifted up upon the shoulder of the sea. She lay down on her strong abdomen and dug her arms into the azure surface which soon gave her great speed upon the slope of water. As the wave began to stand up so did she, her feet stepping nimbly forward upon the smooth wiliwili wood. The sun on its afternoon descent glowed through the wave as if it were made of tiny pieces of blue and green stained glass. She sped alongside the aqueous slope at great speed looking as composed as a dancer with a white rushing wake at the tail of her board—her face beaming, blessed, exalted. Cleansed.

Suddenly, the sound of fierce cracks snapped in the air like pistols. My stomach turned as I spotted Herman and others down the beach at the edge of the water. In his clenched fist he held a long, black cat o'nine tails that he had procured from a British frigate, and now I knew the reason why. With Pua following me as determined as a shadow, I marched down towards him.

Herman looked across the water to the wave-riders speeding towards the beach and turned to Stuart. "This wave-sliding hurtles them down to the lowest depths of depravity," he called to him, as if to explain his whip. "This laughter you hear will one day turn to eternal cries of agony—I can save them from that fate!"

Reverend Goodwin clutched a whip of his own, his face aghast. "Can it be? That pagan water-sprite—is the Princess?" he said, crestfallen, all his efforts to shape her will into obedience suddenly for naught.

"Theirs is a slippery path to redemption," Stuart shouted to them above the crash of waves as the hissing foam tumbled towards his black leather shoes. "On my island, these cursed waves rival rum in their powers of seduction."

Herman was silent and grim, the way he became when life disobeyed his wishes. He had been so proud to show Stuart his accomplishments on Maui.

Princess Leilani's wave transported her directly towards us. Purified, sanctified, exalted from her ride, she laughed and turned her board around to paddle back out. Their rage tripled, the three men waded into the surf up to their knees and the foam of spent waves crashed upon their thighs as she cast a defiant smile over her shoulder.

Then the tip of Herman's whip found its first flesh. An unsuspecting man had come smiling in from the surf, had reached his muscular arm around his board, turned to pull it to the shore, when the cat-o'-nine-tails lashed long red streaks across his back. Shock and surprise seized his face as he realized it was no stingray; it was the man in the wet black wool coat shouting Isaiah 13:9.

A movement along the beach path caught my eye. There came Doctor Thatcher along the turn at the lava point, humming a song with a peaceful face, and as he came upon the bay and saw the commotion his cheerful countenance transformed into a look of horror. He broke out into a run, arms outstretched in alarm.

As my husband pulled his arm back and turned to cast his whip once more, Doctor Thatcher's Southampton accent, often so refined, thundered across the water. "Webster! Have you lost your senses?"

I had already rushed in towards Herman, my skirts suddenly as heavy as lead and my throat full of woman's wrath. "Herman! Stop!" I shouted, stumbling as the ocean sucked on my skirt and pulled the sand out from under the bottom of my shoes. I cried out again as he knocked a woman right off of her board as she was skimming to a stop in the shallows. The water tore by me like a river, drawing me helplessly in towards a mighty churning wave that was heading towards me.

"Herman!" I cried, this time for help. He moved around to see me and gave me a sour look. Then he turned away as if I did not exist to him.

I tried to step back, but my heavy, wet skirts were locked in the clutches of the incoming wave; it smashed me down into its silent depths and my head ground against the sandy bottom. My bonnet ribbons cut into my neck—I scrambled up onto my knees—found the roiling surface with my hands—but could not breathe!—my skirt was twisted up around my face. Another wave snatched me back down into the depths and a torrent of hot fear rushed through my heart.

And then I was being tugged away from the iron grasp of the sea by a force even stronger. An arm wrapped around my corset, a hand clenched above my stomach, strongly and surely lifting me up into exquisite oxygen, and finally to the blessed shore. I sat there, sand in my fists, gasping and coughing and crying. Herman had saved me after all.

Through wet eyelashes I looked up at him. His blurry face came into focus. I coughed desperately and wiped the water from my eyes. The face was not my husband's.

Cruz, the vaquero, knelt above me and then helped me sit up. My nose stung with saltwater as I tasted the sweet air and a sob burst up from my throat. He searched my eyes, the whites of his eyes showing in concern around the hazel center that was the color of greenish-brown seaweed lit by the sun.

I heard a clash of words and turned to see Leilani on tip-toe towering over Herman, her face dripping onto his.

"You will put away your whips or you will leave my island," she said.

Herman smoldered like coals being doused with water. He conceded one step back, turning his head to the side choosing his reply, as Doctor Thatcher gathered together the stricken to lead them away towards his hospital.

Herman turned rudely away from Leilani towards Stuart. "Thatcher would pay a call to Hell to help alleviate the suffering there," he said.

Stuart nodded. "The British have not been firm enough. Praise God we are here."

"Reverend Webster," Leilani ordered, "I am speaking to you. Perhaps it is time for you to sail back to New Bedford."

"I am merely trying to save thy people from eternal anguish," he said, his words riding politely atop a back of rage. "I have spoken to a chief of eliminating this particular sin, and he did not protest."

"A chief?!" Her eyebrows raised in surprise and she gave a little laugh. "Leave now, and I will forgive you for your disrespect, Reverend Herman Webster."

Still and solid as a statue, she faced him until he was forced to step back further, coiling his long whip deliberately as if to say *have it your way, but in time I will win.*

I kept coughing—my throat was raw, still choking. Pua had untied my knotted bonnet bow, cast the hat aside, and tried to help me up with all the strength in her slight body. The vaquero stepped in and gently helped lift me up by the sides of my corset until I could stand. His breeches were dripping, his leather boots soaked. His wet white cotton shirt clung to his shoulders and arms; they were wide, strong, capable. With a nod of his head, he turned to go. I watched him walk away, muscles well-built as he moved easily in the deep sand.

Pua uttered a cry and I tore my eyes from the vaquero to see why. Her brother Thaddeus was galloping in, not on a horse but a wave. The joy on his face twisted into alarm as he saw Herman gesturing emphatically to Stuart and Goodwin with a large, coiled, cat o'nine tails as they walked away from the beach. He saw his friends hurried away by Doctor Thatcher with bloody lashes across their backs.

"Thaddeus will be found out!" Pua moaned.

"They will not turn to look back," I said. "They fear being turned into pillars of salt."

"They would never let him be a preacher if they knew. And then he will never be worthy of Tabitha." Pua said, distraught.

So that was why Mary guarded her daughter so closely. Mission children were raised behind tall lava-rock walls, especially as they grew past an innocent age. It was well known that a missionary girl on another island was sent away from her mother and father—at the tender age of eight—back to America for simply playing an innocent game of Honey-Pots with the native boys.

Pua ran to Thaddeus' side and I struggled weakly towards the path home that led up from the beach through the cocoa-nut grove. A long piece of my indigo hem dragged behind me like a tail. My sleeve was torn, my back cold and bare—the little buttons ripped away. I would take my scissors to the dress and cut it in pieces to be used again, as if all my proud little stitches would mend what had happened on the beach that day.

CHAPTER 3

Article Eight: A Letter From Emmaline

October 9th, 1832

Dear Kittie,

It is nice to be back home, but I miss you and Abigail so. What a blessing it was to be in each other's company.

Stuart told me what happened on the beach the last day we were there, and that you remain upset with Herman. His advice to your husband was to treat you with more lovingkindness, as Christ loves the Church.

This is my advice to you: sometimes husbands act wrongfully because they carry heavy burdens on their shoulders—and so their actions must be quickly forgiven. I worry for you in respect to that intimate matter of which we both spoke, and urge you once again to find the communion that is most sacred between a man and his wife. You say that your husband's lack of attention is the problem, but it is a woman's responsibility to attract his interest. Take those pretty underthings out of their tissue and put them to use, and before long you will finally know the joy of being a mother. Herman was only doing his duty as a man of God. Forgive, forgive, and forgive again.

*From my waves on Honolulu to those that lap upon your Maui shores, I
remain*
>   *Your dearest friend,*
>   *Emmie*

~

Article Nine: The Parrot-Green Dress

I looked up from my mending out of our little window built
into the thatched grass wall and spied Herman walking up
from the waterfront carrying something large and cumbersome. He
stopped, found a better hold and continued on, closer, until I could
see that he was talking to it.

Puzzled, I met him at the door.

"Mrs. Webster, I have a gift here," he said, his face open and
smiling and searching mine for a sign of forgiveness.

He held out an ornate red lacquer cage. In it was a little green
parrot the color of my dress, its feathers as shiny as taffeta.

"Alooooha," came a high-pitched voice. I could not help but to
smile.

Herman knew the Bible by heart, as if he did not trust himself to
speak without it. Sometimes it still surprised me to look at his young,
good-looking face, and then hear the solemn words of old King James
fall from his lips. "I wish to mention Ephesians chapter four, verse
thirty-two," he said, "And be ye kind one to another, tenderhearted,
forgiving one another, even as God for Christ's sake hath forgiven
you."

I bristled, looking at the bird instead of him.

"So thou still refuseth to speak to me," Herman said, putting the
birdcage down. "See here, I bought this curious bird from an East
Indiaman in from Canton. I hope thou wilt enjoy many hours of
amusement from its playful antics. I traded three Bibles for it; the
sailors were most eager to make the trade, assuring me that this creature will edify us with its peculiar way of speaking."

"Aloha, sailor," the bird said in a feminine voice. Then a low, gravelly tone came from its throat. "Sit upon me lap and taste me rum."

Herman went pale. "Thou must teach it to quote the Scriptures," he suggested firmly.

"Thank you, Reverend Webster."

"I have more to say, Mrs. Webster. This hovel is not fit for my wife. I am planning a new home for us made of coral and wood. Thou shalt have a front porch and a shade tree." He smiled with anticipation, awaiting my reaction.

"Thank you, Reverend Webster," I repeated. How I had longed to live in a real home after a more than two years on a dirt floor, and puddles in my shoes after every tropic rain. There was an awkward pause between my husband and I, both waiting for each other. He cleared his throat.

"I urge thee to spend time with thy Bible reading the fourth chapter of Ephesians, as I have," he said. "Be ye angry, and sin not. Do not let the sun go down upon your wrath." He took a deep breath. "I admit, my wrath can possess me. I ask for thy patience. I am a wretched sinner, as my father always told me."

I put down my mending and moved next to the birdcage to admire the many little sliding doors, carved scrolls, and painted gold brushstrokes on the deep red lacquer. The bird chirped and turned her head to the side as she looked at me. Her face was yellow, and her chest was bright green. A small blue-green tuft of feathers at the top of her beak was the color of shallow waters above white sand on a bright morning. She measured just larger than the size of my hand from wrist to fingertips. I opened the cage door and she stepped out on my finger, and with little feet and sideways steps she walked all the way up my arm to my shoulder. She shook her feathers, as if to shake off the past, and then sank down next to my neck, contented.

"About our disagreement." Herman said, his face contrite, and, I begrudgingly thought, rather handsome. "They that slide upon the waves are sporting on God's time. The hours spent frolicking on the waves is time stolen from eternity."

"Is eternity so short on time that one must be frugal with it?" I asked.

"As a woman thou dost not grasp the basic tenets of Theology. Let me illustrate my point. Oft have I toiled over a sermon only to deliver it to a half-empty church. This always coincides on days when the surf is big. But never before have I seen them dare to sport here on the shores right in front of our Mission!"

"The reef and curvature of the coast here seems to fashion pretty waves when the swells are big. Perhaps they have always sported here by Moku'ula."

"When Satan once ruled the land!" Herman burst. He took a deep breath and exhaled for a long moment. Then he continued, calmer, his words measured so carefully each one would fit in a thimble.

"God is here now, and evil will no longer reign. When the natives put away their dancing and games and learn Christianity and civiliza-tion—when these swamps are filled with soil, and orderly rows of corn and wheat grow in its place—Satan will no longer have his foothold."

"The Princess told me that wave-sliding is not mere frolic, but part of being alive; a path, she called it. They believe that being one with the ocean heals, cleanses, regenerates."

"Exactly," Herman said. "A belief, which is the heart of the sin of it. Do not be tempted to sympathize with them, dear wife! We have come here to make them put away false idols and gain everlasting life. Or wouldst thou be happy to have them surf Hell's molten sea of fire forevermore?"

With a flash of tropic sunlight, the door opened and Reverend Goodwin stepped in. "There are horses for all," he announced. "We will start out Tuesday at dawn."

There was to be an exploration party to see the curiosities and wonders of the unexplored parts of the island. Herman walked outside with him to talk of supplies and share rumors of what we might come across, but Goodwin paused in the doorway. Dressed as black as a raven and hair stark white in the sunlight, he turned to look at me. I turned away from him, only caring to see my new pet, but in the corner of my eye I caught his glance; he was peering his way along the long line of blackberry-glass buttons all down my green silk back. I have a foolish imagination, I told myself, shaking off chills of distaste. I am vain. Or at least that is what he would say.

Reverend Goodwin hesitated and then followed Herman out. I watched them through the window as I sat back down to my mending. Herman's body arched high and eager to discuss their plans as he walked, and Goodwin's black eyes and beaklike nose looking like a large bird of prey. I suddenly pricked my finger on a forgotten pin. I stuck my wounded finger in my mouth as I thought how many times, like a sock, can a marriage be mended? Their conversation faded away as they walked towards the mission houses. I watched them disappear, trying to clean my heart with forgiveness; I stared for the longest time, lost in thought with the taste of iron in my mouth.

THAT NIGHT the persistent tradewinds stopped, and our bedroom was left sweltering, so I took off my hot dress and hung it up on a hook along with my cotton petticoats, unlaced my corset and drew a nice deep breath. My cotton chemise was thoroughly damp although I had changed it twice that day. I carefully filled the fine porcelain bowl and set its matching Wedgwood pitcher down softly where it always sat in its place at the corner of the table. The day that Herman had given it to me was so untarnished and bright and heady with feelings of first love. His face had been nervous, and his hands had trembled like his voice as he asked me to marry him. *Yes, yes Reverend Webster*, I had answered, and in that moment I thought I would be swept away from Aunt Sallie's fate, never to be alone and waiting, never to feel unloved.

I had made up my mind, despite the challenges—I would not forever be a woman who lacked intimacy with her husband. I could hardly bear life if it draped me in sad cobwebs of romantic girlish dreams. I put drops of lavender oil in the bowl, soaking a clean washcloth with its fragrance, then pressed its coolness against my skin. I slipped on a white nightgown of the finest cotton organdy, so delicate it was sheer down to my calf where it was embroidered with a thick band of white hand-stitched sunflowers and leaves.

I unbraided my hair, and it fell below my waist. I brushed the shiny wheat-colored waves as I waited for Herman to stop working on his next sermon. But his eyes still belonged to every little black printed letter in his Bible. As I waited, I began packing what I would need for the excursion.

Herman finally looked up from the pages, removed his eyeglasses, turned up the wick to burn brighter with whale oil, and peered over to look at me. I had caught his attention.

"What art thou doing?"

"Preparing for the journey, of course."

"Thou shalt stay here, with the other wives, where thou wilt be safe."

"I am to go along. There are birds to be seen that have never been seen before. There are ferns and flowers to be discovered; the heart of any botanist in London would skip a beat at the thought of exploring these forests."

Herman's anger rose, then I watched him check it. He closed his Bible, extinguished the lamp, and got into bed.

"Then thou shalt come along, dear Catherine," he said, patting the mattress beside him. "I will be most happy to have my helpmate by my side."

I slipped into the clean sheets beside him and softly placed my hand on his hip below his waist. "He that believeth not shall be damned, and how will they ever hear the Word of God without our endorsement from this Princess?" he said, his voice rising. He then reached for my wrist and absentmindedly dropped my hand away upon the quilted space between us. I let it lie there, as motionless as a bird shot down from the sky.

We both lay there silently, he wrapped up in thoughts of his church, me thinking of the seemingly impossible and unique challenges a woman must sometimes navigate.

His body relaxed after I drew away, his voice taking on the deeper, slower tone that I liked. I imagined his whole being—his dark brown hair, those sharkskin-gray eyes, and his lean muscular body—all wrapped up in the sound of it.

No girl I had ever known spoke about lovemaking; who among us would want to give the impression of being related more to Eve than to the Virgin Mary? It was the unspoken way of Christian schoolgirls: each trying to impress one another with saintliness—much like showing off a new bonnet or parasol. Secrets and whispers of mothers and sisters made my girlfriends' wide eyes wise, while in my house there was only talk of ships and lumber and perhaps a muttered curse that slipped out before it was remembered I was in the room.

Having no mother to guide me in my younger years, Emmaline had been my only source for feminine advice. Embarrassed to speak plainly, there was a curtain inside her that drew closed just when I needed to know the most intimate particulars—as if she assumed I knew everything a wife needs to know. In the past two years I had yearned for Herman to teach me but was deserted of his affections. Aunt Sallie had never enlightened me—she could not—for she had been waiting her whole life for love, never knowing it for herself.

"Surfing princesses and goddesses!" Herman's sudden gust of words, in the context of silence, were difficult for my mind to catch up with.

"The latter is a fanciful delusion and the former should be. False idols, carved in a woman's form! Such is this upside-down heathen land we are in, where a woman holds power to cast missionaries away! Goodwin tells me repeatedly that it will be best to have Princess Leilani's blessing—not from the young prince, or the chiefs, or even the Queens, but from her."

What do you say to a husband whose thoughts are like strangers?

"Mrs. Herman Webster, thou art what a woman should be; my own wife, a rib taken from my side, submissive and pure."

I lay there silently staring at the thatched ceiling feeling as if he had placed a heavy stone upon my stomach. A stray thought, as if a little savior, came to me, wild and unafraid. I yearned to be like Leilani and feel the power and life of a wave bring her sailing craft beneath my feet. I wished goddesses were real and that 'Mrs. Webster' was fiction.

I listened to Herman's breath until, to my relief, it became heavy with sleep, and then he began to snore. I turned and looked through the open window at a lonely star and tried to pray. The longer I was a missionary, the harder that was to do.

CHAPTER 4

Article Ten: A Ruffled Pink Night Dress

The sound of trees swishing like taffeta skirts wakened me. I thought it was a lingering dream of gowns moving and spinning at a ball, but as I lay there a gust of wind shook an orchestra of branches outside and whispered through the walls of the grass-thatched hale telling me I was still on an island faraway from home where I had dwelt for two years and three months.

In the dim room came the sudden sound of china breaking onto the hard matted floor and I sat up, startled. Herman was gone, as he often was in the mornings: still up at the printing house—Hale Pa'i— or practicing a sermon up at the church, or praying down along the seashore, as he always told me.

I lit the brass chamberstick beside the bed and peered down in the flickering light. There on the wet woven mat my precious china pitcher lay with its handle broken off. Aloha's cage was swaying from the wind-shaken rafter, and must have knocked it over. I needed fresh water to wash and dress, so I sadly took up the body of my pitcher and set out to get more.

I had slept in my pink chemise. It was edged along the top next to my chest with delicate, almost doll-sized ruffles made of the same fine cotton. I put my gray velvet cloak on over it, for dawn had not yet lit the sky and surely no-one would see me in such an indecent state.

I walked south towards a freshwater stream that flowed through underground lava tubes from Kaua'ula Valley down to meet the sea. Behind me, a faint glow of dawn began to reveal the outline of the jagged mountains that guarded Moku'ula. I passed through a thick bower of closed, sleeping koki'o flowers and reached a pool. As I knelt there, a gust of wind sent the bodies of the unopened pale pink flowers across the rippling surface, looking like little ice skaters.

Suddenly, there was a movement behind me and a burst of warm air on the back of my neck. I jumped, spun, and saw a shadowy beast looming above me in the dim light. It snorted at me, and I was sickly afraid that it was a wild bullock. The living air smelled familiar—like grass and grain and molasses. The dawn light became just a shade lighter, and I realized it was a horse.

His reins trailed past me like a snake as he moved to lean down to drink. I slowly reached out and caught them.

The sky and sea turned from dark pewter to a blue-gray, the shade of my cloak; I blended almost invisible as I spied another figure moving on the other side of the pond; it was the man looking for his horse. He slowly walked up to me and the spirit of the wind whooshed its way into my heart and veins, for there in the growing light I recognized the vaquero Diego Cruz.

"Gracias," he said. "The wind frightened him loose." He gestured to his horse whose velvet mouth jerked up, dripping with water, its hooves dancing skittishly in the gusts.

"You are welcome." I said, glancing down at my pitcher hugged into the curve of my waist, turning to show him the short broken piece on its side that was once part of a handle. "The wind…"

I held the reins out to him and neither of us let go. "Thank you for saving me from the ocean that day," I said.

I felt his energy through the leather and he connected with mine, as if our souls had just begun their first waltz. We stood there a moment longer. Then another. And then, as if an orchestra had stopped, I let go and we both slowly stepped away.

As I walked back, cool air moved up towards me through the low shadows, chilled by the waters of Mokuhinia. Beyond the waves and sleeping ships, lavender dawn clouds atop Moloka'i were changing to butter yellow. A thrill lit up my heart as if something lost inside me was stirring to life. The tall arches of great old koki'o bushes moved above my head, and the first rays of sunlight touched the edges of the pale flower petals with a glow, waking them to open up and receive a new day.

CHAPTER 5

Article Eleven: The White Sprigged Calico Trimmed in Blue

The Mission building that housed Hawai'ian girls faced southwest and was fringed by red ginger plants, its long lanai shaded by generous wooden eves. It lay inside not one but two volcano-stone walls that were dark chocolate brown spotted with gray and green lichen, and it was home to Mary and Charity's Christian Female Seminary, a boarding school where young girls were taken in to learn Godliness and the arts of civilization and propriety.

We had fourteen armed with needle and thread that morning, ready and waiting on benches set against the plastered white walls between tall windows trimmed with French blue sills and shutters. Yards of strong cotton duck had been donated to the mission by a ship out of Charleston, with which we could make riding breeches for the older boys and young men who wished to become vaqueros. They lined up as quiet and proper as soldiers to be surveyed by Mary's measuring tape, as their being admitted inside the mission enclave only happened under special circumstances.

Thaddeus was there, wanting to be fitted for a black cutaway coat like one I had made recently for Herman. I suspected it was his excuse to see Tabitha, who sat arranging sewing notions primly under Mary's watch, stealing glances his way whenever her mother turned around.

The girls were eagerly spreading the cotton out flat and smooth, ready to be cut. I leafed past my sketch pages of dresses that looked like ruffled flowers, then sat with pencil and paper staring at a blank page. I always fell into my designs, delighting in possibilities, but that day I struggled trying to remember the cut particular to the Californio horsemen. I couldn't focus on exactly how the design of the riding trousers would be constructed; my thoughts kept wandering instead to a certain vaquero and how he wore them. I looked at the tip of my pencil and tried to concentrate. The trousers were close-fitted like pantaloons, buttoned tightly from hip down to knee, and then they grew uncommonly wider as they went down to fit around the boot, long enough to meet the bottom of the heel when sitting in a saddle.

A sudden pull in my chest lifted my head up from the paper and who should I see but the vaquero Cruz being ushered across the yard towards me by Reverend Goodwin. A light shiver brushed down my arms as they headed straight for me and up to where I sat on the wooden porch.

"Sister Catherine, let me introduce you to Señor Cruz. As the Queen has ordered that her riders will have proper pantaloons, he has agreed to advise you on the matter." He looked down at the horseman's legs and added, "But no silver buttons, of course. I know you will design something more practical."

"I am pleased to meet you, Señor Cruz," I said holding out my hand, for naturally it could not be known that I had already met him twice before, once in my clinging, wet blue indigo torn at the chest, and more recently in my nightdress.

I was now respectably presentable beneath a crisp white organza apron over my white calico dotted with sprays of pale gray-blue roses and trimmed with French blue edges. No longer trying so hard to earn missionary approval, I wore curls at my temple again and arranged the rest of my hair more becomingly as I once did up at the crown of my head.

"My name is Diego Alejandro Fernando Vicente Cruz," he said in that strong, warm voice, "But I am known to my friends as Diego. If it pleases you madam, call me Diego." He was taller than I, and he would still be a nice height even out of his thick leather boots.

Shocked at my thought, I took up my cloth measuring tape. Reverend Goodwin stayed. His square jaw dropped like a marionette as he prepared to speak further.

"The Princess has repented of her nakedness and surf riding and wishes for new dresses," he told me as I wrapped my tape around the vaquero's slim waist. "We must engage her immediately before she requests them from others and we lose her favor. There are merchants quite eager to gain her favor with fancy European wardrobes, and a French brig has just anchored which will contain goods from Europe. I do not have to tell you how critical it is to have her turn to us American missionaries for the things she desires."

"My shipment of fabric never arrived," I said as I struggled to remember the waist size I had just taken. Diego made my thoughts blur. I pressed the pencil hard, wrote 32, and then carefully reached around him again to measure twice. I brought the tape together at his side. He smelled of tobacco and oranges.

Reverend Goodwin was nettled. "My dear, what kind of dress-maker has no fabric?"

"The ship that carried my new goods was a whaler. I heard she passed by our Sandwich Isles in her haste to get to the sperm whaling grounds off Japan."

"But thou must have fabric! It is your sole duty here!" Reverend Goodwin insisted, his brow furrowing, fingers holding his chin as he thought. I touched Diego's waist with the end of the tape and stretched it way down the outside of his leg to his spur. It slipped from his waist and as I reached it back up he softly placed his fingers over mine to help hold it. They were calm and strong.

"Ah! We may have a solution," Goodwin said, and I quickly pulled my fingers away from under Diego's.

"The Royals have a storehouse. When the great king was alive in the decade past, he built a storage house to put the many goods given to him in trade for sandalwood. Perhaps there are bolts of silk and satin from Canton. I will seek permission to go there and we can make some use of their wasted earthly treasures."

I put the measuring tape around Diego's knee and held it there by placing my hand against him. Almost imperceptibly, he leaned into my palm. Then I slid my hand down to take in the width of his boot. His spurs were sharp silver Spanish stars.

Then Reverend Goodwin left, and I looked up into Diego's face. His chiseled lips turned soft at the corners. "Señorita, will you be with the expedition?" he asked.

"Yes. I wish to see the beautiful flowers and birds," I said. "I would like to sketch and paint them with watercolors, as I do my dresses."

"Muy bonita," he said. The way he looked at me made me wonder if he meant flowers were beautiful, or I.

"Mrs. Webster, have we more thimbles?" Tabitha asked, suddenly beside me, and I realized she was repeating her question.

"Thank you, Señor Diego," I said primly. "Come, Tabitha, I will show you where they are kept, and let me help you find the thickest and strongest needles and thread."

When I turned and looked back across the yard I caught Diego staring at me. He tipped the straight brim of his hat and then he disappeared around the corner of the mission house.

CHAPTER 6

*I*t was arranged that I would be transported by a double-hulled canoe around the southwestern cape of the island and then taken by litter across a field of sun-baked lava. I was embarrassed to be seen upon such a pompous conveyance, but traveling thus was common for women, and I soon realized that I would not have survived the excursion otherwise.

Four porters beneath me carried a long, thick bamboo pole on each shoulder, and fastened tightly atop these poles were the legs of a sturdy chair upon which I sat, swaying along; a Japanese parasol was attached atop the chair's high ladder-back to provide shade. On and up we went over a barren plain of tree stumps as we ascended the lower slopes of the volcano.

From my view up across the heat waves I spied it, built of lava rock and set into the mountainside. The Royal Storehouse was a tomb of riches gained by trading away the forests of ʻiliahi—sandalwood—that had once covered this dry plain. How many birds had sung in their branches, and where did they fly to on that day when their world came crashing down?

The Queen's men stayed at the door as I stepped into the inky, mildewed darkness. The air smelled of age, as if those who last breathed it were no longer upon this earth.

I lifted the lantern and gasped softly. There, all around me were massive piles of forgotten goods that deadened the sound of my square-toed shoes as I found a narrow, winding trail in the shifting yellow light. It shined on a large, black ebony carriage with red velvet curtains. There were stacks and stacks of porcelain china vases, bowls, and plates. There was an open crate revealing a treasure of green crystal goblets that glowed like emeralds in a sharp beam of sunlight peeking through the doorway. I walked further back until it all towered above me: unopened boxes upon boxes stamped Dutch East India Company and others burned with Chinese symbols. A silent harpsichord sat with dusty keys. Pelts of dry sealskin lay stacked upon each other that once lived, sliding through the clear, sunny waters off the coast of Alta California.

And then I stopped and smiled. There before me were bolts and bolts of Canton silk, damask, linen, and cambric. Satin kimonos embroidered with gilt and silken threads glowed in the yellow light. There were ruby, amethyst, amber, and sapphire folds of luminous velvet woven from the threads of silk worms. And I had once thought that my thirty folds brought from New Bedford were coming to save them.

I set the lantern down upon a wooden crate and reached for the velvet, dug my fingers into it, soft as worm webs and rose petals. It melted from my fingers.

I pulled the bolt out into the sun, and then another bolt, and then another. It was all ruined. All the sandalwood stripped from the hillside—once so lush with ferns and birds and shade—had been traded for this rotting silk.

CHAPTER 7

I brought my cloth measuring tape around Princess Leilani's waist. We stood on a dais covered with woven makaloa mats, visiting pleasantly in the happy, languid afternoon breeze.

Entering royal Moku'ula had been as intimidating as always. I had been paddled in by four imposing native men along canals and fishponds and across Mokuhinia lake to a wooden dock, where beneath a grand native open-air structure with a tall pointed roof I had found the waiting Princess.

She was surrounded by her servants, several chiefesses, and a society of flatterers that flutter like moths around any royal circle. They looked at me sideways, some with admiration and some with suspicion as I settled on the soft, finely woven lauhala mats patterned with palm shadows. The ocean air flowed in over the waterways keeping us cool from the persistent sun. The flag of the Hawai'ian Kingdom with its British Union Jack and a red, white, or blue stripe for each island softly snapped in the breeze above us. As my sharp scissors began cutting through plain muslin to create a new pattern I fell into the peaceful, calming work that Aunt Sallie had taught me so well to do.

"Tell me," Leilani asked just like the women did in Aunt Sallie's studio, "will this new dress be the latest style? When will I have it?

"I must make amends for my surf-riding and be more civilized," she went on in her well-schooled English. No-one taught as thoroughly as a missionary, and none learned anything more quickly than the Hawai'ians.

"Princess," I said, as if asking for a secret a missionary would never know. "How are you brave enough to master the waves? I often fear for your life."

She laughed with delight. "How would I not master them? They have been part of me since I could stand. They are part of my *mana*— my life force."

I cut a sleeve pattern from muslin and held it to her arm, marking where I needed to revise it to make it fit exactly the way I wanted it to. "Make me a dress with strong mana," she said as she fingered a ruffle on my calico dress. "Sometimes I do not feel it in these clothes, as if I am trying on a dress that doesn't fit. For the last year it has been strongly suggested to me that I think about marrying a Christian man on another island who lives inland, without even a little peek of the ocean. He doesn't even wave-slide." She let out a soft, scoffing laugh.

She struggled on to make sense of it all. "I must have every advantage and bear myself like any other sovereign and help lead our people in these times—we are like a small fish, fearing the mouths of larger ones." She glanced up at their flag, so similar to that of the British East India Company. "The United Kingdom protects us, yet respects us as we stand independent. My brother plans to draft our own constitution inspired by theirs."

I removed a pin held between my lips to fasten two cut pieces so that I could baste them together. "You have a way of making anything you wear serve you well, Your Majesty."

"It serves me well to be dressed in a Christian manner; they say that by ruling in the name of the Christian God my kingdom can stand shoulder-to-shoulder with any who come to challenge us."

A minute went by filled with silent sounds; my fingers pushing needle and thread through muslin, feather fans stroking the gentle wind, her eyes turning to stare out at the ships at anchor. "I have granted a Captain Warwick, of the brig Archangel from Liverpool, an audience with me," she said. "There is word that he has the dresses I ordered months ago."

I must have looked startled, because she reached down and hugged me as I sat on the thick pile of mats. "Don't worry, dear Kittie. We do not need pins and thread and cloth to be friends."

"We leave on expedition tomorrow," I promised, "but I will have your new dress in two weeks time."

She smiled. "I will look forward to it. A dress from you fits perfectly, and I like how the design holds your mana."

It perplexed me that my spirit could somehow live on in something I had created. I folded and tucked the idea up neatly into my sewing basket along with the muslin pattern-pieces.

Then the Princess ordered food to be brought out for us. We used heavy silver forks to eat fluffy cooked fish seasoned with finely cut seaweed and sea salt, ate purple poi paste from a smooth wooden bowl, and sipped cocoa-nut juice from red glass goblets. The gentle surf broke in the distance and a cool breeze reached out to us across the water canals.

I took these waterways home; they were her kingdom's roads, and well suited—no dust, no need for carts—as people and goods moved smoothly along to their destinations. I sat in a large, wide canoe built to float serenely on the shallow water. A steersman sat at the stern, and with well-built shoulders he guided the craft along quiet waterways that wound past grass houses and verdant fields of growing taro.

From somewhere along the shore came the gentle sound of the 'ohe hano ihu—a nose flute. Little Pua had told me of their belief that the flute's haunting song was the pure essence of the soul because it was played by the breath of the nose, whereas air that came from the mouth could be polluted by words. That it wasn't because words were so unclean as much as the breath, or Ha, was so pure. That right there inside each one of us lived the sacred breath of Life. Herman preached that we were natural vessels of impurity, contaminated since Eden, shameful and low, and he made sure no one ever forgot it.

The water carried me peacefully along, and even as I was lulled by the haunting song I sighed with worry. I looked down at the clouds in the liquid sky and said a prayer.

I still had nothing to make her dress with. A merchant had told me that a ship had rounded the Horn carrying his goods, some being textiles, and should arrive in a fortnight. The only plan I could think of was to wait for it, and then sew day and night as soon as I had my yards of the silk, or cambric, or fine cotton lawn that would be a dress fit for a princess.

CHAPTER 8

Article Twelve: A Yellow Scarf

The expedition began in cold silence. Herman stared straight between the ears of his horse and would not look at me. I had won, and I looked up in wonder at the early morning light showing faintly through the towering black trees, joyous that I had come along after all.

I had been standing by the horses, looking for my mount, when Herman pulled me aside and said in a low voice that only I could hear, "Why, thou art here—I did not notice. You will stay home and sew the dress."

"But I have not yet the fabric! And you said I was to be included."

"Surely something could have been salvageable from the royal storehouse," he had said, excited for the expedition to start, too impatient to temper his words with lovingkindness. "Thou art failing not just as my wife, but also in your calling. Thy Princess still cavorts in the surf and ye neglect thy job as her dressmaker. The other mission women accomplish a multitude of chores in a single day, yet ye seem to require a month to sew a single dress."

"I cannot always create something in a single day," I said. "Even God needed seven."

"Thou art blasphemous," he hissed right into my ear, loud enough for it to hurt. "I think perhaps ye intend to be the wife of a disgraced missionary. Wouldst thou prefer to be the wife of a man in shame? His new occupation perhaps a postal clerk, or a pig farmer?"

"Not if he loved me."

A man's will can be like an invisible wall. How to navigate around it and find your own way is a skill difficult to master. He could physically force his decisions if he chose, and it takes sound logic to pierce through his imagination of how he decides the world should be. I ignored him and looked around for the horse that had been appointed to me.

Keola, one of Thaddeus' friends, smiled at me and started to lead me to my horse when Herman swept over and shoved him away to the shock of all present. This was precisely when Princess Leilani had arrived to see us off on the big excursion.

"You will cease to touch my people so rudely," she commanded. Herman had no choice but to stand down and let me come along.

Under her measuring eye, the party continued to make ready to depart. Diego came towards me leading a beautiful buckskin mare with a creamy golden coat and long black mane and tail. A woman had the disadvantage of sitting sidesaddle and there were none to be had, but he had fastened a second stirrup on the left side for me. As I settled up on the horse, he moved to the right side and tied the right stirrup securely so that it would not flap about. I looked down at him. His hands were strong, yet gentle and polite. He checked the girth, and then ran his palm kindly along the horse's neck. As he handed me the thick leather reins he pressed a golden yellow scarf of the finest wool into my hand. I did not understand why. When he had walked away and no-one else noticed it or claimed it, I tied it about the neck of my chestnut brown riding habit.

· · ·

WANTING to be as far away from Herman as possible, I rode up at the front of our equine procession with Thaddeus, Keola, and Diego, and from them I learned a great deal more about the island. They had taught Diego the Hawai'ian art of stringing of flowers into lei, and they all wore the braided fern and flowers around the crown of their large-brimmed hats woven from dried grass to resemble Diego's sombrero. A blend of two customs became something new as different cultures made friends.

I studied Thaddeus' ease upon his horse. Showing no visible movement with his hands on the reins his horse seemed to follow his mind, avoiding a rock, a ditch, a branch in the trail.

He told me about his lost father. "He is a great vaquero, in San Diego," he said. "Maybe why I like to ride horses. May be why he stayed far away, becoming a Californio."

Ships take a person to faraway places, different and unknown, on journeys often so perilous or wandering that there is no guarantee of returning. Once you find life in a new world, the life you once had fades. One changes so much that the other becomes another lifetime ago. Was it was beginning to happen to me?

As we rode along they talked about the fruit of this native tree, or the benefits of that fern. To the sound of stories told to the rhythm of hoofbeats thumping along the trail and as birds called down from the towering trees Keola described ancient warriors who once used a secret path straight through the mountains from the eastern side, a passage generally thought to be impossible.

We rode our horses between hanging vines and through the deep vegetation until I could hear the faint sound of water. Soon we came upon a deep pool, dark jade in the morning light, into which cascaded a waterfall that spilled from atop a cliff higher than a crow's nest. Flowers of lavender, white, and yellow reached towards the sun. Ferns, like furry little animals, curled upwards to embrace the mist.

We continued on until Keola brought us to a sudden stop. Hand hanging in mid-air, he listened intently. We all strained our ears until he let his hand fall back down to his reins, and he turned and said to me: "I thought I heard the singing. I wanted you to hear it. The voice of the forest."

"The—voice of the forest?" I said, not knowing how else to answer.

"Deep up in the sacred heights they sing. Maybe you'll hear it, by 'an by." He looked around, as if to feel the forest, and then said almost to himself, "When the voices are alive, we are alive."

There in that moment I could believe anything Keola wished to tell; I had not felt such a magic sense of wonder since I was a child. Here I was, Catherine Helmsley Webster, deep in an ancient forest in the middle of the Pacific Ocean, so far away from New England that I hardly cared to recall it at all. I breathed in the living scent of the trees and only wanted to be exactly where I was.

We rode deeper into the island, past large rocks carved with ancient symbols. One reminded me of Leilani: a figure on a surfing board with rays of light coming from the head.

And of course there were the birds, with extraordinary patterns of feathers and hues like little dresses from French fashion plates. Whenever we made stops to water the horses and stretch I took out my pencil. I leafed through my sketch book past dresses to a blank page where I recorded the birds, flowers, ferns and the rock art of the surfing goddess as faithfully as I could.

I was lost in my artwork when Diego passed by me long enough to say, "Muy bien, Señorita. You are gifted." I tore my eyes up from the paper, only to see his broad back walking away.

At night by the campfire he serenaded us with his guitarre. His fingers touched the humming strings and brought out exquisite melodies that carried me away with visions of warm California breezes under great oak trees, of air damp with the breath of the ocean flowing inland in at night, of haciendas where orchestras of guitarres played to the rhythm of dancing feet and swirling skirts. Once, when he looked up at me as he played, I touched the yellow scarf around my neck and smiled. His smile in return glowed brightly in the firelight.

When it grew late, Herman curtly told me to join him in our tent. "Come along now, we will go to bed, my wife," he said, quiet enough to sound proper but loud enough to perhaps be heard as a good husband that always slept at home every night.

Thankfully, he fell asleep quickly in his usual position, flat on his back with hands crossed on his chest like a corpse. I lay there listening to the faint sound of Diego's guitarre as those that were still up enjoyed the glowing embers of the fading fire. At length the camp grew still, but his guitarre played on in my mind as I finally fell asleep, but I slept lightly.

I WAS AWAKENED BY MUSIC. I felt dawn rising and I sat up, listening. This time it was not a guitarre; it was soft, like thousands of faraway angels. It sounded as if the trees were singing.

Herman was still dead to the world. I pulled a blanket tightly around myself like a cloak and stepped outside upon footsteps slow with wonder. At the edge of our camp the trees parted to show the waning moon hanging in the sky like a little boat.

I smelled the scent of cigarillos and in the dim light Keola and his friends sat with Diego by the horses. "Listen," came Keola's voice quietly towards me out of the blue shadows. "Kāhuli. The land shells that sing. The voice of the forest."

Then he softly uttered a chant:

> *Kahuli aku*
> *Kahuli mai*
> *Kahuli lei ula*
> *Lei akolea*

I had gathered a handful of the shells on our exploration. They were each a little work of art, like miniature porcelain painted by fairies—shaped like sea shells, and perhaps more colorful. Each one was unique with swirls of candy stripes—periwinkle, yellow, ivory, persimmon, and black.

The ethereal song continued as the forest mist grew lavender with light. I wandered from our camp and found myself surrounded by soft, pale, tiny globes like pearls clinging to tree trunks, branches, ferns. Pink and cream-colored shells glowed in butter light cast by the approach of the morning sun, each delicate shape and pattern beckoning me. They were vibrating in lush waves like conch shells do, but each a sound so tiny and soft that it would have been barely audible if not for their vast numbers chiming in together finding resonance and harmony. Like a million tiny violins it came from far away and deep within the vast tropical forest to surround us—a marvel, like delicate piano strings left open and humming that find the tones of a chord.

Diego drew beside me and we both stood in awe. He offered me his arm. A single bird began to sing, answered by another, then another—and they joined in the symphony of the Kāhuli.

Diego and I reluctantly walked back towards the campfire where Keola and the other horsemen sat. No words were spoken between us. There is another language that lies beyond words—more elegant, more sacred.

Diego pulled out his guitarre and touched the strings, chiming along with the forest until the song began to fade in the first rays of the sun. The fire was stoked, a coffee pot put on. Horses and people stirred. I did not want it to end.

When we returned home to the mission, I realized that I had forgotten my homesick habit of counting the days. I suddenly remembered Leilani's dress, and so with Aloha on my shoulder I set out down towards the wharf to speak to the merchant and see what could be had.

He greeted me with a grimace and muttered, "I 'ave no goods. The ship was lost. Stove by a whale, or never made it 'round the Horn." His face was wide and his red cheeks were framed with thick salt-and-pepper sideburns that wandered down along his jawline to his chin, or at least where that once had been as a younger man.

Aloha flapped her wings. "Damn ye to Hell," she squawked.

"Quite a mouth on that one!" He laughed. "I'm sorry, Mrs. Webster, but I cannot show you any fine fabrics."

"But you must have something!" I said.

He scratched the whiskers along his chin, staring at me. His teeth were black at the gums. "The best I have is blue-striped ticking."

Reverend Goodwin had pressed Herman at breakfast as to how the garment was coming along, and even Leilani had sent a messenger to ask when she might try it on. But the only material I had at hand was the invisible kind, once storied to have been used to fashion The Emporer's New Clothes, for no amount of style can keep a dress made of ticking from looking like a mattress.

CHAPTER 9

Article Thirteen: My Mother's Hymnal

On Monday when the church was empty I sat down at a shiny new organ. I began to play, smiling at the sound of the breathy bellows, still damp from its voyage as it sang a soothing sound of home faraway.

"Bless you, Catherine," Charity Thatcher said, unashamed of her tears. "It has been so long since I heard the sound of a hymn played on an organ." She and her seminary students were sweeping the floor and sorting stacks of freshly printed Bibles to set out on the pews. Happy as a brown robin, she had been singing along in delight as she fluttered gently in charge of her brood of young girls.

Then the sound of boots and silver spurs joined with the chords and melody, and to my delight in came Diego with his guitarre slung at his back.

"I have invited our Vaquero; he is a Catholic," Charity said. "Mary is of the mind that he will not be allowed into church, but I think that if she heard him play a hymn on his guitarre she might remember that

Jesus welcomed all. Would you teach our Californio something from your little hymnal?"

My mother's hymnal was the reason I began sewing pockets in all my dresses in the first place. We had a painting of her hung above her favorite chair that had been stained in my mind for as long as I could remember. Her oil-painted eyes were soft, her smile kind, and she wore a black ribbon tied around her head. Her hair was arranged in a high topknot, she wore a pale yellow, empire-waist dress, and in her kind hands was the hymnal. Ever since the age of four I had carried it around with me as if I were holding her hand. The little book had followed me from childhood nursery to Female Seminary, from singing its melodies in a New Bedford church to this one halfway around the world.

I smiled at Diego shyly and fingered through the small pages. I stopped at an illustration of angels and played the song next to it. I found Diego to be quick, and soon we were playing in unison.

Charity called over from the far corner of the sanctuary. "Oh, dear Catherine. The organ and guitarre sound like a Heavenly orchestra." Then the joy of a new idea sprang to life in her voice. "Girls! Would you like to learn to sing? We can begin a choir!" They talked excitedly, no longer paying any attention to Diego and me.

He stood close to the bench that I sat upon. We did not know what to say. He toyed with the guitarre strings, fingers sliding up and down the neck, not really playing it. I ran my fingertips across the keys, not pressing down all the way; it was more of an affectionate gesture.

"Please play us another!" Charity called out. I thought of my favorite hymn, found it, and began to play.

Were the whole realm of nature mine
That were a present far too small
Love so amazing, so divine
Demands my soul, my life, my all

I stole a glance at Diego. He was softly touching his guitarre strings, learning the song by ear. Soon he began playing it in earnest and the sound of us lifted my soul.

Love so amazing, so divine
Demands my soul, my life, my all

I never imagined how beautiful the song would sound on guitarre. When it ended and the last echo of our instruments echoed away to a pregnant silence I swallowed away a swell of tears. A thought came to me as I reached up and felt his yellow scarf around my throat.

"Diego, I meant to thank you for giving me your beautiful scarf. Let us make a trade: you may borrow my little hymnal. Perhaps if you learn all the songs within it the missionaries will be pleased."

The unspoken truth of it was that his presence was only tolerated because the Royals wanted his horses and knowledge, but to the American Board of Foreign Missions a Catholic was never welcome. It was not long ago that missionaries on O'ahu were severe in their efforts to keep a ship of Catholic priests from disembarking; they were permitted rations of fresh water and foodstuffs and sent right back over the ocean from which they had come.

I was embarrassed at the way my fingers trembled as I handed my hymnal to Diego, so I quickly pushed it into his hand.

"The cover is damaged, Señorita," he said, rubbing his thumb on the hard, seawater-damaged leather. I was almost content just to sit there listening to the way his voice resonated from his cheekbones, then down into his throat where it sounded low, in that place where smiles and secrets live.

"My dear mother had kept it perfectly, but I regret that it suffered a kiss from the ocean on our voyage over," I finally said.

"She surely misses you," he said.

"She passed away when I was born. Her devotion inspired me to answer the call as a missionary. That, and the urging of my friend Emmaline at school."

He put the hymnal inside his vest and stood to go. "Gracias. I hope to see you soon. Come down to see the riders work with toros if it pleases you."

"I cannot be seen anywhere beyond the mission, for I am expected to be working on a dress for the Princess."

"I remember the Reverend was speaking to you of this on the day you measured me, Señorita." I must have looked quite hopeless, because he leaned in, waiting to hear more.

"I have no velvets or silks for a fine dress," I sighed. "I am pressed on all sides to produce it, and I have nothing but thread and a muslin pattern to make it with."

Diego was silent but his eyes were full; it was hard to read what he was thinking. Then he bowed and was gone. Charity and her girls gathered around the organ like a flock of happy birds, eager for their first singing lesson.

Charity eagerly arranged her skirts as she sat down to play. "Catherine, go take back up your dressmaking duties," she said. "I will tell no one that you were here. Oh, to hear this played so beautifully," she beamed at me. "Thank you."

The sound of a C scale beginning its ascent up the keyboard echoed behind me as I walked through the church doors and out into the empty day.

CHAPTER 10

"You have outdone yourself, Mrs. Webster," Reverend Goodwin said with a creaky smile shifting across his hard lips.

"A good balance between proper and becoming," Mary said.

"Most delightful," smiled Doctor Thatcher.

"You have a lovely gift with dressmaking," said Charity.

"My wife is a blessing," boasted Herman.

The Princess turned around with the look of enchantment that is always worn on the face of a woman who has just put on a beautiful dress. Her handmaidens sighed in awe and envy, and the young boys who brushed the air around her with feathers to keep away flies momentarily forgot their duty.

The bodice and skirt were made of perfectly fitted aquamarine velvet, and peeking out at the neck and sleeves and hem where the soft blue fabric stylishly permitted it were waves of frothy white silk. The neckline was low, like a ballgown, which suited the climate and set off her beautiful honey-brown shoulders. She wore a blue velvet ribbon around her neck, and her hair was pulled into a loose braid in which little white blossoms were woven.

"Guard yourself from vanity as you wear it, my dear," Reverend

Goodwin told her. "Remember Matthew, verse twenty-eight: And why take ye thought for raiment? Consider the lilies of the field, how they grow; they toil not, neither do they spin: And yet I say unto you, that even Solomon in all his glory was not arrayed like one of these." Having said that, he stood back and smiled at his achievement. "They would salute you in any royal court of Europe, dear Princess."

Leilani looked over at him, her hand expertly leading the thick skirt as she turned. "Do you really think so, Reverend?" she asked quietly.

"You may dress like a European royal," Mary said, "but a princess of France would never cavort naked upon the ocean waves. Your highness engages in a shameful activity that will keep her soul from entering Heaven."

Leilani dropped the heavy hem and stood still. "A princess of France would never surf-ride if she had the chance? Do you mean to say that they look at our sporting in disdain?"

"I mean no offense," Reverend Goodwin said uncomfortably. "Thy kingdom is to be admired, but I'm afraid Europeans would consider wave-sliding quite heathen and thou wilt not to be taken seriously. They may not all realize that the Sandwich Island population is now one of the most literate in the world—I estimate that our efforts have increased it to 91 percent."

"Yes, I know" replied Leilani. "My people are quick to learn."

"We have been blessed to accomplish much here," the Reverend said with a little bow. "Do not thank me, all praise goes to the Almighty. Now, about that matter we had discussed of building new churches, with your royal permission, circling the island..."

I wondered if the feather fly-swatter brushed his head on purpose as Leilani and her retinue walked away. I turned around to look back at her as our boat slid away from Moku'ula with its palace of grass-thatched roofs standing tall like the letter A—she was a splash of blue and laughter under feather standards and palms that waved in the soft breeze coming in from the ocean.

My relief was great; I had accomplished the dress. The fine, white silk was sacrificed from an unworn petticoat of mine that Aunt Sallie had lovingly made; there was just enough, once I had cut it all up. And after all my searching and praying, I had discovered the startlingly blue silk velvet wrapped in a soft leather bundle on my doorstep early one recent morning.

There can be no mistakes in cutting or especially stitching velvet—if a seam is wrong and taken out it will always show. With careful design I had managed to cut it so there was just enough for the over-skirt and Leilani's generous bodice and with the scraps I had made bows. No expert would ever have guessed that it had once been the prized cloak of a vaquero.

CHAPTER 11

Article Fourteen: A Pendant, In The Shape Of The Sun

SEPTEMBER, 1833

*A*nd did I show Diego the vaquero my appreciation? It is not always easy to find a bridge between two worlds. Sometimes it appears when least expected, and other times it is scarce to be found.

One day, most of the California horses were loaded onto a ship and all four vaqueros sailed with them. It pulled anchor and disappeared off to the Big Island to help teach the riding and saddle-making skills of the vaquero there. Eight months passed with no news of them, and not even Pua knew when Señor Cruz was planning to return to Maui.

If Diego came back, I was uncertain I'd have the chance to see him again, for my freedom was sharply restricted: such a great number of ships with lawless men had begun to anchor at Lahaina that I was rarely permitted outside of the mission buildings.

Herman had made good on his promise and built a house for me on the hill near the Mission with a commanding view of the harbor. It was made of lumber from the Northern coast of California, painted white, and boasted thick amber bottle-glass windows taken from an old ship; a captain had once looked through them at the stern of his vessel to see a churning wake cut through deep billows of the sea. Now Aloha's cage had a view out to Lahaina Roads where a great many ships were preparing to sail back around the Horn; for it was fall, and in those latitudes December was summer, the season holding the most hope for a safe passing.

I stood next to Aloha staring at the shapes of the islands of Moloka'i and Lāna'i in the distance. I could see the *Averick* testing sails and fastening barrels tight. She was a whaler bound back for Nantucket, a Captain Edward Swain—a good Christian man with his wife aboard. Having dependably brought the fifth company of missionaries out to Honolulu, he would surely take on a certain precious cargo and see it safely delivered to America.

Aloha twitched as Herman burst into the room. "And how are ye faring today, my beloved wife?" he asked, irritation showing through his transparent words.

"Fare thee well, and take ye plenty rum," Aloha said, ruffling her feathers before setting them smoothly back into place.

Herman glowered at her. "How is thy work with the Princess coming along? Has she learned to surrender her will to our Lord God in all things?" He took a pause that put dread inside me. "I hear the natives are gathering to watch for surf—out of our sight—far up North, beneath the cliffs at Honolua. Dost thou know this to be true? Ask thy native girl."

He drew near and looked down at my half-sketched and watercolored work spread across the table. "What, pray tell, is this?" he asked. "Painting pretty skirts striped with colored ribbons? Dost thou need to waste time as a dilettante when a simple draft will do?"

"These are not dresses, they are land shells," I told him. "I collected them to record what I saw on our expedition last winter."

He gestured fiercely, causing Aloha to lose her perch and flap against the sides of her cage. "Surely thou dost not think that thy work could be worthy of the printing press," he said as he took one page and threw it into the fireplace. I gasped and grabbed his arm as the edges began to curl brown and smoke. The fire grew brighter, and then it was gone.

"How do you dare?!" I cried. "What darkness has been brewing inside you today to be so cruel to your own wife?"

"Forgive me, Catherine." Confusion, rage, and guilt fought their way across his face. "I have tried—thou hast a fine house for a missionary."

My voice rose higher. "It is not a house that I want as much as a husband, my equal, who sees our love as worthy, who does not desert me at night."

"Perhaps I am not worthy of thee—and yet—I have been patient. Thou spendeth idle time playing artist, while I toil to save souls!" He looked at me squarely with desperation in his bloodshot, shining eyes as he reached for his Bible and held it up: his reason, his commandment, his badge.

"Can ye not see that some days it feels as if we are losing the battle? If we fail, souls will be lost to the fires of Hell! Yea, they will burn there for eternity with our names upon their anguished lips, saying 'Thou couldst have saved us, Reverend and Mrs. Webster, but thou didst not try.'"

"But I want a husband," I said flatly and slowly as if his mind and ears were dull.

"Have I not been a good husband to thee?!" Frustration and the faint echo of tears rang from his voice.

He drew close, staring at me like a gray-eyed wolf. His shirt stank of old sweat. "Thou art as lovely and pure as an angel," he said. "How can I behave like a beast of the field towards thee?" He dropped his Bible down on the table as a dark and frightening passion leapt from his eyes as if Herman was gone, and someone—something—else had taken up his spirit. "Very well, I will make thee my wife, if that is what thee require." He dug his hands into my arms and forced me against the dinner table. Little pearl buttons fell like hail onto the floor as he roughly ripped off my pelerine and grabbed my breasts as hastily as a thief.

There are two buttons near the hips in front of most men's trousers. When they are unfastened, there is yet another button revealed in the center of the waistband that holds the pants from being undone. Herman had his fingers on that one, starting to push it through the buttonhole. I struggled, grabbed the edge of the table, bent my knee and my square-toed slipper found a soft foothold—and I pushed him away with all the might of my strong leg, sending him stumbling backwards. It was too late to accept him as the lover that I had once so yearned for.

"I have counted the days," I said. "Our three-year term is over. It is time for us to pass back around the Horn. Where are our sea-chests to pack? I expected we would be preparing for our journey home by now, and instead you have built this house. I suspect it is not a monument to our marriage, but more a monument to the Mission, a more permanent foothold than a grass hale for which to claim this island."

He was recovering from shock and pain, found his breath, and stroked the pages of his open Bible, flipping through them as if looking for something. It was his way of not looking me in the eye.

"Our term has been extended indefinitely," he said.

It felt like a paper cut. Stinging, I turned away, searching for words as I opened the door of Aloha's cage. "You did not tell me," I finally said. "Your word is worthless."

He hurled his words at me, "Thou art a worthless wife, as worthless as the dead flowers and empty shells ye attempt to paint!"

"Worthless husband, worthless husband," Aloha squawked as she flew out of the cage and landed up on the top rung of a tall New Bedford ladder back chair.

"Some souls choose flames over Salvation, and so waits the oven for this creature," he said darkly, reaching for her tail feathers. She snapped her head around and bit him with her strong beak. He stepped back, furiously searching his hand for blood.

I went to my dressing table and took up the armless English china pitcher I had always treasured and still used despite the missing handle. I held it up as high as his face, making sure he recognized it was the wedding gift he had given me. And then I let go.

The sharp, broken pieces of bone china shattered down all around and between us. The painted scene I had loved was now a horse head here and a bit of a castle there. The sight of it cut my heart. It could be mended, but it would never be perfect again—yet it would have a story to tell. Perhaps how it had survived a perilous journey so far from a world where it once belonged to live a life barren of comforts, a poignant reminder of home, only to be shattered. Perhaps how something beautiful and precious can be thoughtlessly destroyed.

We would never be what I had once dreamed we were. In truth, we were enemies. I took up my sword. "You touch my bird again and I will tell the Mission Board that I suspect a large and growing Webster family scattered by you all over this island."

He laughed clumsily in the direction of the doorway and he turned to go. "Suspicious thoughts still brew in thy unstable mind. That is a delusion they would never believe. With the multitude of lascivious sailors in this port it is mental derangement to point a finger at me. They would think ye a strained missionary wife, her senses made dull in this indolent climate."

Herman paused at the doorway. With a look like a bolt of lightning shot in my direction, he pulled the brim of his tall hat down level with his eyes, then ducked out into the sunshine.

I left the pieces of china on the floor, postponing the humiliation of me having to sweep them up. Tears of anger and desperation drove me to curl up in bed with a quilt, and I pulled close a needlepoint pillow given to me as a wedding gift by a woman at the New Bedford Ladies' Tea Society who had worked on it with such earnest wishes for my happy matrimonial life. Through blurry eyes I read: *Happy Is The Home Where Love Abides.*

I turned it face down, pinned it with my elbow, and as I wiped my face my fingers tripped across the delicate gold chain around my neck. Upon it was my pendant as warm as my skin, lying on my bare chest. The golden amber gemstones reached from its yellow diamond center in the shape of a sun; it caught the light, and as little rays of gold danced on the walls and ceiling the words came to me:

I shine with the might of one thousand suns
I cannot be broken or lost
He spends cruel words dearly, at his own cost

I repeated it over and over until the strength of the words sank deep down inside my heart. Gradually, my tears stopped. I sat up on the edge of the bed. Aloha fluttered in and sat on my shoulder, softly nibbling away a stray tear.

"Pass us a pint of the kill-devil," came her queerly human-sounding words.

I stood up to stare again at the ships, spotted the *Averick* among them, soon to be all at sea. I put on a clean dress and began to hastily pack the only trunk I had at hand, my dear old pine dome sea chest.

CHAPTER 12

haddeus was the only one I could find to help me with my
trunk, and that caused me great distress for I knew I was
leading him straight into desolation. Cruelty was stalking me on all
sides and I had to flee—I could not take time to weigh what was right
and what was wrong. Perhaps he would not see Tabitha as he made
sure my trunk was loaded onto a rowboat sent in from the *Averick*,
while we took another shore boat for passengers.

I found Tabitha standing at the edge of the surf, her face white and
stiff. Reverend and Mary Goodwin held her arms and she strained
against their firm hold. The scene was more horrible than I had imagined it would be.

"But I prayed—all night long—for God's mercy—that you as my
own parents would find compassion," Tabitha said, looking as
shocked as a young deer the moment an arrow pierced.

"It is love that sends you away to America," Mary said with lavastone face. "It is for your own good. There with family, you will have
all the advantages that we spoke about."

Tabitha's face crumbled into despair and tears fell down her
cheeks. I turned around and there stood Thaddeus, frozen.

Reverend Goodwin faced him. "Keep God on the throne of your heart, Thaddeus," he told him. "Accept His will."

"Am I just another native boy to you?" he asked like ice. "Once I lead my own church, would I not be as worthy as any to ask for her hand?"

"You will marry your own kind, Thaddeus, and then thou shalt be ordained," Goodwin said.

Tabitha was wilting under the weight of her tears, and Mary Goodwin touched my arm. "Please Catherine, see her out to the ship. I cannot bear this cross any longer." With that, she brushed past me, headed straight back home with her poke bonnet turned away so no-one could see her face.

I put my arm around Tabitha as our small boat dipped roughly through the sharp waves out toward the waiting ship. Her young shoulders shook, still as small and delicate as a little girl, as she repeated "Oh, Thaddeus!"

"There now, Tabitha," I said, feeling helpless for words. Thaddeus was still standing ashore, his face locked on Tabitha's, but soon he was so far away we had to squint to see him.

"Mother and Father are sending me to live with relatives in Boston," spilled words from her small, red, bitten lips. "Mother says that serving God is much more important than living at home. When I am seventeen, I may return and will be permitted to learn the Hawai'ian language and allowed to teach the natives. Until then she says I must mingle with industrious, educated people and enjoy the advantages of civilization."

She was such a serious girl, having spent every day of her life studying the Bible, forbidden to talk with the islanders. Then, as if the double row of high stone mission yard walls came tumbling down her real feelings rushed out. "Mrs. Webster! How could my own parents be so heartless? Do they not love their own daughter? Tell Thaddeus to wait for me," she pleaded. "No—for then he shall never have the church he wants so badly."

"I think he only wanted one so that he could have you," I said softly, and she bent over with fresh sobs.

Over the sound of her crying I became aware of the sound of the waves slapping and echoing against the giant barnacled hull of the ship rising up at our backs. The sailors fastened Tabitha securely to a strong armchair and then hoisted her up and over the railing onto the deck where I watched her dissolve in the arms of Captain Swain's wife, a sweet woman who would chaperone her reliably to the door of a home in a strange country she had never known.

"Are ye to go aboard?" a seaman asked me brusquely, his mind already on the oceans ahead.

So there I had it: my opportunity to escape back to America. Away from Herman, back to dear Aunt Sallie, my father and my brothers.

I thought of my trunk that Thaddeus had abandoned on the beach. I thought of Aloha on her perch, looking through the window for my return. How could I have been so distraught as to forget her? I wanted to go back to my familiar things: the precious belongings in my trunk, my tea china, my dresses, the warm bread I had set out that morning on the green table to cool. I thought of my mother's little hymnal that Diego still had in his possession. Would he ever try to return it to me?

I imagined the shame of arriving back to New Bedford as a single woman just like Aunt Sallie, with only an echo of love to last her for the rest of her life. My fate would be that of the spinsters who move like ghosts in a world where life revolves around family, babies, and church.

I looked back across the clear blue water at the majestic emerald peaks that rose above Moku'ula and something moved deep in my soul. There was yet more life here for me.

I was uncertain which thought it was, or maybe all of them, that made me shake my head no and sit back down on the hard boat bench. A chorus of shouts sounded from above as canvas sails unfurled, snapped like whips and then filled silent and hard with wind.

The *Averick* groaned away and I let the rowboat take me back to the island that somehow, not quite, but oddly, for now, felt almost like —home.

CHAPTER 13

The sea-monsters arrived in the night with a sound that rumbled through the thick walls of the mission houses as if giants were rolling great water-barrels along the rocky shore. Early the next morning we walked north along the pounding shoreline past empty villages and we gathered together up on the bluff above Honolua Bay like a murder of crows, black coattails and skirts whipping in the breeze. Beneath us came waves of the deep, the largest I'd ever seen.

Surrounding us were possibly every soul on our side of the island; they stood assembled as if for church, all facing the mighty sea. Pua came up to my side. "The crowd here is called *'aha ma kaki ka'i,*" she told me. "They are all here to watch the *he'e nalu*—wave-sliding."

Herman stood with his back to it all, jealous of the ocean. He struggled to find his own audience as he preached, succeeding modestly until another collection of waves came in and all eyes would sweep back to behold the stunning might of the ocean. The intended thunder of his words was stolen by the wind and the giant thump of each wave crashing; every syllable, like a tiny leaf, was played with and then tossed away up into the misty sky. Herman's voice grew higher in pitch, sometimes loud but with at least every other word missing.

A loud crack like falling timber sounded down on the reef. It was a *Kīko'o* board, its strong, dense koa wood snapped in two. Its rider was nowhere to be seen.

Then a swift double-hulled outrigger canoe darted into view with a sail that grasped at the wind like a sharp lobster claw. It cut a path between the waves and out to a location far out past where the strongest surfers gathered—after paddling with great effort—at the most advantageous place to catch the largest swells. In the canoe was a young chief wearing a red malo loincloth, his leg muscles naked to his waist—lithe, flexed, fearsome. Mary Goodwin turned her head so that the long sides of her bonnet acted like blinders on a carriage horse, to block the indecent sight of him, and like always, making her view of the world only what she wanted to see.

Farther out, the water was darkening into lines of swells trimming the point of the island. An enormous swell stood up and the outrigger paddled swiftly with it. Out leaped the chief with a surfing board, dropping onto the watery slope, lying on his stomach digging deep strokes with powerful arms, his position well-chosen, and he joined up with the cresting wave. A collective cheer sounded all around me as he stood up on his board and sliced down the face of the terrible giant until it disappeared out of sight into the bay that lay beyond the edge of the rocky cliff.

Pua was on tip-toes, her young voice close to my ear. "To leap from canoe with a surfboard is *lele wa'a*," she explained. "On a day like this, the Royals will wave slide with the people, because they can be taken by canoe far enough out to catch the ones that come in like mountains. Those belong to them."

From somewhere down on the coral reef beside the booming sea rose up the thin sound of a lone voice singing an ancient chant. I recognized the old ocean-priest, the *kahu*, that always prayed for Leilani's spirit when she took to the surf. The salty mist in the air filled my nose as I took a deep breath. Sure enough, there she was, bravely paddling her way out to the faraway spot where only the royal canoe had been.

Pua saw her too and inhaled quickly with fear. "Look!—without a canoe she has made it through the warrior waves—see now—she has reached the *kulana nalu*—the smooth rising place where she can begin her ride."

Herman's voice, thrown around by the wind and the sound of waves, was for a moment audible. "Heed the Book of Jonah, verse three! For Thou hast cast me into the deep, in the midst of the seas; and the floods compassed me about: all Thy billows and Thy waves passed over me!"

An enormous wave rose up in front of the Lilliputian figure of Princess Leilani, and then it became a wall, two stories high. She paddled with all her might up to the very lip where it would throw her backwards into its mashing jaw of white water. Just as it crested, her long board pierced the lip and she dropped down out of sight behind the steep face.

Herman's eyes darted from his Bible to the sea and he began to shout with victory in his throat. "They that worship false gods will be cast under deep waters! The Almighty will smite idol worshippers!"

Indeed, Leilani did have a surf idol, but few were privy to it. I had seen her the evening before at sunset as I had gone to check the fish traps. Up from a lava cove had floated the sound of a wild, ancient song in a minor key coming from Leilani's throat. Then I spied her out on the edge of a lava precipice that looked down upon the churning waves. Beside her, draped with a lei stood her beloved surfboard, and placed on the very edge of the cliff was a carved wooden figure with abalone eyes, its body tied with several long dark feathers. The wind blew into Leilani's face, her hair flying back in the breath of the waves. Something solemn and powerful told me I was intruding, so I had walked on, listening to her voice growing stronger before it faded in the distance.

Some kind of force was running through her now, for Leilani—her strong arms and unmistakable lizard-tattooed legs bare and shiny, her hips bound with a skirt of black feathers—turned her board around on the face of the largest peak of the day. It began to crest with terrible height behind her. Then, now upon her feet, down she slid, her speeding board trailed by white lace trimmings, her body weight firmly steering, the feathers flying at her thighs and whipping behind her, her arms stretched out wide like a graceful ballerina. Shouts of awe and approval came from every voice on the cliff and in the water. And then they fell silent as she reached the trough: the wave was closing in over her, and would crush her in its hollow fist. She steered away from the deadly waterfall that was breaking behind her, but was swallowed up in its roaring white mist.

"Eve disobeyed, took the apple, and so doomed all mankind!" Herman cried triumphantly. "God did not intend for women to have their way, and therefore made the feminine body weak so that all of her kind must submit to the protection of men. God hast judged her! She hast met her deserved fate!"

I looked at Pua's face. It was strangely calm. She looked up at me. "The Princess will be like the Ka'upu bird that slides just above the waves. She will not be taken." I looked at the snowy-white mountain of spinning water in dismay, wondering how Pua showed faith stronger than a missionary.

Then, out from a rainbow veil shot Leilani! She stood proud and tall on her speeding craft, arms outstretched as if she were flying and then she raised her hands to the sky before she disappeared around the corner of the cliff into the bay. A chorus of shouts and cheers seemed to come from the very cliff itself and then many islanders began to move down to the bay to congratulate Leilani, not only their princess but also their new surfing hero.

Our group of missionaries and converts turned to make our way home. Herman's face was pale; I had seen faces with more life painted in oil on canvas. He strode past me, flanked by a handful of faithful followers, one of which gave me an unexplainable stab of alarm.

She was an islander, with long dark tresses and she wore an indigo cocoa-nut tree dyed into the side of her neck as if a hand reached up with its frond-fingers to clasp the side of her face. All of New England would judge it barbaric, but I found that it did not steal from her beauty. She carried a little babe whose face was lost in the garlands of flowers that hung from her honey-brown neck down past her voluptuous breasts. As they passed, the maiden locked her eyes on mine. She paused and stood before me. A strong breeze blew the flower petals from the baby's face and it stared at me with large, unblinking eyes that filled me with horror. They were exactly the same uncanny shade of silver-gray that belonged to my husband. I looked into that innocent gaze as my own innocence shattered into sharp little pieces that stuck into my heart. The babe gurgled and laughed at me. I do not know how long the girl-woman, the babe, and I shared this communion of eyes but as I looked up into hers with a furious question she looked down at her little one, nodded, and then walked away down the dusty path.

I reached beneath my white cotton pelerine to the jeweled sun upon my breast as I walked alone, rhythmically, desperately, reciting my chant:

I shine with the might of one thousand suns
I cannot be broken or lost
He spends in his folly, at his own dear cost
I shine with the might of one thousand suns
I cannot be broken or lost
I cannot be
It cannot be!

CHAPTER 14

Article Fifteen: A White Lace Handkerchief, Yellowed By Teardrops

That night it was as if the missionaries had never come. Kukui-nut torches burned wildly against the twilight sky and hands relentlessly pounded an ancient heartbeat upon tight sharkskin drums. The full moon had just risen over the volcanic mountains to the east and began to shine a path brightly across the Mokuhinia waters that surrounded Moku'ula.

We were gathered away inside the Mission walls, yard gates shut, children sent to bed. Reverend Goodwin began the evening prayers but his words sounded nonsensical and faraway. Still shaken, I felt as if caught beneath a great wave, unable to hear, to breathe, tumbled. I sat with my eyes wide open despising Herman's pious eyelids and expression. At amen he leapt from his chair, saying that he must go make sure that the church was securely locked.

"I must go guard against this wicked feast and bacchanalian revel. Evil will be expected to follow, as it has before," he said.

"Hear the drums," Reverend Goodwin said. "It is the wild heartbeat of a native soul, a heathen sound that throbbed for hundreds of years with no love for Jesus Christ or the civilized world—it is the passion of pagan sorceries and an unordered world. It speaks of ancient generations that lived and died without uttering a single prayer."

"'Tis the sound of human flesh pounding against man-eating sharkskin, its murdered spirit being drummed back to life," Herman agreed as he took up lantern and hat, and leaving those frightening thoughts he then vanished out into the night.

I slipped out of the kitchen door and crept softly down the wooden steps to follow Herman, seething with both curiosity and fear of what I might witness him do. I stayed just out of his swinging lantern light, and like a shadow I followed him as he hurried down along the path.

A grove of large trees like a giant's lantern reached their high umbrella limbs trying keep the golden fire-glow from spilling out beyond into the purple-blue night. I lost sight of Herman, but there on the dark edges I could anonymously search for him as I witnessed a scene I could someday tell my grandchildren about, if I ever had them under my sorry circumstances.

Inside the native cathedral of great trees the islanders crowded; in the center danced troupes of men, and then women, who shouted a rhythm of their own when the drums paused for a breath. Men stamped their feet to the pulse with dog teeth rattling at their ankles. The women were bare-breasted and wore short *pā'ū* skirts and feather anklets.

I didn't see Herman anywhere—perhaps he had gone straight over to the church. The performance held me captive. A quartet of musicians created mournful hollow tones with *'Ka 'eke 'eke':* holding these thick, bamboo stalks vertically upright in each hand with a loose wrist, they let the sealed joint of the bamboo end bounce down upon a hard mat. The largest was thicker than my arm in circumference, and the musicians held them lightly, fingertips buzzing from vibration. The tops, sawed open and hollow like an organ pipe, let the alternating tones call out, echoing upward in the night air. Each bamboo tube was of a different length—two feet, a yard, and taller—producing the notes of a minor third in varying octaves, resonating together in an eerie yet beautiful sound, centuries old.

I kept searching the crowd for Herman. The drums paused, and then began again faster in cadence with my quickening heart. I drew closer to see the dancers, their bare knees parting the curtain of ti-leaves that made up their skirts. Then—abruptly—the drums slowed to a sensual cadence and one young woman stepped forward, commanding the eyes of all. She moved one hip, then the other, with a slow, purposeful shake. The fronds of her skirt fell aside as her bare thighs appeared, each in concert with the throb of the drums. Shell anklets chattered sharply in time with the rhythm above her shapely feet. She turned her head and I saw upon her neck and cheek the tattoo of a cocoa-palm. It was her. Bitter jealousy surged through me.

Then from the corner of my eye I noticed a figure standing in the cover of the dark grove, stiff as a cane, intensely watching her, his face flushed like a glowing ember. He wore a tall black stovepipe hat, his expression transfixed and unguarded, and so taken with the performer he was unaware of the torchlight that revealed his face. I believe that I could have danced naked before him and he would have absent-mindedly pushed me aside, for it was Herman, and the way he leaned up and forward locking his eyes with the tattooed woman made me know for certain that her babe was his. He was smitten. It was plainly written like a love letter all over his face, a face that I could expertly read even in the dim light, having studied it for over three years.

THAT IS how I came to be lost, wandering desperately along the edges of Mokuhinia where the tiny waves lapped and the amber lights danced in the silver waters. And that is where I was found by Princess Leilani.

An echo of laughter still rang in her voice as she discovered me. "Kittie, is that you?"

She had come from the direction of the celebration and was still wearing her skirt of long black feathers beneath a short feather cape; a bounty of flower lei were stacked high to her chin. A man pulled her away teasingly into the half-shadows where they passionately embraced. With a short laugh of pleasure she came back towards me, pulling him by the hand. It was the tall young chief, the one who had leapt from the canoe and conquered the Honolua waves with her.

She pushed him back away with a promise in her motion, and he and a jovial crowd of attendants reluctantly melted into the darkness.

"Your highness? I did not recognize you." I said, quickly wiping away any sign of tears.

She paused, and her joyous voice fell dead. "I will confess to you, Kittie. I have danced and I have taken the rum. You will think me a pagan." She self-consciously touched the bower of lei to make sure they covered her naked chest.

She led me to a wooden dock that faced the island, then dropped to sit upon its edge. "You see I have taken a lover. The pull of the surf and the tide in my heart makes it difficult to desert him for any Christian man Mary Goodwin tries to arrange for me. I suppose you will think that beneath all my elegant silks and French ribbon there has always been a lost soul."

"That's untrue, your highness. On this island I have come to realize that the most savage heart beats beneath the black tailored wool coat of a certain missionary." Pained, I glanced at the faraway scene. I remembered the new coat Herman wore the day he first knocked on Aunt Sallie's door. Later she had remarked that the fabric was of poor quality, but I had insisted that it was the heart beneath it that counted.

"I thought you were aware. It is known that your husband has reasons to ask God for forgiveness. I have learned that the civilized are not without their share of sins; they have just learned to break their own rules in artful secrecy. This discord inside perhaps makes Reverend Webster so *huhū wela loa*."

She moved her bare feet in the water, feeling it with her toes. The tattoos moving up her legs looked like a water lizard rising out of the lake. I sat down on the dock beside her, took off my shoes and we sat in silence for a while, stirring the water with our ankles. My ankles, never touched by a man's hand.

"Tell me," I asked at length, "all the while that Herman stands before the congregation preening as a holy man, does everyone know he is such a significant sinner?"

She nodded. "I have never seen a sailor with eyes that peculiar pale shade—of clouds that cling to the lower slopes of Haleakala, and I know that in each *ahu'pua'a* there lives at least one gray-eyed child."

To think that Herman had betrayed me in every neighboring fiefdom made a pang of nausea rise from beneath my corset. *Did you notice my new husband's beautiful eyes, Aunt Sallie?* I had said so long ago. *I shall enjoy staring into them for the rest of my life.*

I leaned over the water, throat dry, stomach boiling.

"I'm sorry," she said. "I thought you were content." I pressed the corners of a handkerchief to my eyes and she stared up at the moon. It was waxed full, heavy with light.

"Can you see Hina-papa'i-kua there, the Goddess of the moon?" she asked compassionately.

I did not know quite how to answer; I was overcome by the shadows of Herman and the night. "I see the 'man in the moon,'" I contradicted her.

"No," she said kindly, as if I were a child that did not yet understand. "The moon shines on us when we are surrounded by the darkness, there to show us the way out."

That I had just been thinking of my own darkness startled me, as if she had read my thoughts.

"Hina-papa'i-kua is a woman," she went on. "This is how they tell it where I grew up on the far eastern side of our island: Hina lived by the sea at Ka'uiki where she was made to pound kapa like a slave by her very wicked husband. What kind of man acts like a fierce warrior making a shameful fight against a gentle flower blossom? This was her husband. One day he was so cruel that she rashly fled up the rainbow path that leads to the sun, but was not prepared for how unbearably hot and difficult it was; she realized that in her hurry she had brought no water or any of her cherished belongings.

"She was forced to slide back down to earth where her husband was waiting for her. *I am sorry*, he told her, *I will change and be a good husband*. Come back to live with me. But soon his hate and cruelty returned, worse than before. Hina was discouraged, but she decided she would secretly prepare and pack a calabash with all she would need so that the next time she would succeed. The very next evening, he came home in a foul mood, and he beat her. She seized her ready calabash and ran towards the moon. He chased her and pulled at her foot as she struggled to climb the moonbow. She was slipping off when she turned and knocked him in the head with her calabash! Smart she had her calabash this time! Through this victory she gained great mana, and now watches over all women, ready to offer strength and help to all that call on her."

"It is a nice story to believe in," I said.

"It is true. The board she pounded her kapa on can still be seen today in the shape of a long black rock above the surf line below Ka'uiki."

Leilani's face glowed in the moonlight. She emanated an uncanny strength.

"What is it about this place that feels so unearthly?" I asked her, gesturing all around me.

She lowered her voice reverently. "Moku'ula and the lake that surrounds it hold sacred power. There are passageways here, a tear in the veil between this world and the next."

"But people cross over to death everywhere in the world," I said.

"This is not just a place where mortal souls pass: it works both ways. Here, when the time is right, our Kūpuna can more easily reach through from the other world and touch us, giving us wisdom or point us the way we are destined to go."

She reached her arm around my shoulders. "Kittie, it is well for you to leave Reverend Webster if you desire. Climb the moonbow."

"But it is not done! To be his wife is what is expected of me. My life would be destroyed." I held my handkerchief to my cheeks.

"I have many things expected of me," she said. "I feel as if I am being torn from my ancestors. I had prayed and resolved to be a good Christian until the big waves came. Did you see me from the cliffs today? I felt cleansed of all guilt and shame. The Divine force of life protected me, and my mana is stronger for it."

She pushed her palms down the stiff, long skirt of feathers as thick as taffeta petticoats, her eyes seeing only those moments on the wave. "I flew like the ka'upu bird that glides above the surface of waves! My skirt is made of the seabird's feathers, and, like the ka'upu, I did not get wet."

A handful of silent moments passed before Leilani continued on in a confession that turned quickly back into passion. "At night after I put down my Bible and say my prayers I dream of the murmuring sea and I long to be awakened in the coolness of dawn to take up my board when *'Uo* or *'Uhā'ilio* is smooth and the breakers curl in the softest blue. I love the way the morning light reaches through the mountains and shines on me as I fly on the wings of sea. My soul feels blessed."

"My husband sees wave-sliding a sin, but he cannot know; he is made blind by his own."

"I try so hard to follow what is right," she said with clarity and strength. "But surfing is my greatest pleasure and my life force. If you surfed, you would understand."

She rose from the dock and placed her heavy accumulation of lei on my shoulders. "Forgive me, Kittie, if you think I should be forgiven," she said, then she touched her forehead to mine, turned, and dove neatly into the black water. She must have swam far beneath the surface, for I never saw her emerge.

CHAPTER 15

SPRING, 1834

Article Sixteen: A Letter From Emmaline

April 28th, 1834

Dearest Kittie,

Stuart confided to me a conversation that men usually keep to themselves. As he and I both have interest in the soundness of your marriage, he told me that Herman speaks like a man in love! His letters are as poetic as a man like him can be, waxing on about how lovely a woman you are and how much he desires you. I suppose every man's pride tempts him to talk with his brothers on that subject, and we must admit that women do too. Of course it is in a proper tone with meanings only implied, but he quoted Song of Solomon Chapter Seven Verse Eleven, 'Come, my beloved, let us go forth into the field; let us lodge in the villages.' You must have found private time away from the busy mission houses, finally sharing your womanly charms with him.

I am working on a gift for you, and I will not tell you what it is save for that it is tiny and I have made the delicate lace myself. I say a little prayer with every stitch, that it will clothe the fruit of lasting love between you both —a Holy, eternal bond that God intends for us.

We are returning to Maui soon to deliver the new printing press that has at last arrived by a ship out of Boston. We had almost given up hope of ever seeing it.

My hope for seeing you and Abigail once again will now come true as well.

Emmaline

CHAPTER 16

Article Seventeen: Woolen Slippers Made From A Faded Black Dress

I suppose the black wool dress was to blame for my undoing. It owned a nod of approval from Mary with its long sleeves and high neck, and it covered every part of my body except my red face. On the sands of Maui on a sweltering day it was unbearable. I simmered in it under the Devil's Sunshine—as Herman called it—that beat down upon the sweltering beach.

The sun fell down from windless heights and there were no trees nearby to offer shade. I sat in the sand with my cotton petticoats arranged beneath me like a pillow but the searing heat soon set them baking.

The Goodwins had ordered another dress for Leilani. A thick fold of dark navy silk with thin black vertical stripes had just arrived on a ship from Canton and I was charged to quickly produce a very proper dress in time for the coming Sunday when visiting missionaries would be there to appraise the progress made with the Princess's soul.

Beside me was my sewing basket with dress patterns packed

inside. I stood up against the pull of my skirts made heavy with heated sand, shaded my eyes with my hand, and looked for Leilani.

She had promised to meet me at her island hale for a fitting, but when I got to Moku'ula I was told that the waves had begun to stand up, and that she was out upon her outrigger, so I determinedly trudged down through the deep sand to find her.

I wiped my dripping forehead with my coal black sleeve and finally caught sight of Leilani out on the water, her craft moving in a swift, airy soar along an ice-blue wave. I walked to the shoreline, thirsting for its coolness, thirsting to be her in that moment. My shoes became wet and because of the lovely coolness at my feet I didn't care.

Leilani spotted me and soon her canoe-like boat with a sail swiftly reached the sand and ground to rest just beyond the reach of the waves.

"I forgot we were to meet," she apologized with exhilarated breath. "My outrigger called my name; this is a day meant to live on in hearts. Come out with me, Kittie; the sea commanded me, so I must command you."

"You promised a dress fitting, Princess," I protested. "I cannot join you in sin—and I might drown. A haole, much less a woman, does not surf-ride."

"Women have been surfing since ancient times," she said impatiently.

I opened the buttons at my throat, freeing my pale white neck naked to the sun. A neck never touched by my husband. Somewhere in the depths of wild green forests or out on a blazing reef was another throat; tattooed, sensual. Her femininity had won over mine.

"Princess, with all respect, it is just not done," I insisted. "If I am seen my life will be made very difficult."

"Kittie, I am sorry to say you act just like the rest. Missionary women are a queer kind, hardly women at all; they let other minds think for their own and they can be like timid crabs that hide in the sand."

"You cannot know what it is like! I must endure my lot in life—I must be Mrs. Herman Webster or find tragic ruin! Would you have me gossiped about and ridiculed? Doomed to a life of loneliness and shame?"

She put her hands on her waist and leaned down, wrestling with her thoughts as if in pain. A moment later, she looked up with disdain in her eyes, and her smile suddenly belonged just to her, not shared with me.

"Your majesty, you know I'd lose my culture, my way of life, my self!" I continued. "Can you try to imagine it?"

"Yes, I can imagine that." Her eyes shot me a tortured look.

"I cannot swim in the sea, as you know," I said, but the sea no longer held such a frightening threat; I was slowly dying on land.

My eyes had become so blurry with sweat I didn't know she was close until her hand touched my arm. It was cool and wet. "Come, Kittie," she said more gently, "and you will understand me, and we will tell no one. And then I will let you fit me for your new design. I hope it will not be a missionary kind."

"I regret to tell you it is a very missionary kind. They will approve of you."

"Your spirit is weak when it is ruled by their thoughts, Kittie. Come out with me and you will find your mana."

"I am fine the way I am." I crossed my arms. "Thank you."

"You are fine hiding yourself as the obedient wife of the faithless Reverend Webster?"

Speechless, I looked away at the sapphire ocean. It made me want to cry. Then I darted towards the outrigger, yanked up that hot, hated wool skirt, and climbed in.

She smiled and leaned against the weight of her boat, pushing it out through the slushy sand. It gained momentum, she hopped aboard, and it suddenly lifted, buoyantly carrying us smoothly above the aquamarine shallows like a sleigh over newly fallen snow.

"Take off your petticoats—they will pull you down if you fall in and you'll drown if I can't find you," Leilani ordered as we sped away from the shore, and that thought made me quickly do so. "Take up the rest of your dress between your legs as my maidens do and tie it about your waist."

That done, and my dress unbuttoned down to the top of my corset I was free. The cool spray from the bow felt divine on my face and chest and bare legs.

Leilani paddled us toward a lump rising out of the water that looked like the back of a whale. Fright splashed coldly on my burning courage but she confidently dug her paddle deep and trimmed the sail; sure and swift, we swept above and over the swell and farther out past one larger that almost broke upon us.

"Sit still and hold on—here we go!" she called as we turned and began to slide towards the beach as a wave built up behind us. I had never felt such fear and pleasure all at once.

Faster, faster we slid until something miraculous happened. A sacred force rose up beneath and through me as the outrigger came alive. Living Spirit had taken it over and lit me too. We spend along the wave as it curled into a little waterfall behind us and I laughed with joy.

We slid down several more, each no less thrill than the one surfed before it and by the time the hull ground up back against the sand I was still soaring inside. Feet on the draining sand, exalted, I reached up with wet fingers to touch the blue sky. My wool dress was sagging at the seams and we both laughed at it: gray with salt, ruined, never to imprison me again.

"Now I will make good on my promise and we shall do my dress fitting," Leilani said as we walked along the dry sand, not so hot at all, and I looked down at the patterns and my sewing box as if they were strangers.

CHAPTER 17

Article Eighteen: A Letter from Aunt Sallie

Tucked inside of:

Article Nineteen: The White Muslin Dress

That was not the only time I went out with Leilani in her wave-sliding canoe. In her regal, commanding way she easily bargained that from that day forward no new dress would be created without my first joining her out on the waves.

It is curious how the ocean can become a part of your blood, can call you back again and again like opium and make you need it like a drink of cool water, how its bliss can stay inside you all day long.

One day Leilani handed me her paddle and showed me how to steer. I found it an art difficult to learn but was thrilled to try, and when I put us in danger she would correct our course.

Many a time when we were swept back on the sandy shore by a farewell wave, I would look around in fear dreading to see a seething

Herman walking steadily towards me, doom and anger measured in every step—but my joyous sin miraculously remained a secret.

THAT SPRING BROUGHT MORE whaling ships than ever before. Boston, Nantucket and New Bedford whalers anchored in Lahaina Roads, their bare masts as thick as a forest.

Pua and I were on the beach at low tide where I was teaching her letters and arithmetic with my finger in the hard, damp sand. We would pause from time to time looking up to stretch our necks and watch the ships sail into our archipelago, stun'sls loose to catch the light breeze like pillows before the bow. It is a grand sight to see a ship flying under all sails—main, topgallant, royals, skysails all billowing—making its way down to Lahaina Roads with long, brightly-colored pennants streaming at mast-top telling the path of the wind.

I looked away from the ships to see little Pua crying. I gave her my handkerchief and took her to sit down in the shade of a breadfruit tree.

She gazed at the ships as if she had expected them for some time. Her unblemished young brow, always so serene after picking flowers or coming in from a swim in the surf, was troubled.

"*Palaoa* Hunters," she said, her fingers brushing a small, smooth whalebone fishhook that always hung about her neck.

The whale ivory was occasionally found in our waters, and rare was the Palaoa, or sperm whale, that washed right up onto the shore. An intact, large sperm whale tooth was precious, and only worn by the royal ali'i. The word palaoa appeared in the Kumulipo, or Hawai'ian Chant of Creation—their book of Genesis. The palaoa had spiritual significance to the natives, but meant only money to American whalers.

The whaling ships found Maui an opportune place to reprovision before sailing west in pursuit of the sperm whale. A handful of *koholā kuapu'u*, or Humpback whale, had only recently appeared in Maui's waters being run off the coast of California and Chile since the discovery of whaling there. Our protected archipelago was a welcoming invitation to the koholā looking for a gentle place to give birth, for during the winter months it was quiet, as most ships were still rounding the Horn.

"Palaoa—my *'aumakua*," Pua said, tears filling the big eyes in her little face that looked even smaller without her smile.

Now 'aumakua was a word I was quite familiar with, as it is a central aspect of the native belief system. To employ us on our ocean voyage so long ago, we had studied Hawai'ian language and practices and were told that 'aumakua was a kind of idol worship that held that certain spirits take up residence in living animals or even objects found in nature. In New Bedford we had been told that the Sandwich Islanders were begging for us to come and deliver them from the horror of eternal death. I had been told to imagine wild heathens struggling to stay up on a precipice at the edge of the earth where the oceans fell off steaming into a bottomless fiery abyss, their voices screaming in hopeless agony and fear.

"'*Kūpuna* are ancestor spirits," she said quietly. "I was my great-grandmother's favorite, and her spirit is in the Palaoa. I am not afraid to die."

"None should fear death when Heaven awaits them," I said.

"I do not want Heaven without my *kūpuna*, and they lived and died before the missionaries came," she said, her eyes growing larger in her troubled little face. "No Heaven for me. My spirit will become free to protect my loved ones; we will be nothing but love and light and peace."

There must have been a proper missionary reply to that, but I was lost for words. I sat with her in the shade, nothing else said, helplessly content to let silence take over. Pua took my handkerchief and pressed it to her face. I squinted out at the ships.

Suddenly I stood up and walked towards the water in the searing sunshine, my hand shading my eyes as I peered at one particular ship. I knew those decks, I knew the rigging, I knew the flags, I knew the carved wooden figurehead. It was the *Fair Wind*.

. . .

By the time I got back to the Mission I found Mary and Charity elbows deep into a new barrel of donations from the New Bedford Church, and there was a large package addressed to me wrapped in oilcloth and bound up in dressmaker's ribbon. Too excited to wait, I opened it right there on Mary Goodwin's long dining room table. From within the sharp scent of aged lin seed oilcloth bloomed the smell of roses, and out fell a sachet of petals from a cloud of fine, almost sheer white Swiss muslin: it was a gown, and with it a letter from Aunt Sallie. The dress was exquisite. It lay snowy white draped across the length of the dark walnut table while I read her letter.

November 2, 1833

My Dearest Kitten,

I have made you another muslin dress—this one may be my best creation, I must admit, because every woman who has come into my studio has stopped to admire it on the dress form.

Did you know that Marie Antoinette once had a dress of muslin? I saw a painting of her wearing one when I was in Paris, and she had on the straw hat with the blue satin ribbon like the one we bought you. The style of the dress, being French, has outlived the ill-fated queen by decades. I was so taken by the painting that I made a detailed sketch of it down to the pink rose she was holding, and I am satisfied that I have replicated it exactly, save for a few little stylish updates that you know my nature cannot resist. I believe that working with muslin is a test of a dressmaker's skill, and I hope you will be pleased with my efforts. The sheer fabric lends well to ruffles, and when you wear it the lightest breeze will pass through the garment and keep you cool.

I cannot thank you enough for sending the exquisite cuts of native kapa-cloth. I am taken by the tiny flowers stamped upon it, and how do they ever make dye that is such lovely brown, blue, green, and red? The printed design is bold and artistic, a clever fusion of both dressmaking and printing arts. I am experimenting with the exotic material—don't you think a lady might enjoy carrying her personal items in a handbag made of the cloth? No other lady will have one just alike and it will be the start of many a conversation. You say it is made from pounding fermented bark? Like velvet or satin, I suppose it must be kept from rain or snowflakes. I have a nose about this kind of thing: before long I expect these kapa reticules to be quite the fashion in New Bedford, so I may need more of this kapa-cloth!

You must wear this gown for love, as it was made with—

All my love,

Aunt Sallie

I looked up from the swirls of ink made so personable by Aunt Sallie's own hand, seeing her before my eyes, wondering if she looked different now: her hair style changed, her back more bent forward from sewing, her face older?

Charity touched the lavish sleeve longingly as Mary scrutinized the dress. "The cabin boys who brought these over also delivered an invitation," Mary told me. "As the *Fair Wind* has returned, they will be delighted to receive us this very Friday night! Our fellow missionaries will arrive just in time to join us."

She pulled a dress from the barrel. The shape was thin, the style long since passed. "This will be quite suitable for me to wear. 'Mrs. Coggins' it says inside. I once knew her. There was news that she had passed away only last year."

She held a jade green dress up against Charity. "This would be lovely for the special evening," she told her. "I have a good linen apron that can hide this hole in front."

"I do say, an apron is not suitable to wear for a party aboard the *Fair Wind*, Mary," Charity said. "I should like to wear one of the lovely dresses that Kittie made when she first arrived. They have been folded away far too long, and this is surely the kind of special occasion they were saved for."

Mary shot a guilty look in our direction. "Heavens, we do not need to look like a fashion plate here on this battleground. I sold those dresses some time ago to a merchant ship in order to gain money for our church organ. We can look quite presentable in these donations."

She then grasped a handful of my white muslin dress, wrinkling it in her fist. "Is this for the Princess? She needs nothing so frivolous. Perhaps you can remove some ruffles."

"This dress is mine," I told her as I gathered it up along with the letter. "For Heaven's sake, God made these islands hot, and long-sleeved black wool fashions were not designed with this climate in mind. I thank God for Aunt Sallie who made it for me, and I shall wear it tonight."

Mary stood grasping for the right Bible verse to counter with, and Charity helplessly gave me a sad look of empathy, desperate to fix the situation.

I paused at the door. "And, I will not remove a single ruffle."

CHAPTER 18

Our chase boat came up alongside the *Fair Wind* and a rebel wave pushed our rail against her mighty hull, scraping it in greeting. As we waited to go aboard I looked up past the barnacles up to the waterline and thought of all the seas she had sailed since I had last seen Captain Swift.

The late afternoon sunlight flashed on *Fair Wind's* shiny brass fittings and glowed up in the canvas awnings that were draped like an airy tent above her deck. She was magnificently dressed in colors: from bow to stern fluttered American and nautical flags of blue and yellow and red and black-and-white check.

It wasn't just the gaiety coming from the ship that made my heart beat faster: we were a large company of missionaries in the boat, together again once more. Abigail and Henry had journeyed from the middle of the island, and Emmaline and Stuart had sailed over to help install the new printing press at the Hale Pa'i printing house up at Betsey Stockton's school on the hill above Lahaina.

Emmie, Abigail, and I chattered merrily as if we were still schoolgirls in those olden days back at Miss Willard's Female Academy. We clasped each other's hands in support as we were hoisted up the side of the ship in the gamming chair. It was a half-barrel fitted with a seat and rigged with four ropes that were drawn through pulleys up on the yardarm. Many women had been tipped into the sea using this conveyance, but the only other choice was to climb up the side of the ship like a man, without the advantage of wearing trousers. Of course we were accustomed to the gamming chair, but never used one without first saying a little prayer.

The sound of the waves swishing and clapping against the side of the ship faded as we approached the rail, and from across the deck came voices, fiddle, and melodeon. It floated cheerfully down over water-barrels and coils of rope, and faded past us towards the surface of Maui's blue bottle-glass water below.

Then a lone man's voice began to sing; loud and full, his baritone voice commanding the attention of all.

It's a damn tough life full of toil and strife
We whalermen undergo
And we don't give a damn when the gale is done
How hard the winds did blow
'Cause we're homeward bound from the Arctic ground
With a good ship, taut and free
And we won't give a damn when we drink our rum
With the girls of Old Mowee

I was giddy from friendship and smiles, glad for recess from sermons and chores. The lyrics were not for Missionary ears, yet I couldn't help but laugh with happiness. Emmie didn't. I searched her face for the glint of light that had always lived like a smile in her brown eyes. What trials and cares had she endured since I saw her last, that her once lighthearted nature could be so lost?

Then from up in the rigging and along the yardarms where the sails were tightly furled rained down the voices of sailors, thick with harmony as they joined in a hearty chorus:

Rolling down to Old Mowee, me boys
Rolling down to Old Mowee

We're homeward bound from the Arctic grounds
Rolling down to Old Mowee

The song grew louder and ended in a lusty shout as we reached the ship's railing. I could feel *Fair Wind*'s blood coursing, and Captain Swift was her heartbeat. He made her alive. Long ago on our journey over from America he had gone ashore in a port off South America leaving the *Fair Wind* remarkably lifeless, as if she had suddenly become an empty shell.

We gathered safely up on the main deck and there he was, striding up to welcome us. He gave a short signal to the musicians who promptly began to play a hymn. His authority and comportment commanded all, and then he looked directly at me and smiled.

"Welcome, old friends," he said. As he shook hands with the men and bowed to the women he kept checking in my direction. And then he was there, right before me.

"Mrs. Herman Webster," he said. "I have sailed the seven seas, and have the good fortune to be back upon your shores."

I could see the voyages on his face, as if he were a figurehead at the bow of a ship. The lines were carved deeper, his youth faded by salt-water and wind and sun. Faraway continents had dressed him in the finest: an ivory silk Canton scarf tied about his tanned neck, his shirt a shade of cream, his vest the color of vanilla. His British coat was a deep blue and boasted rows of gold buttons upon his stocky chest. Beneath his slightly crooked nose, his square chin was shaved smooth and his ever-so-slightly thinning brown hair—strands lightened to honey from the sun—was brushed forward attractively as was the latest style, as if a wind blew at his back. He bowed above boots of Spanish leather, then lifted his head, his eyes darting all across my face seeking to take in my every feature that I feared had changed in three hard years.

"You are even more beautiful than before. How have you kept yourself?" he asked intimately as if he knew all of my struggles or hoped I would find some to divulge, eager to be my confidant. "Gone is the girlish, frightened young missionary that I once delivered to her post. In her place is a woman."

Herman swept over to my side. "Captain Swift," he said. "Hunter of the great leviathan. How many barrels of oil hast thou been blessed with?"

"Seven hundred on our way here, Reverend, and we pray for many more between here and Canton, and even more before our return to New Bedford in the fall. And how many native souls have you collected?"

"Only God knows the exact number," Herman said, "And each heart is worth more than a barrel of whale oil, I assure you."

"Most certainly, yet I compare you missionaries to nothing more fitly as whales—the great ones eat up the little ones," the Captain said as if he had just sipped a drink of straight bitters.

"Thou wouldst do your soul a great favor to quote the Bible, not Shakespeare," Herman said.

"I think not. Yet I do try to practice compassion, a trait which can sometimes be found within your gilt-edged pages," he answered. "Put yourself in a native's place, as if the leviathan were hunting you, and imagine it: *such whales have I heard on o' the land, who never leave gaping till they've swallowed the whole parish, church, steeple, bells, and all.*"

Mortified, Herman turned about face, pressing his fingers sharply into my elbow to steer me away with him. Detesting his touch, I pulled my arm from his grasp.

Captain Swift saw it. I glanced back at him as we walked away. "A pretty moral," I whispered to him as he stood, arms crossed, with a big smile on his face as if he held a better hand of cards.

"Pretty indeed," he said, eyes taking me in from hem up to my long bare neck.

I had found that I had kept my same measurements left with Aunt Sallie, for the white dress fit perfectly. Its translucent ruffles were bordered with a line of thin white silk that seemed to float from the gossamer material in a wavy cloud above the neck, sleeves, and skirt. One can see through the open weave of muslin, so Aunt Sallie's design took that into account and layered it tastefully, tripling the fabric in places where modesty was required. Extra bands of muslin criss-crossed my chest and continued past corset and chemise, showing a tint of my skin beneath before it ended at the edge of each shoulder. The stylish placement of the white ruffles caught the blue and yellow colors of light in the late afternoon sun.

The train of my skirt swept across the clean-scrubbed decks as my friends and I strolled along, surveying the scene. The royals, chiefs and chiefesses were holding court on a platform above the main deck. Leilani's lover, the young chief who had victoriously surfed the big wave after leaping from the outrigger, stood lithe and strong as if he were ready to pounce. His head was shaved on the sides leaving a long mane from his forehead to the nape of his neck and he kept his bare, tattooed back to the missionaries.

All the mission men gathered at the stern eagerly seeking news from the first mates and captains of neighboring anchored ships. A cook and his cabin boys were busily setting up food and tea on a table outside the galley door. The sailors that had not been permitted ashore were up high on the yardarms lighting candles in lanterns still lit by the sun which hung low in the sky between the two islands across the channel, casting everything in a golden glow. A majestic parade of clouds, the same color as the sails and lanterns, moved across the blue peaks of Moloka'i island.

Emmie, Abigail and I paused at the bow of the ship where the three of us looked at each other and embraced once more.

"It seems an eternity since we were all together," Abigail said, her hair still the color of a New Bedford Autumn. Her large, darkly circled eyes bulged to take in every detail of the ship so grandly refitted as if she were on her maiden voyage; the *Fair Wind* was a much more successful ship since we once knew her.

"I am relieved to be off the island," she confided softly. "We were nearly killed by another wild bullock on the journey here!" Fright moved across her face, remembering. "I love my Henry, and cannot desert him, yet sometimes I just feel as if this island will make me come undone."

She reached inside her skirt pocket and took out a small glass vial of opium. "My nerve tonic," she explained. "My husband prescribes it for the times my senses are overwhelmed, which, on this island so far from home, is often." She lifted the little bottle to her lips and tilted her head back. A glint of sunlight at the horizon shot through the dark liquid setting it aglow like a ruby. "I especially like to take my medicine before sermons," she said. "When I listen to the Word of God I can practically see angels hovering, and—the hymns! I feel as if I can truly understand how exquisite is the voice of music."

"Emmie," I said, "Abigail and I see each other when we can manage it, but you have been on O'ahu a cruel length of time. I tried to sail over to help you when it came time to deliver your baby, but Herman would not hear of it. He actually pursued me all the way down to the wharf and told its captain to surrender my fare."

"I had the help of the other mission wives. But you, Abigail, how did you manage in your time of sorrow without a white woman to help you?"

"I made haste to be there," I interrupted. "Abbie had not told me she was close."

"I'm sorry Kittie," Abigail said. "I did not want you to see me in distress; I was not myself. And after all, Henry is a doctor. We must promise to be more faithful writers."

"Who has the time? Emmie said. "It is all I can do to write every few months. We must work harder than the men if we wish to save souls after we are done with keeping children, the house, the washing, the mending, the cooking—and more, as we all know."

"Ladies, you grace my ship with your presence," Captain Swift suddenly appeared beside us. "Was it just yesterday that my *Fair Wind* brought you to these Sandwich Isles? I give you credit," he said, looking at me. "I feared you would beg to be sent home. You should see New Bedford! It has thrived since you left. There are many stately homes now on the hill overlooking the harbor. I am building mine, and it will be the finest of them all. It will have many windows, and a rose garden."

Emmie had always been alert to the designs of men, especially those of Captain Swift, and had falsely accused me of encouraging him during our voyage so long ago. She stared at me firmly and then pinned him down with her eyes. "I am sure that your wife will enjoy it," she told him.

"I have been away at sea and have had no time for courting," he replied, and went on. "There is talk that New Bedford will soon boast a train station." He turned to me. "If I am correct, it is your father and brothers who host the renown New Year's ball every year. I attended once; his shipyard warehouse was decorated in pine wreaths and garlands, and there was a large evergreen tree lit with little candles. I am sure you recall those happy occasions. Sleighing parties? Dances?"

Abigail sighed, wistful, her eyes staring at faraway memories.

"Hold the apple in front of us and tempt us to bite," Emmie said, "but we will not be lured away from our purpose here. Saving souls is work that lasts forever; holidays and entertainments do not. Good evening, Captain Swift." She took my arm and turned away to dismiss him, leaving the Captain in our wake. I stole a glance back at him as he stood with his arms crossed, his eyes twinkling as if he were planning his next chess move.

We stood at the bow to watch the sun as it set in glimmering orange and peach, the shafts of light through the clouds like golden trumpets.

"Even the sunsets here are brazen," Emmie said.

"I long to see a delicate lavender sundown across a New England countryside," Abigail said dreamily.

I could not join with Emmaline and Abigail's thoughts as easily as I once did. "Yet, remember Psalm 91?" I said. *"The heavens declare the glory of God; and the firmament sheweth his handywork.* Does not the Bible say something in Psalm 65 that even souls here at the ends of the earth know that the dawns and sunsets proclaim the glory of God?"

"Then all the better that we are here to let them know exactly who God is, my friends," Emmie said.

The scent of beefsteak on the fire wafted up on the lazy air. The lanterns strung between the masts grew luminous as the sunglow slipped away. The musicians began a rowdy jig as we walked down the old familiar decks towards a banquet of imported delicacies and fresh island food. In a sudden moment the air was charged like a bolt of lightning and a hush fell across the ship. I looked all around for the reason, and then I understood: Princess Leilani had just arrived.

Reverend Goodwin stood up straight to face her, proudly pressing his ever-present Bible against his chest. Herman stared and nodded slowly to himself, satisfied. Mary peered past fingers pressed together against her nose in prayer. The young chief spun around with a fierce look of hurt as mighty as a Honolua wave about to break. My mouth fell open as I saw Leilani standing on the deck caught in the glow of large burning whale-oil lanterns.

From her dainty pointed slippers to her silk bonnet she was a picture of refinement, modesty, and Christianity. Gone was the young woman glowing with the life of the ocean, who had ruled her outrigger and who had carried her tall surfing board with strong, tattooed arms.

She was covered in the new dress I had made for Sundays sewn from dark navy silk. What had made her hide her golden arms inside its tight dark sleeves? I had been talked into fashioning it from shoulder to wrist rather frugally—not too extravagantly big, as was the new fashion. Her ample waist was made unnaturally thin by a corset. She wore a high-necked indigo pelerine of Mary's like a little cape that conservatively ended below her breasts. Her large bonnet was black, her face almost lost in its dark shadows. In her hands she clasped a Bible. She wore no flowers.

"Well done. Quite a transformation you have made," Captain Swift said low in my ear, startling me. "You've taken all the God-given truth out of her." The pride glowing joyously from one missionary to another reached me and burst into ashes like a lock of hair.

"I had nothing to do with it. I am more surprised than anyone here," I said numbly.

"Your fingers did not push thread and needle through her dress? Is there not a tiny drop of your blood pricked and hidden somewhere in a seam? I'd say you have blood on your hands."

I wanted to push him over the railing of his own ship. I was already sinking fathoms down—I felt cold, and I couldn't breathe.

Leilani regally cast her gaze across all, and for the slightest moment her eyes tripped on the young chief. With a flicker of pain her eyes darted away, then continued across the faces crowding the deck, avoiding mine.

With all attention on her, the captain pulled me behind a hedge of coiled ropes and furled sails. I let him, so that I could curse him with all the words I'd ever learned from the men in my family. For that moment, maybe more, we were alone.

"Damn you."

He laughed. "That is your best curse? You draw one of your own needles for a sword?"

"How foolish of me to try," I said, embarrassed. "I am no match for the vileness and depravity that so often spews from your mouth."

"Catherine, hear me. Your three-year term has been fulfilled. Leave your husband here and sail back to America with me. A divorce is not impossible; your family and friends will forgive how you found your way back home to them."

I turned away towards Herman but could not move. No longer could anything make me go to him.

Captain's Swift's voice was close behind me. "Your white dress is as beautiful as a wedding gown. Wear it on the bright morning some day when we will wed."

Then I felt something warm on my bare neck. It was his breath. Shock and anger prickled down my back as he kissed the bone at the top of my spine where my neck rose high above my collar. His lips injected laudanum in my blood, pounding in my temples, pulsing elation through every vein. Searching for gravity, I looked down at my dress. It is curious how some dresses can hold wishes.

My corset was perhaps too tight—I felt dizzy when he placed his hands roughly on my bare shoulders. I could feel a texture of fine sandpaper, like the skin of a shark, as they stayed heavy on my skin and did not slip away.

So I whirled around. "Captain, I think I have a say in the matter and I do not consent to your affections. My answer is no."

He pantomimed a sword stabbing his heart. "I concede," he said. "That single cruel word hath won the match. But it will not be our last duel. I will have the most beautiful wife in New Bedford."

I looked down again at my naively hopeful gown. "I will wear it one bright morning when I go to meet my true love," I murmured to myself, and then as if a cold wave had splashed up over the railing I shook my head and fled from Captain Jonathan and the privacy of the *Fair Wind*'s folded canvas wings.

"Oh there you are Kittie," Abigail appeared, smiling serenely and taking my hand. She lifted her large eyes up to stare in wonder up at the luminous stars making their appearance one by one in the cobalt sky. The nervous look on her face was gone, and without the pinched look between her eyes I hardly recognized her. "I am sleepy, and we are going back. Charity and Mary saw that more rum and wine have been brought out, and they have called for our boat."

I SAT ALONE by the edge of our little craft as it headed for shore. Emmie and Abigail conversed in soft tones with their husbands while mine sat with the rest of the men at the bow discussing the news that they had just gathered.

I looked up at the night sky thinking about the Captain's attentions towards me, pondering what a kiss by him might feel like. Had Herman's coldness driven me to imagine such wickedness? Yet I found I could no longer quite imagine the Captain's lips as I perhaps let myself do once or twice before. Perhaps thrice, but no more than four.

That was before I met Diego. I kept seeing his mouth—his brave jaw, the soft shade of his smile. Such an unexpected yearning for him rushed into my heart like the moonlight water streaming alongside the rail.

But Diego was away on the Big Island and would soon return to Alta California. I was a missionary's wife, wed to a man whose lips could only quote scriptures. It was my fate to live out my life stranded on an island carrying a distant memory of a lonely woman once in the days of her blooming. There were surely beautiful, young unmarried daughters of the great Alta California ranchos who were building their dowry, combing and coiling up their long hair to slide tortoise-shell mantilla combs into its depths. Who wore exquisite dresses bought with the riches of tallow and hides, who looked coquettishly past their ebony fans for a man just like Diego. He would build a family there, a life. Yet he could have at least had the courtesy to give my mother's tiny hymnbook back to me before he left.

The dark sea lifted and dropped our boat as a large swell passed beneath, ushering us to shore. I gripped the railing tightly as if to moor myself. In one evening almost everyone, every feeling, and every belief I'd known had shifted. I hugged my elbows and tried to imagine that somewhere inside myself lay an anchor. I yearned to discover what was within, to not always feel the torrential pull of those around me.

Suddenly, I could see their spirits more clearly than I could see mine. Herman wanted to feel forgiven, clean, approved, worthy. Emmaline wanted success equal to any missionary man. Abigail simply wanted home. Mary wanted justification for all that she had sacrificed. Princess Leilani wanted to be accepted as a modern ruler. And, plainly, Captain Swift wanted me.

CHAPTER 19

The rains came and stayed, as if God was trying to put out Hell. Emmie and Abigail left. The *Fair Wind* sailed west towards Celestial shores. And the Princess no longer surfed. She let Reverend Goodwin visit her royal residence regularly and all invitations to me had stopped.

One day Herman, Goodwin, and two visiting missionary men carelessly walked right in across my clean floor with red mud on their boots, and thinking that I nor any other woman was near, were laughing and talking of me as if I were just a card in a game of whist.

"We can find other work for my wife now that the Princess has finally been converted," Herman was saying. "We no longer need my Catherine to sew frivolous gowns. Perhaps she can offer her talents to modestly add to the Queen Regent's wardrobe, or make the ruffled shirts that the Prince keeps asking for. She could assist at the Printing House by cleaning up and alphabetizing sorts. She still has thread and needles, a small measure of good sense, and a few qualities remaining that were first presented to me."

One visitor chuckled sadly. "I regret to admit that my wife has lost the physical qualities that the Board once selected her for."

I stood fixed around the corner of our bedroom door, my mind scrambling to make sense of their words.

Reverend Goodwin let out a good-natured sigh. "Well, be grateful men, that ye had the opportunity to choose; they presented thee with a carefully selected list of potential brides, complete with every attribute from pie baking to hair color, from comeliness to having a missionary mindset. In my case, I was already married and so qualified for service."

I looked down at the white embroidered pelerine on my chest. Its fine lace edge shook with each heartbeat. I had heard the men in my family talk but never stopped to suspect that there was a breed of men who shared course, unspoken camaraderie in which its members, a circle who sought to feel powerful, lived in a separate world in which women were just instruments.

There had been rare times in my life when my anger overtook me like a burning sun. In those moments it was a wild light within me, barely manageable, and I could hardly stay master of it. Sometimes it made me weak and sometimes it made me powerful. This was her zenith.

I walked in and looked at them all. "Did I hear correctly? That it was the Mission Board who presented me as your wife, Herman?" I faced him so squarely that he took two steps back. "Why did you not inspect my teeth and hooves the day we met? Was there money exchanged as well? I believed in your lie of true love, never knowing that I was trading my very life for this experiment in the Sandwich Isles."

The men quickly scraped up their looks of shock to reassemble their faces into an appearance of pity. Herman put his hand on my shoulder, pressing his fingers into my back, his cold eyes piercing me like metal harpoons. "Mental Soundness should have also been on that list," he said, "and in that thou dost not qualify."

I did not let him take me down. "Some men, unlike yourselves, do not join like schoolboys to play a game of being powerful, because they know true power already lies within themselves."

The men exchanged glances, eyebrows high, as they slowly stepped backwards to quickly evaporate from the room.

"Go back to thy bedroom, stay there, read thy Bible, and do not come out until I bid you," Herman said to me, searing the air with a demeaning sound in his voice. "Thou shalt not speak to me so brazenly again!" His face was red, his eyes brimming with humiliation.

"You were talking to the other men as if women are horses, or pawns," I answered. "Is it true that you chose me from a list? To qualify you as a foreign missionary? If only I had known before you proposed that you were never worthy of me."

Sometimes one can eloquently state the truth to a guilty heart, but it slides right off its armor and the target remains unconvinced. His lips broke into a jagged smile. "No, no, my dearest—men will talk amongst themselves, as perhaps do women. It is a trivial thing, and masks—protects—the deep and true feelings he has inside. I must have the good fellowship that a brotherhood provides. We spare the fairer sex information that they would find unsavory. We confide in each other important news."

"You are growing more detestable by the day," I said as he put his tall black hat back on his head. "You have sacrificed our marriage to lust and a cause that can never be won. Neither I nor this island will ever belong to you."

Rage flickered across his face before he put on a mask of composure. "Thy nerves are frayed. A man must be above emotion. Thou dost accuse me of being an ogre, but I point out to thee the fact that I will now disregard your insults and calmly walk away."

"Turn back around and talk to me!" I cried, but he remained coattails as he fastened his cape and ducked his stovepipe hat that bumped the doorframe as he left.

I stood with Aloha on my shoulder watching the rivulets cry down the wavy glass windowpanes and through the open door came the scent of wet flowers, deep, wild forests and volcanic earth that would never be tamed.

CHAPTER 20

JULY, 1834

TWO LETTERS

Article Twenty: A Ship-to-Ship Letter From The Celestial Seas

It came to me hidden deep in the middle of a thick fold of pale pink silk that was the weighty gift of a million silkworms, beautifully hand-embroidered with white cherry blossoms and light blue butterflies—fine enough for the kimono of a Chinese princess. A letter sent openly to me from him would have surely raised eyebrows and been ruinous to my character, causing me great suffering. But fine fabric, should it be needed to seduce a chiefess or queen, was an appropriate gift to the cause and the parcel would naturally be addressed to the mission dressmaker. Only she would be the one—confident in her craft, curious of the yardage, the quality, the possibilities—who would unfold it all out flat on her worktable.

June 15, 1834

Dear Catherine,

What cross devil makes me pen this letter to a married woman?

We found the sperm whaling grounds off Japan and made seven hundred more barrels. The Fair Wind's hold is getting full—but she feels empty. The decks once graced by your footsteps feel only the heavy boots of my men, and that once made her content. It is no longer enough.

I beg your forgiveness for my behavior when we were together last. You are a lady. But all women have an Eve in them, and I will discover yours. I may be a man who easily wins feminine treasure, but you are the one I will seek and finally marry.

I dreamt that your beautiful face and the curves of your body were carved as my masthead and all Neptune's wooden angels were jealous of you. I look around mast and rope half-expecting to see your face. I get angry at myself for searching for a glimpse of you, as if by wishing it I might turn a corner, hand on a brass fitting or rope, to suddenly encounter you on the deck as I last saw you, standing in that white dress still lit by a departed sun.

I will have the boy at the crow's nest scan the horizon for any ship headed east towards the Sandwich Isles—we'll trim our sails, hove to and exchange mail. One day the Fair Wind will return to claim you, and you will cast off those matrimonial chains of church and land; I do not live by any other laws than those of ship and sea.

Time is passing like the sand in my ship's hourglass and I consider the speed and direction of my life—I have wandered long enough. The grains of sand tell me to set the clock, record the longitude to chart a better course. You'll quit that damned Mission and sail with me back home.

Cpt. Jonathan Swift

Article Twenty-One: Another Missive From Emmaline

June 29th, 1834

Dearest Kittie,

We have made good on our vow to be better correspondents, haven't we? I enjoyed your recent letter, but you did not answer my question. Have you and Herman found matrimonial comfort with each other? I thought surely you had, until I saw the distance displayed between you both on our last visit. Study your Bible, namely the Song of Solomon, for as it is written in Chapter two, verse six: "His left hand is under my head, and his right hand doth embrace me."

Obey the Bible in this manner and soon you will be tightly knit to your husband with a little family of your own. I myself, having a growing brood of children, must not indulge so freely; yet as my mother once told me, as long as Stuart and I keep our closest physical affections in the first and last week of my month, we shall have no more babies for a while and all we want of each other.

I am no good at keeping surprises and I must tell you I have finished making you the gift of a christening gown. Write to me with the happy news as soon as you find you are with child.

Emmaline

CHAPTER 21

Article Twenty-Two: A Map of The Journey of the Soul

When Emmaline and Stuart sailed off they had left a young printer from London named Cornelius. Because the printing press was such a powerful tool, a clever or fascinating topic for a printed piece was always something to strive for.

Cornelius and Herman had been sitting at our dining table for hours working on an idea that Thaddeus had originally conceived: they were devising the greatest illustration of a soul's voyage to ever to be etched in copper, inked, and pressed to paper.

"It will be a map of the soul's journey!" Herman exclaimed. "I have often thought that life is like a voyage and in the end one reaches either Heaven, or Hell. As if our lives were a ship, and each man its captain, this map will clearly illustrate the eternal consequences of his choices."

"Quite brilliant," Cornelius said in his British way, his accent sounding like clear bells and dainty teacups. "What about Heel-Tapping Inlet?"

"Yes, a deceptive route that only leads south towards the Sea of Despair." Herman said. "But sail north through the Straits of Temptation to Fair Skin River and Cold Water Creek, and there one will find the passage to the Land of Heaven!"

"And far down here might lie the Straits of Rum and Brandy."

"Rum and me brandy," Aloha added. I sighed at her and smiled, threading my needle, as I sat with Pua in the good light by the window making lace muslin ladies' caps and mending riding breeches.

"Wife, that creature is the mouthpiece of the Devil. I have a taste for fowl tonight. What say ye, Cornelius?" Herman never joked.

Cornelius looked uncomfortably at Herman and decided it best to continue on. "I say we put Generosity Rocks and Idleness Isle just above those, for both can alter the course of a ship towards the Sea of The Wicked."

"And North of that, the Divine Sea of Eternity," Herman said.

"Of course, Reverend," said Cornelius, eager to please.

Cornelius was Herman's shadow now that Thaddeus had abandoned his apprenticeship, ever since that day Tabitha sailed away.

I knew the whole story, and many more, through Pua. I often smiled at how much news could come from such a little person.

She said that in his anger and grief Thaddeus had put down his Bible, taken up a *reata*, and joined the bullock hunters—the *paniolo*. The Regent Queen of the yellow-feathered cloak had named them thus; at first calling them *españiolo*—for the vaquero were both *española*, or Spaniard, and Californio.

"The proper pronunciation is Español, your Highness," Mary Goodwin had corrected her, but since the letter "s" was not to be found in the native language, and coining new words for new times being naturally the Queen's prerogative, from that point forward the two words española and californio were fused together and all bullock hunters were called 'paniolo.

"Did you know that one of Mrs. Goodwin's seminary girls stole away with a French Captain bound for Chile?" Pua whispered as we knotted and cut our threads from the delicate caps and folded the thick canvas breeches.

"I knew of Mary and Charity's despair the day she went missing, but they have no idea of her circumstance and whereabouts. They will be heartbroken; I think we will not tell them."

"I have another secret nobody knows." My heartbeat paused at something in Pua's voice. "One day through an open window I heard Mrs. Thatcher and Mrs. Goodwin talking. Princess Leilani had a baby inside her when she rode the big wave at Honolua, but then later she lost the baby. Doctor Thatcher told Reverend Goodwin and he told Leilani it had been cursed because she was a wave-slider. He told her that God made it happen. After that was when she gave up on waves and began wearing Sunday dresses."

Stung with heartache for Leilani, I jumped up, waking Aloha who fluttered through the open door of her cage to my arm. "Scallywag, scallywag! Son of a biscuit eater," she squawked, a favorite outburst of hers sometimes performed for no apparent reason.

Herman slapped his pencil down loudly and looked up. "Mrs. Webster. I have yet to hear scriptures come from that blasphemous beak. Rid us of the bird, or I will."

With Aloha firmly clutching my shoulder I stuffed the painstakingly made caps into a basket, and Pua and I left the stifling house.

We strode in the heat of late afternoon down towards the shore as more news spilled from Pua. "I heard the vaqueros are leaving the Big Island," she said as she struggled to carry the heavy stack of riding breeches.

Pua chatted on as I traded her the wicker basket for the breeches. "They are done here and will sail back to Alta California. And Mrs. Goodwin's best hen has gone missing. She was very sad—the hens are her pets."

"Have the vaqueros already sailed? Will they re-provision here?" I asked, making my voice sound careless.

But Pua was distracted. "I am sad that there are not enough eggs for a pudding," she continued on and did not stop talking about pudding until we were down where the cool ocean breezes came in past the ships anchored at Lahaina Roads.

Many schooners, barks, and brigs had sailed away, and Lahainatown had quieted down. The *Fair Wind* was to return in September according to Captain Swift to stock up on provisions and leave to cross 'round the Horn in that December summer. We could reach New Bedford by Spring and I would have a stately new mansion, a carriage with a matched team of horses, the means to buy whatever delighted me, and enough wealth to gain society's acceptance… or so he had said. He was given to proclaiming the future as if he could command fate, and me, just as he commanded his ship. Of course I had not yet told him I would desert my station and marry him, and even if I did decide to find my way home, his was not the only ship on the sea.

We reached our destination to call on the merchant's wife who was so eager to purchase the ladies' caps that she didn't notice they were crumpled; she put a Spanish dollar in Pua's palm and another in mine.

"Shouldn't the money go to the Church?" Pua asked.

"Keep yours, Pua," I said. "You have earned it; you will always be able to earn from your sewing if you wish. The time and the muslin were mine to give you."

She had a new light in her eyes and a happy step as we left the mercantile. Our next stop was the 'paniolo grounds to deliver the riding breeches where we arrived to a terrible sight.

A rider lay in the dirt, unable to stand as an angry young bullock faced him and lowered his sharp young horns, hooves pawing the ground.

They had been practicing how to capture bullocks in an arena fenced by lavastone and wood. People often came to watch this new entertainment and Pua and I had slipped away from the mission buildings more than once to see it.

It goes like this: a rider will sit ready on his horse, his fingers twitching and rubbing the rope, or reata, that lies coiled in his right hand. Then a young bull calf is released from a corral into the arena to the good-natured shouts bursting from all around. The rider then throws the wide noose at the end of his reata up into the air above his head and he and his horse charge towards the calf.

His first goal is to get the noose around the neck of the creature and so capture it, but like a harpoon sunk into a whale he is now tied to a powerful force. This is where he depends urgently on his horse. The rider lashes the reata around his saddle horn that is built wide and strong enough to take it. Up on the slope of a volcano it would be the thick trunk of a tree. The bull would be left there until weak enough to be approached and killed. Beefsteak for all, and one less animal to send someone to Doctor Thatcher's hospital.

Early last spring a young, motherless bull calf had been caught from the wild and his life spared despite some argument as to the wisdom of it. He had grown up in captivity, and in time was considered gentle enough to keep, his background gradually forgotten.

Today was the day he suddenly grew up. His hide rippled upon muscular shoulders, and he lowered his head, his once calm eyes now viscous, demonic.

The rider's reata had missed, and the bull had charged, sending the horse trotting away towards the reassurance of the gate as the man still scrambled drunkenly in the red dirt.

Pua and I gasped as we both recognized the young 'paniolo in the dust with ripped breeches trying to stand up on a wounded leg. It was Thaddeus. With sickening intent, the young bull snorted and charged again straight at him, muscles rippling under his oily black coat.

My own cry stopped in my throat as a reata darted through the air —sure and swift—and its wide, circular noose fell with precision down over the bullock's head. The rider leaned back, he and his horse a singular force bracing deep and tightening the reata like a guitarre string and the beast slammed into the red earth not three paces away from Thaddeus.

The stallion sank its rump almost to the ground and his ears flickered in surprise as the force of bull made his hooves skid forward. But the horse and his rider stayed sure and strong. He then dismounted gracefully while his horse lowered his hindquarters to the earth, backing up, keeping the rope taut, and when the bull was tied the rider calmly slit the beast's throat, as if it were all part of a day's work.

Shoulders back and satisfied, he stood straight to the cheers of all as Thaddeus was helped up. I only saw the top of the wide, flat brim of his hat—until for one piercing instant he looked up and smiled directly at me before them all.

The air suddenly tasted of sunlight and sugar. It was Diego.

CHAPTER 23

"*O*, it is a polluted land," sighed Mary. Her fingernails clicked on the bottom of a china bowl as she washed her hands at the sideboard, barely splashing in the shallow water that she had poured so frugally.

"I came upon the Queen and her chiefesses playing a game of whist today—so absorbed was she in her sensual delight of cards that she waved me away—and the young King is down by the shore, sunken in intoxication." She dried her hands, put a pail with table scraps for her hens by the kitchen door, set a stack of plates on the table for the next meal and then sat down, looking wilted, fingering the carved handle of a wooden spoon.

"Have you heard lately from Tabitha?" I asked, thinking that the subject might cheer her.

"Ere will I hear, but not soon enough," she sighed. "And we have lost one of our favorite girls. I taught her, trained her, invested in her education with all I had to give. She was a shining example of our efforts here. And then she just vanished."

She clutched the spoon in a fist and ground the end of the handle into the table. "We must double our efforts. That Vaquero is back, and he had the audacity to propose that he perform his guitarre in church on Sunday. I am disappointed by Charity's encouragement of the idea. That heathen Catholic cannot leave soon enough—we must protect the integrity of our Protestant mission here at any cost."

A chorus of laughter broke the dark mood in the room as Mary and Charity's younger children came running in with a wooden toy.

"Where did you get that?" Mary scolded them.

"At church, from the merchantman," one confessed.

"Children, toys only encourage you in fictitious play," Mary said, "which in turn produces deceitfulness and lies."

Disappointment and guilt fell onto their little faces. "Give it to me," she ordered. "Now, go memorize your Bible verse for the day." She dropped the toy with the happy painted face into the woodbox by the fire.

"Catherine, I would like to see your latest gown for the Princess. My husband said your dressmaking services are finished, but I told him you are needed as much as ever, for she must have modest, simple gowns, with high necklines. And, your own wardrobe must be remade now, as it is the wrong example. You must rip apart all your dresses at the seams and remake each to resemble the restraint and simplicity of ours."

Married to Herman, sentenced to live on an island deserted of love was almost too much to bear, but destroying all the dresses that expressed my happy nature and reminded me of Aunt Sallie would be the last nail in the coffin that held all my younger hopes and ambitions.

"I think not Mary," I told her, keeping my head high. Little did I know the humiliation that was waiting for me the very next morning.

IT HAPPENED down at the stables. I went down early after breakfast to deliver a new pair of riding breeches for Thaddeus, hoping in exchange to catch a glimpse of Diego before he sailed on, but found Herman and Dr. Thatcher there, borrowing two horses.

Diego appeared around the corner of the barn carrying a saddle. We both stopped in mid-stride when we saw each other.

"Thou art leaving us, yet hast thou captured and killed all the wild bullocks?" Herman was asking him.

Diego placed the saddle up on a horse, calmly adjusted the girth and stirrups, his hands smooth, expert, musical. He turned to Herman and faced him, sizing him up.

"Perhaps, el clérigo. You might find more."

"I pray not!" Herman said.

Dr. Thatcher mounted a sorrel gelding and patted its neck. "With these horses, we will reach my patient quickly and be back home by dinnertime," he smiled. "I have encountered the bullocks when on foot, and it was dreadful. Horseman, I am most grateful for your skills."

With a muscled arm, Diego held the bridle of a blood bay as Herman mounted it unsteadily.

Herman looked down at Diego. "The Lord God will protect us," he loudly told Diego, his volume intended to help Diego better understand English. "Wait! Californio, bring me a whip."

Diego looked down and slowly shook his head as he ran his palm over the bay's rump as if he wished it the best of luck.

"He doth not understand," Herman said impatiently, looking around for help and seeing me for the first time. "Wife there! Tell this horseman that I demand a whip. Is there not a single strap in this crude stable?"

I looked away. Diego's jaw muscles tightened as he slowly checked the saddle one more time.

"Mrs. Webster! Do not simply stand there like a dullard!" shouted my husband. "I will procure a whip in the future and use it on thee to drive out thy disobedience!"

Diego's eyes lit up fiercely like the sun caught in a hand mirror. Dr. Thatcher looked down at his horse's brown mane in embarrassment and cleared his throat. "Brother Webster," he said, "let us make time soon to pray and share devotions over Ephesians 5:25."

With great effort I breathed in deeply, speechless, trying to imagine a light within me. I stood as tall as I could so that Herman's words could not make me feel small, but the air around me smelled bitter.

"God has made man master of both beast and woman!" Herman insisted loudly. "Have we run out of whips, Californio? But of course he doth not understand me at all." He raised his voice even louder towards Diego and added, "We must pray to God for thy soul upon my return."

Diego looked Herman right in the eye. "We have no whips for hands that sin against horses," he told him. "You deserve to hold neither whip nor your wife."

Stunned, Herman said, "If I have my way, celebrated Royal Vaquero, thou wilt surely be punished for thine impertinence." Then he kicked the reddish-brown flanks of his horse, sending it leaping forward.

"I will certainly have counsel with your husband, dear Catherine," Doctor Thatcher sadly assured me before turning his horse away.

Herman's long, dark coattails flew behind him in the day's first breeze. This startled his horse, and they soon passed Dr. Thatcher at a runaway gallop.

Diego's straight back was rigid with anger. Down the path under the breadfruit trees his students were approaching, singing and talking, ready to start a new day. I walked to the far side of his horse and put my face into its mane. Diego, his hand along the horse's neck, walked around from the other side and leaned close to me. In that instant, we were alone. He looked into my eyes with great compassion.

"Do you love your husband?" he asked.

I shook my head, letting my tearful eyes tell him all.

He gently reached his forefinger to the edge of my lips in the most tender and sympathetic manner, and slightly, gently, pushed up the corner of my mouth as if he could make me smile. Smiles had always been armor to hide one's true feelings, or weapons in the war for souls, but Diego's smile was a gift. It was catching. Slowly, I managed a little smile back.

The paniolos arrived, and the moment was over. I looked down and realized that I still held Thaddeus's mended breeches. I pushed them at Diego and left before anyone could see me.

A distance away, I turned around to look at the vaquero Diego one last time. To have such an intimate encounter was more than I had hoped for, and to have another soul, almost a stranger, understand my personal anguish was something I would treasure forever. And then, as if we were still connected, he turned his head and for a moment his eyes reached out for mine.

"Farewell," I said, across the crowd of horses and people between us. I knew he had read my lips when he mouthed the same. And then we both turned away.

I walked back to the mission houses, my heart full to the brim yet knowing that when the day wore it off I would again long to have just one more last chance to see the man who had once looked me in the eyes and saw my heart.

If my soul had a map, it would depict a hopeful little ship on a lonely voyage battling the stormy Sea of Matrimony. It would stop at the sheltered Bay of Diego, long enough to find enough provisions for its spirit before it sailed forward again past the rocky Straits of Broken Threads to the Ocean of Disappointment, and then on until lost in a lifeless paper sea.

CHAPTER 24

Not far outside my back kitchen door lay the waste pit. I was throwing out an empty bottle when a scrap of paper from its depth fluttered up, lifted by fingers of air that placed it lightly down upon the toe of my shoe. I took it gingerly and meant to cast it back into the refuse when certain words caught my attention. So I paused to read what was penned between its two ripped edges.

"—that the American Board of Commissioners for Foreign Missions is funded by the Confederacy is not our concern. There are those privy to this knowledge who think it disillusioning to learn that our cause here is paid for by slave labor—they say it troubles their conscience that our great works for the Lord here in the Sandwich Islands have been financed by the suffering of these African slaves. While this more or less is true, if church members at home would part with more coins at offering, or when the time comes that the Mission is self-sustaining, this will no longer be the case. Until this comes to pass, it is not a fact to be advertised."

I felt like I'd swallowed lead. Through Thaddeus I had learned that the Church's first foothold on Maui was not gained by the might and cleverness of their missionary men, nor the almighty printing press, but by the freed African slave Betsey Stockton. She had learned the Hawaiian language before most of the missionaries, and because the powerful Queen Keōpūolani liked Betsey and wanted her to teach the prince, the missionaries were allowed to come to Maui. The influence of Thaddeus' beloved teacher was so strongly evident in the learned minds of her students that they rivaled the knowledge of some who had come to teach and save.

I smoothed the paper out on the dining table, read it again, and then placed it in my pocket. I went about my chores on into evening as the note burned a hole in my skirt. All night I dreamt scraps of dreams: of whips, and songs sung low in mournful molasses voices—then I was in a hot field picking cotton as a slave master cracked his whip above my head. Suddenly, his face changed into Herman's. I sat up quickly, tore the tangled bed sheet from my legs and lit my chamber stick. Herman was gone. Dawn was approaching.

MY FIST TREMBLED as I raised it before the Goodwins' door in the blue light. All was quiet. I tried to breathe. I hesitated, summoned more courage, and then knocked. I heard a shuffle; the door creaked open, and a lantern was pushed towards me through the doorway. Reverend Goodwin peeked out, still wearing his nightcap. It was a white cotton sleeping-hat, which in the island climate he wore more out of habit than need. At home in New England, the coldest hour is dawn, the stove is cold, and a sleeping hat is necessary. But a missionary man clings doggedly to his habits as if they were an edifice to fortify his spirit against the uncivilized land he lives in.

"Why, Mrs. Webster?" he said, squinting his eyes, ushering me in. "What brings thee here at this hour?"

I thought I could hear Mrs. Goodwin rising and dressing in the other room. I had hoped that she would still be asleep.

Our conversation continued in quiet tones. "Sit down," he said, his face waiting expectantly as he stoked stale embers to build a cooking fire. Only last week this man had preached a sermon on God's mercy, so surely he would be grateful to know, and he had the power to make right such an injustice.

"Tell me, Reverend," I said. "Was our passage by ship, all the Bibles, and even the flour to bake our bread purchased by the agony, tears, and suffering of human beings?" I shoved the paper towards him and he fumbled for his spectacles, then held it up to the light.

He must have read it twice because he remained standing there for the longest time, stroking his chin.

"Catherine," he finally said in a patient tone, "This is one reason our printing press is so important. It prints tracts that will rouse the sympathy of many back home and they in turn will donate to our cause."

"But how can we be even temporarily dependent on money given by slaveholders? It is tainted by the suffering that produced it."

Reverend Goodwin looked about, and seeing that the door to their bedroom was still closed, he reached out and removed my bonnet. I cringed at the personal nature of his gesture. He placed his dark, sun-freckled hands on my head like preachers do with babies or for souls praying for salvation. One palm cupped my forehead and the other hand rested on my crown as he pressed his long, jagged finger-nails into the base of my skull.

I jerked my head back so that he could no longer touch me, my face hot with unfounded shame. It was then that I thought I heard a tiny soft wooden creak at the bedroom door. I had thought it was closed—yet was that the shadow of the frame or a crack in the doorway?

He spoke simply and slowly, as if I were a child. "The world is built by sin upon sin. We are in the world, but not of it, and it is not for you to question the decisions that men make. Let us not cast the first stone; for you cause your own share of injustice."

Had he truly read the letter in the dim light? He was not making sense. "What injustice do *I* cause?" I asked.

He stepped closer, reached for my arm, and his breath struggled and hissed across his parchment teeth as he found his next words. "My dear—like Eve, thou were created especially to gladden a man's heart. Pray, and read your Bible more, for thou art an easy tool for the Devil to use. Perhaps ye were too pretty to be considered a missionary."

Pretty, as if I only existed inside the word. It was sometimes an obstacle that always took me by surprise as I went about my life as any other human being—then sometimes abruptly pulled up short to realize all my efforts overlooked and my human contributions tallied up based on something I had nothing to do with, rather than everything I worked so hard to produce.

I shot up, pulled my skirt away from my feet and bolted towards the door. His jaw dropped, his eyes were shocked, deprived, as I deserted his little sermon.

"Thou mustn't flee—" he said, as if I had teased him with an apple and a bite lay stuck in his throat.

"What about this letter?" I turned. "What of the chains of iron and the bleeding stripes on the backs of poor unfortunate souls? Why did we travel to the ends of the earth to save, when we could have tried to save those at home?"

"Thou hast ears to hear but do not heed my words," he whispered, throwing the shred of letter into the fire. "Thy feminine charms are but trickery. May God punish your wicked nature!"

I strode out through the Mission gates towards the sea, furious, wondering exactly why it was that Reverend Goodwin could look only at my appearance instead of the burning facts that he did not want to see.

THAT MORNING WAS hectic and all the little mundane things that could go wrong did. A meal followed by a sermon was to be held in the main mission dining room—it would be full with visiting missionaries, a sea captain, a handful of chiefs and chiefesses, the merchant and his wife, and Cornelius the printer.

I was setting the table just before people arrived when I found out that some of the dinner napkins were ruined with holes chewed in them by rats—so I made do and put out the clean, untouched ones which would have to be shared.

Reverend Goodwin was still preaching his long sermon based on the book of Judges in the hot room as Charity and I finally cleared the table, carrying away plates, silverware and napkins to make room for Bibles.

"And Delilah said to Samson," he quoted, glaring at me like a rejected suitor, "Tell me, I pray thee, wherein thy great strength lieth, and wherewith thou mightest be bound to afflict thee." His head kept turning to follow me as I moved around the table. "Delilah was a temptress and sought to undo him."

I had the table almost cleared when Reverend Goodwin pulled his gravy-spotted napkin off of his lap and peered through the hole chewed in its center. I had set it out especially for him. As he began the final prayer he twisted it in his hands like the Bible verses he wrung to serve his own thoughts.

Charity joined me out in the kitchen and we began in on the mountain of dishes. "Let me and the other women wash these," she said kindly. "You did so much to prepare the meal. Perhaps you can set out the pie tins and rolling pins."

I paused on my way to the storeroom and stood quietly by the open door which gave a wide view of the sea, scanning for sails and wondering if there was one less ship anchored out at Lahaina Roads, one with a course set for Alta California.

Sermon ended, the women gathered into the kitchen to help clean up and bake sweet potato pies. Mary looked over at me tartly, the way a woman gazes upon another who has aroused the interest of her husband. She was a wife made poor by a man frugal with his love.

I looked down at the flour I was stirring to see that it was covered in worm webs.

"Mary, where is the flour that came in last month?" I asked quietly, not wanting our visitors to notice. "This is infested with weevil eggs."

"That is what a flour sifter is for," she said loudly. "The maggots make a special treat for my hens. We can be thrifty with our goods and deserve a chicken dinner on special Sundays."

Looks of surprise and guilt played across their faces as they stirred in butter and salt. "Of course, Mary," said one. "You are a Saint."

Mrs. Goodwin did not deny it and proudly scraped the rock hard flour into another bowl, handing it to the woman who took it with reluctance.

I tried to scrape the webs off on the rim of the bowl but they clung to the rough wooden spoon. The batter was not yet finished, but I was done.

I could bear it no more, but knew just where to run.

CHAPTER 25

$\mathcal{I}$ stood knee-deep in the calm azure water of the cove that lay cradled by massive shoulders of black lava rock. The most western promontory on the island was only reachable by a thin trail that ran through the thick tropical forest. It was choked by wild sugarcane and embraced by flowering vines falling from a ceiling of tall breadfruit trees that opened like a curtain to reveal the sea.

Imagine an enormous length of seashore where the entire coastline stretches up to turn a corner; the empty waves, and a great silence, save for them. Then imagine the peace of a little cove, protected by reef and an enormous brown lava cliff jutting out into the water like the great bow of an iron ship.

I had never seen a soul there and had begun to think of it as abandoned. Its borders were too sacred to trespass according to the natives, and still a territory of Satan's according to Herman. Which was why I had never seen anyone there. Which was why I was drawn to it.

There I could hear myself think. Away from the busy mission, and the way my faith in it was breaking like a wagon driven wildly by Reverend Goodwin over a field of rough lava, Herman seated beside him cracking a whip.

There on the beach I felt safe from the human strays and sailors with teeth of yellow brown grinning with lusty smiles in Lahaina-town, down where ships met shore sparking a friction of thoughts and needs and unbridled deeds at our crossroads of the world.

The horizon was a sharp line where the pale midday sky met the deep indigo of the distant ocean. I stared out at it until it calmed me, took my deepest breaths and waded out into the calm water, pantalettes rolled up, skirt gathered up high in my arms. I longed for wave-sailing with Leilani but I hadn't seen her out on the ocean since that evening on the *Fair Wind*; she had been taken under Mary's wing to learn the Bible and civilized arts and she mostly stayed on her sacred island where I could not go un-summoned.

Beneath the clear surface, bright-colored fish of lemon yellow, iris blue, parrot green, with patterns of stripes and polka-dots swam curiously around me, and one bravely nibbled my ankle. It tickled. I laughed softly.

Far off in the distance, I could see the island of Moloka'i. Beyond that, farther than the eye could see, was the isle O'ahu where Emmie was. I ached for her friendship. The water beckoned, cool and clear. I stepped in deeper up to my thighs where the water darkened the edges of my crumpled skirt.

I did not hear him approaching until his fierce voice barked right behind me, casting my smile to stone.

"'Aina kapu!"

I whirled around. It was the young high chief, the one who mastered the wave at Honolua, the one who kept his back turned to missionaries that night on the *Fair Wind*, the one who lost Leilani because of them. Behind him stood his fierce retinue, their arms crossed, eyes glittering. He looked even more frightening in close proximity, clothed in an unbuttoned Admiral's coat, ti leaves, kapa cloth, and sunshine. The tattoo on his cheek was a bird set in a circle. A pattern of black triangles, corners touching, was inked across one side of his chest.

"Yes, I realize this land is forbidden," I admitted. *"E kala mai 'oe ia'u."*

There was no hint of forgiveness in his face—only the grief and fury of a lover robbed of his beloved. Had he known of the unborn child? In his eyes lived a vertigo made by changes that had blown into his world and I suddenly realized he saw the invasion made manifest in me, the trespasser. The kingdom he loved had been a prize taken under England's wing and jealously desired by other countries. His people were becoming almost lost in a crowd of whalers, merchants and adventurers that all sought to take something. But it was the missionaries who wanted more: their heart and soul.

I apologized again, my voice sounding so awkwardly formal, lightweight. My body felt as heavy as an hourglass when time is up, my blood draining down towards my feet like sand.

"You are murderers and thieves," he said, taking a step towards me. "You look at our appearance and judge us inferior. You massacred our grandparents at Olowalu."

His accusation was a blow. "Please, do not look at my skin and think me one of them," I said, remembering that evil and oft-hushed event that took place not many decades past south of the very shore that I stood upon.

He did not reply, which made me more uncomfortable than if he had. I went on. "You need not tell me what that feels like to be judged wrongly, as unequal. I know what it is to have someone look at me as a woman and do the same. Cast your anger towards a more accurate target and look your enemy in the face: there are those much more deserving of your hate than I—those who have not come in goodwill like myself."

The muscles of his chest and arms flexed, undecided, ready. "But by taking their beautiful woman, I will throw a spear to their hearts." He reached out for a blond temple curl that fell from my bonnet.

Fear twisted my stomach. I had to be careful. "Being a woman, I—I am vulnerable to your strength," I began, "yet how is that much different from your beautiful, mysterious, desired island—defenseless to the men who have come for spoil—and not strong enough or yet hardened and cunning enough to protect itself?"

He dropped my curl but moved in even closer, sharks circling in his eyes. He seemed to rise up higher as he cast his eyes down at mine. "We are not defenseless, and neither are you," he said. "You speak like we are endangered."

We faced each other in a silent exchange, strange equals. My heart pounded on, louder than the waves, until the chief finally crossed his arms and glanced down, then up, then away, dismissing me.

They stood unmovable—like lava stone, watching me go as I walked away with trembling knees.

CHAPTER 26

Article Twenty-Three: The Pink Silk Corselet

I left the hot sand beach behind me and melted into the forest's kind shade. When I reached the tree where I had tied my horse I found only broken branches and deep hoof-cuts in the earth.

It was a long walk back. The trail began to cut inland bringing me along the shore south of the forbidden boundary where an outgoing tide had left the surface of the sand as smooth and crisp as a pie crust. Several ships were tacking at angles up the channel towards the open sea and I shaded my eyes, straining to see any flags or clue for one that might be bound for Alta California. I wondered if in the hold of one of them there might be a band of stallions and mares settling in for a long voyage, shifting uneasily, yearning for solid land beneath their sensitive legs.

That was when hoofbeats whispered in the sand behind me and I nervously spun around to see who was approaching.

And then he was there. Without a word, Diego reached down

towards me and I took his arm—bent at the elbow as solid as a rung on a wooden ladder. He kicked out of his stirrup to let me step up with it, lifted me up, and in the next moment I sat behind him holding on tightly as his horse moved beneath us, galloping away. He sat erect, chest up, as if nothing in the world could ever make him afraid. My hat blew behind my back and his horse spooked at my bonnet ribbons flying like banners atop a ship's mast as we bolted through the air. Reaching down to hold on tighter, I felt the strength of his stomach muscles. It jolted me to suddenly be so very close to a man that I had tried so hard to let go of. An unknown kind of joy whirled through me.

WE RODE inland along a stream until we stopped by a waterfall that cascaded into a pool trimmed with ferns and mountain-apple trees. The fruit was ripe.

"May we stop here señorita?" Diego asked. Herman had never uttered the word "we."

Diego was waiting for my answer. We. I paused as if one foot was stepping out over the edge of the waterfall. I looked up at the apple tree. From the back of the horse it was easy to pick one; I reached up and one fell willingly, heavy, into my palm. I weighed the apple and then took a bite. It tasted sweet.

I nodded.

He helped me down from the saddle, dropped the reins, and his horse reached down and nickered happily into a patch of grass. A light breeze laughed in the treetops above. A bird warbled high up, and far away another answered its call. Water splashed into the pool sounding bright on the surface and low from its depths.

We were silent.

I sat, cool air filling my skirts and petticoats that billowed down to rest on the shadowed moss and stone. I untied the ribbon at my throat and slowly placed my hat upon bright flowers. He joined me and we faced each other, both catching our breath from the wild ride.

"Are you recovered?" he finally asked.

"Yes."

"Gracias a Dios—I have found you. I must give you something before I leave, for I will sail back to Alta California as soon as the bloodstock returns from the Big Island." He reached into his cape and produced a small, newly-bound leather book.

"Open it," he urged.

There on the pages inside I recognized the familiar treble clefs and staves and musical notes, the illustration of angels on the frontispiece, and the elegant ink inscription: "This belongs to…" in my mother's own hand.

"You mended my hymnal!"

Warmth and comfort fell on me like a soft blanket as I lovingly touched the little pages. I pressed it closed, holding firmly the strong leather cover that now protected what was inside.

"A vaquero can do more with leather than making saddles or bridles or the reata," he said. "Gracias—thank you for lending me your little book. In time the leather will deepen to a dark brown. I hope in that faraway year and faraway place you will look at the cover and remember me."

My fingers left the smooth leather, paused in mid-air, and then with butterflies in my chest I touched the top of his hand. He moved his hand above mine, lightly feeling my hand as if to memorize it.

"I will remember," I said, daring to reach up to touch the side of his face, not wanting time to ever erase the shape of his chin or the color of his eyes. I felt his jaw muscle move. Then, my gesture having given him permission, he softly stroked my cheek and his hand came to rest on the side of my bare head.

"I should take you back," he said softly, like a question.

"The Mission isn't going anywhere," I said, the wry truth of it spilling out, each word a heavy pebble. "I will be back there soon enough, thinking of a man I will never see again. I would not like to forget his shoulders," I said, reaching my arms along them and then around to feel his strong back.

He gently took the book from my lap, placed it carefully inside my bonnet, took off his soft wool serape and draped it across thick grass dappled with sunshine that had found its way through the canopy of leaves above us. Then, fingers spread wide beneath my corset, he gently guided me down.

He was close above me, his flexing arms taking his weight. A balmy breeze set flowers falling down around us bringing their lush fragrance. His lips were just above mine.

"I should not want to forget your lips," he said tenderly—and then he gently kissed me. He pushed away to better look into my eyes, searching for my blessing, asking for more.

"Let me not forget your kiss," I answered, pulling him back to me.

How sweet a sin could taste. Inside the moment of that kiss, I knew deeply what was surely about to happen between us. My mind spun as I tried to recall Emmie's womanly advice; I tried to count my days of the month, but days turned to kisses and then I lost count of them all.

I had often been nervous at the thought of ever being with a man, but the woman that I suddenly became with Diego knew instinctively, easily, what to do. We were two worlds crushing together with all the want of having been so far apart. The shadows of leaves danced across us as the sun shifted along its afternoon path.

In time we lay still, nose to nose, sharing our breath like Hawai'ians, his hips still lost in my white lace petticoats. I looked up in wonder at the sky and the sunlit trees that were his halo. He cradled me in his arms, pulled me to his side and I rested my head inside the curve of his shoulder. We stayed like that, listening to the forest.

"I should not want to ever forget lying with you," he finally said with a smile curving the edge of his strong mouth.

I was no longer the woman in the plain dresses, the smothered spirit, the obedient mind, the muzzled mouth, the conquered woman.

"I am afraid I am forgetting it already," I teased. I had become a bird, fierce with freedom.

He raised his eyebrows in mock indignation and began slowly

unfastening each button down the front of my dress, struggling with them like a man does, wondering which one would cause my protest.

I laughed, waited on a few more buttons, then pushed him away and got up, stood at the edge of the deep pool, smoothly undid the rest of them and slipped off my dress. Wearing nothing but my pink Chinese silk corselet, I sank into the agate water. He dove in after me and I playfully swam away towards a hollow echoing splash sounding behind the waterfall. I moved along the edges of its force to discover a passage to a little cave lit by rays of sunlight shimmering through the curtain of water and dancing upon a wall of lava-stone.

"Found you," he said, joining me, arrested for an instant, eyes wide at the sight of the wet pink silk almost invisible against my skin. He stared, transfixed by me with awe and desire, a look that only a woman in her fullness knows.

We circled, then in a rush drew close again, my arms around his neck and knees hugging his waist.

In my heart I was no longer the sad wife of Herman Webster. All my resolve to be perfect was terribly and beautifully broken. A tear spilled out of the corner of my eye. He kissed it away as if to make certain that no matter how lonely or gray my days would go on to be, a timeless smile would always remain within me.

CHAPTER 27

OCTOBER, 1834

Article Twenty-Four: The Pale Yellow Calico

The church boasted two thousand in attendance, by Reverend Goodwin's count, on the first Sunday in October. Every pew was full, the aisles crowded, and the windows were open so that all those gathered outside could hear.

I sat restlessly on the hard wooden pew next to Charity Thatcher, turning the pages of my hymnal as Herman took his turn at the pulpit. His lengthy work on a new hymnal translated into Hawai'ian was being debuted that very day fresh off the printing press, and because of that modern wonder the church was supplied with an abundance of the new hymnals.

Herman proudly announced a page number and fumbled in his

pocket for his silver pitch pipe. He checked his breast pocket and then remembered his right pocket where he always kept it. Vexed, he pulled out his empty hand and proceeded to lead the congregation in an off-key Praise God From Whom All Blessings Flow.

Ho'onani i ka Makua mau,
Ke Keiki me ka 'Uhane no,
Ke Akua mau ho'omaika'i pu,
Ko keia ao, ko kela ao
Amene

I preferred to look at my own little hymnal as I already knew the native words by heart as he had recited them around our house many times. I touched the beautiful illustration of angels.

My fingers felt ashamed. For weeks the horror of what I had done crept along the edges of my mind trying to fight the happiness that Diego had left inside me. I had tried earnestly to repent, but like Abigail and her laudanum my mind kept returning to what it craved.

I studied the ink angels, so pure and perfect, but their image dissolved into a picture of Diego and me at the waterfall and his halo of sunshine as he lay above me.

I turned the hymnal page, just as I had tried to do with Diego, but my resolution had been weak and quickly broken. Emmie's womanly advice proved true and I had safely avoided the danger of pregnancy. The vaqueros had stayed on, still waiting for their best stallion to be shipped back over to them from the Big Island, and they used the time to show the paniolo how to make saddles, bridles, and play guitarres. Up the steep slopes of the great volcano, they returned to hunt the terrible wild bullocks that still reigned there.

Charity looked over at me and smiled, unaware that it was not a hymn I was seeing on the page. I saw Diego and myself the morning we met before dawn near the freshwater stream by Moku'ula and how we stole away down the beach until we found a tiny little cove just big enough to hold us, surrounding us by lava on three sides, opening out to the dusky blue sea and sky. I had worn only my most delicate underthings beneath my cloak, their packing tissue crumpled up the night before and thrown into the fire, and I remembered the way my soft skin slipped under the whispers of feminine ruffles and lace and the strength of his hands. I remembered the yellow moon setting in the pink-lavender west like an old paper lantern as we lay cradled in soft white sand beneath his wool serape.

Charity nudged and pointed to a page in her hymnal. I was on the wrong hymn. I flipped pages and joined her in song, but my eyes drifted from treble clef and notes falling off the staff into the soft mane of his horse as I ran my hands underneath it to hold fast to its powerful neck. Diego had sat behind me holding my waist as we rode bareback, taking me along a narrow, secret trail he had found through a fragrant forest of flowering maile vines. I thought about how his hair and skin had smelled of leather, and the sea. He had touched me as lovingly as if I were his guitarre, running his fingers down my smooth white stomach more tenderly than the way Herman had ever caressed his Bible pages, and I was finally as treasured as Herman's beloved typeface and gold-edged paper.

I was sitting up straight propped up by my tight corset, transfixed with a secret smile, unaware that the singing had stopped. Jumping awake, I closed my hymnal and let it rest on my lap in the folds of my pale yellow skirt. It was a dress made to be happy in, with round, wide, soft bias-cut sleeves—the shape of a bell—that began just off the edge of my shoulder, then sweetly tailored close and tight from elbow to wrist, a style that surely made any wearer feel serene and smart. Tiny sprigs of green leaves were printed on the sunny cotton skirt that Diego had once reverently smoothed back down over my knees one afternoon when we had stolen away inside the top of the church steeple. We could see the entire land and coast, but no-one could see us; we were higher than Lahainatown but the belfry's upward reach ended far below our hearts.

Surely I had committed great sins, but I could not wholly feel the shame of it. I looked down at a blank page in the endpapers, wondering what would be illustrated upon it by my imagination after my next stolen hour with Diego, whenever that would be, if that would be.

"Heed the will of the Lord," Herman called loudly, interrupting my thoughts. "There are some in this very assembly who should be ashamed. Who here wears the mark of the Beast, those tattoos that forever brand thee as Satan's own?" He clutched the thick lapels of his frock coat, one that I had sewn with an unfinished pocket. Whenever he lost things he would chastise me for my poor workmanship and I would just smile.

"Who continues to spend wasted time playing in the sea?" he continued. "When the waves rise up our church is empty, my prayer-fully wrought sermons go unheard, villages are deserted and Bibles lie forlornly cast aside. Hear this: not long ago a man at 'Uo went out surfing and he was found floating with only the upper half of his body remaining!" Herman's voice echoed along the walls to the back of the church. "At this very moment monstrous sharks await beneath the waters to take more wave-sliders down into Hell!"

He continued shouting the wrath of God from the pulpit at sweet, dismayed, browbeaten faces, and the repugnant old Reverend Goodwin walked through the assembly with a bamboo stick, sharply rapping the shoulders of any who had fallen asleep. My head spun to make sense of how the greatness of creation—the stars at night, and the mystery of life—could fit into a religion constructed by man. I had never questioned it back in New Bedford, but lately it seemed to me that putting mankind's rituals and typeface and rules upon what is Great and Divine, in order to devise a religion, seemed to dampen the life of it—like trying to shut sunlight inside a box.

It was dizzying to make sense of it. The church spun, and the wooden pew felt hard even through my thick petticoats. My corset strings felt like they were shrinking. Darkness speckled the edges of my vision and my face was icy. Charity noticed me swaying and put her kind arm around me. It was a women's lot—not the first time one of us had fainted in church. The sermons were long, the days were hard, our corsets were tight.

I sat there reeling, clutching my hymnal against the bodice of my yellow dress, pressing it into the row of sharp mint-jelly-green glass buttons. I looked down to see a line of button-marks pressed into the cover as I pulled it from my waist. I kept staring. My waist.

Suddenly, I knew. Right there in church, to add another layer of sin upon it. I felt a quickening inside. I was with child.

Article Twenty-Four: The Cotton and Whalebone Corset

The mission houses were soon behind us as my guide, Keola, led me forward. They had spared me the nervous mare, the one with a short neck and a jarring trot. My journey to Abigail's side of the island was the escape I had been yearning for, and I was far more skittish than the horse; my heart beat wildly inside my hard corset like an animal trapped in a cage. I had laced the bars of whalebone tightly to hide my secret, hoping to postpone as long as possible that day of reckoning and judgement that surely loomed ahead.

The grand vista of sea and distant islands as we rounded the southern promontory gave my troubled mind only flashes of merciful distraction, like tiny glass shards of sun. If I found sweet forgetfulness in sleep or a random moment, my predicament slammed back into my thoughts so ferociously I could barely breathe. There was not a soul in whom I could confide, and I weighed carefully the consequences that would come from telling Diego; like a runaway horse, I was bolting away from him and my life, seeking space enough to think before the reality would destroy our lives.

Abigail had just borne a daughter, which providentially gave endorsement to my sudden trip. Keola led me past expansive fishponds and up the isthmus to the eastern side of the same mountains that loomed above our town of Lahiana. The ancient volcanic range was considered impossible to cross, and only the fabled King's Bird-catchers who traveled from tree to tree in search of precious feathers were its only trespassers.

To my right the massive shoulders of Haleakala volcano disappeared inside a blanket of high clouds as the road led north up to the Adamson mission. It wound through an old grove of koa trees, and the rich scent of earth and leaves cleansed by rain lessened my nausea. Through the branches emerged a freshly whitewashed building made of lava rock and koa wood. A sense of comfort greeted me. Sitting at the north end of the isthmus, Henry and Abigail's mission had a harbor of its own which was less popular than our Lahaina Roads, making it removed from the traffic of so many ships and people.

Dr. Henry appeared on the porch to welcome me, wiping his hands on a towel, interrupted from his medical duties. Abigail would soon embrace me and give me the comfort and advice I was desperate for—the thought made me want to cry. A calmness settled down upon me as the puzzle pieces assembled together: a good doctor, a trusted friend, a remote location.

The first thing that I noticed about Henry was that his kind, cheerful face had grown a deep-set look of worry. "My dear Abigail!" he called down the hallway as he led me towards her room. He turned and smiled at me, his eyes kind, and compassionate—a trait that any good doctor does well to have. They made a person want to fall at his mercy; to trust their life to him, to save them, to keep their most intimate matters secret.

"Abigail," he called again as we reached their bedroom door. "A great blessing has arrived!"

I rushed through the door into an airless room, eager to see her face. I squinted in the dim light to find her features, but they blended like an island chameleon against her white pillows, white gown, and white sheets.

"Kittie," she whispered, turning to look at me with a pale face and a hazy smile. With great effort, she held a small bundle towards me. "I have a daughter."

"Abigail, how precious!" In an instant I was beside her, eager to see the tiny infant wrapped inside.

Her long, ashen fingers weakly pulled a veil away to show me her treasure. What I then saw choked me with a silent shriek of horror.

Shiny black worms, engorged and thick like Satan's fingers clasped and writhed against the baby's delicate and tender body. A trickle of scarlet slithered down white newborn skin. I shot Henry a distraught look.

"They are but leeches," he reassured me. "They will drain the infected blood and help the babe. She has a fever."

Abigail looked at me with an anxious smile. "Kittie, you really shouldn't have come. Henry knows just what to do, and how could you have spared the time? I have maidens here to help me pack my things; I had feared I could not do it by myself." She closed her thin, blueish eyelids in relief.

"Abby—you're leaving?"

"She will sail home to Boston on Sabbatical as soon as she is well enough to travel," Henry explained. "It is a hard life here. I fear I am to blame. My only consolation is that she will be safe in the bosom of her family, and when I am finished with my contract and another doctor comes to take my place I will follow her." An assistant called him away, and as he stood in the doorway he said, "You see, I am relent-lessly needed. I am grateful you are here."

"Abigail," I said, pushing on through waves of nausea, "we had promised to be there for each other—I hadn't known that you needed me so. Have I have failed you as a friend?"

"No, I have not been myself, and did not want you to see me this way. Look, Kittie, she has my eyes, and Henry's lips."

I pretended admiration, trying to hide a look of revulsion as she took a handkerchief and smeared the trail of blood from the baby's pale pink rose-petal skin.

"Rest, Abigail. I will check on your boys," I said, feeling failure at deserting her so quickly, glad for a reason to escape the room.

They were in the kitchen, watched over by a young native girl who rushed to embrace me. Then she smiled shyly and slipped out the screen door.

Abigail's little boys, oddly quiet, were playing under the kitchen table, so I knelt down to say hello, feeling the soft air sigh from my billowing skirts. They stared at me with eyes as round as saucers, and the older, three years of age, snatched a cork from his tiny brother's mouth and began to suck on it. The younger wailed and began crawling over his wooden building blocks to play with an empty glass bottle with letters stamped into its square sides. I peered closer, took it from him, and held it up. The light touched the blue glass and set it aglow. It was laudanum.

The little one suddenly stopped his crying and curled up to nap on the worn gray-painted wooden floor. I tried to take the cork from the boy's mouth, but after being scratched by his sharp little fingernails, I gave up and began absent-mindedly stacking his blocks as I wondered what to do. He sat next to me making little sucking noises as he stared at me, unblinking, with large, pale blue opium-bottle eyes.

CHAPTER 29

I spent six unsettling days with Abigail and began to understand why she had not wanted me near. She was not the Abigail I knew, but rather a living dead, sometimes sleeping with her eyes open, or awake and very cross at me until she realized it was I who was pressing a cold cloth to her forehead, wiping drool from her chin, or feeding her bread and butter and soup. Her Hawai'ian helper had attempted to ply her with native remedies, but Henry, a licensed doctor with the best American medical training, had declined what was thought of as barbaric practices and did everything in his knowledge to help his wife. He gave her regular doses of opium, and mercury, and treatments with his best strain of leeches. He was afraid the island water was tainted, and so instead the only liquid he gave her were small doses of brandy-and-milk.

Day by day the climate of niceness faded as my presence was grown accustomed to and the Adamson's domestic situation became a most personal and awkward scene. On the morning that the dwindling supply of laudanum completely ran out, Henry gave her his last crimson drops of straight opium, praying that his box of medical supplies were with the ship that had just dropped anchor. By the next afternoon, Abigail was shaking and wailing as Henry shouted cruelly at a sailor to go check for his goods. I was shocked at the gentle doctor's harsh outburst, and was relieved when two sailors hurried up to the door with a wooden crate stamped: DR. HENRY ADAMSON, ABCFM MAUI, MEDICAL SUPPLIES.

I LEFT before my intended stay was over. I grieved for Abigail and mourned that she had not the presence of mind to listen to my woeful plight, and that she might not even be there long enough to shelter me even if she had been able. So I kept my secret. As I waited days for Keola to arrive and fetch me, my anxiety grew.

Early one morning, giving up on Keola, I abruptly saddled my horse and bade farewell, bargaining with my guilty conscience: I had made Abigail promise to stop at Lahaina first—there we would strengthen her and the baby with good care and lovingkindness, and then bid her farewell with love and tea and cakes and gifts before she undertook her voyage back to New England.

CHAPTER 30

ithout Keola I was not exactly sure which road to take. Unable to withstand the rough gait at a trot, I slowed to a walk to ease a cramp in my stomach. The road grew steeper and wound along a rushing stream. Instead of reaching the flat isthmus of the island I found myself in a thick forest of koa and sandalwood trees that clung to steep, verdant slopes.

Feeling deeply fatigued and uneasy that I might be lost, I finally stopped and dismounted to rest in a small ravine. I led my horse to drink from the stream and unfastened the buttons at the neck of my brown cotton dress. In the misty air crept a feeling that something immense was near. I looked up, the air cleared for a moment, and through the trees I spied a massive pillar of stone, higher than a castle tower.

Beyond that stood impossibly steep volcanic peaks. The sun had just left its apex and was traveling over the range leaving blue shadows and I suddenly knew where I was: the sacred I'ao valley. If I were to follow the sun west over the mountaintops like a bird I would be home. I recalled Keola's tale as we had ridden along on the expedition, of a secret path of the ancient warriors that was the only trail leading west through the extinct volcanic mountain range. If by miracle I found it I would be back at Lahaina in only a few hours' time. Half the day had already been spent. I did not want to be alone and lost at nightfall.

A scramble of hooves broke the stillness as my frightened horse jumped, her head high. Had she feared a wild bullock? Only the sound of birds, miles of birds from ancient treetops. Suddenly, only the faraway chorus could be faintly heard as the voices closest to me fell silent.

I sat upon a mossy rock and hugged my little valise as if it could protect me. The clouds were settling down low all around me swirling like ghosts in the aging light between the shadows of solemn trees. A single bird suddenly burst into song nearby, making me jump, then it landed on a stone thickly fringed by ferns. Its body was yellow, with soft olive-green wings, and she had a thin, curved beak that was longer than my little finger.

"Hello, *'Akialoa*. If you have so much to say, then tell me what to do now?" My voice sounded faint, trembling like my cold hands. Another yellow-green bird perched down beside it, and they chirped and warbled to one another. White fog knelt quietly on the thin rocky path I had followed, cloaking the forest about me. Abruptly, the two birds fell silent.

The misty air moved like a whirlpool before my eyes. A figure began to take shape, darker gray against gray, and then another, and another. Emerging from the fog, silently approaching me, were the most barbaric men I had ever seen. I blinked. They did not disappear. Their finger and toenails were longer than the beaks of the 'Akialoa, curving into claws. Their limbs were athletic, sinewy, powerful. They wore feather lei around their necks, and small mantles made of thousands of feathers about their hips. They stood silently, eyes staring fiercely from tattooed faces. So the tales of the Bird-Catchers living in these mountains were true—an elite group of the island's most gymnastic men, selected by the Maui Chief to procure precious feathers, a currency that had always been more valuable to them than gold.

Then their leader turned and made a sound like a birdcall. His voice echoed against the steep mountains, and brought more magnificent feathered men like him standing in front of me.

"Aloha," I told him. "I am seeking to return to Lahaina. *'O au mikanele lilo*… I am a lost missionary."

The bird-man held his tattooed hand out to me, fingers reaching forward like talons. There was once a time when I would have refused such a frightening offer; but there was also a time when I never would have admitted that I was a lost missionary.

THE QUICKEST PATH home was from branch to branch; that was how these bird-men traveled. My horse was set loose to find her way down to the mission and I was handed and swung, carried and passed as I clung to the bird-men, trying to not look down.

Gradually, I noticed I was taking deeper breaths, as if my corset stays were loosening their clasp around my lungs. I smiled in wonder, feeling like a bird in flight. We flew so close to a waterfall that its mist exhaled cool moss scented breath on my cheeks. Then instantly we were wrapped in sunlight, and through the canopy of leaves with mountain peaks below me and treetops above. Poised hundreds of feet above an emerald valley, I caught a glance of my toe reluctantly leaving a thick branch, and for a long moment only air and a wisp of cloud lay beneath it. In this situation I had to put all my trust in the man that carried me. And then came a heart-stopping moment as he paused. He let go with one arm, and I feared he meant to drop me to my death. He stealthily moved his hand out, and in one motion his long fingernails skillfully clasped a bright red bird that had perched close to us. He put it in a net bag at his hip, smiled at me, and with a birdcall from his throat we continued on.

Then, sooner that I had expected, my feet and valise were set down on solid ground again where the mountain ravine opened up west towards the sea, and with much aloha exchanged they disappeared back into the forest.

.   .   .

GLAD TO BE BACK on my side of the island I walked faster and faster in the hot sunshine, scanning the coast and the faraway ships in the late afternoon light. Had Diego left? The land sloped gently down towards the harbor, gravity and nervous hope ushering my tired body as fast as my skirts would allow. Down towards the lush green coast I went with bones as heavy as anchors but I would remember for the rest of my life the time I was an island bird, when I was terrified but held safe, flying far above the earth and all its worries.

CHAPTER 31

THE FOURTH WEEK OF OCTOBER, 1834

Article Twenty-Five: The Unfashionable Rose-Dotted Lawn

The stone was bare when I returned. I checked it hopefully the next day, and the next. Nothing. Had Diego left?

He and I had devised a system of placing a cocoa-nut prominently upon a large lava-stone that was smoothed by centuries of waves; it was a signal that we would try to find each other after sunset at the reef where ghosts of lava reached up in frozen splashes to form weird shapes and figures.

A bright emerald taro patch lay just inland between the large stone lapped by the sea and the Mission houses. Sailors and adventurers loitered along the freshwater channel that separated the missionary buildings from Moku'ula. The sound of hammers and voices of workmen came from the construction of Hale Piula, a new Western-style summer palace being built next to the royal compound. Long boats carrying water barrels floated inland and back out to the ships, and stray sailors were often found lying drunkenly along the sand in the morning light. I had to take care not to be seen wandering down there alone, but conveniently, the brazen cocoa-nut that invited me to a sinful tryst could be seen clearly right from the front porch of the main Mission house.

The stone had been bare for nine days before at last a green cocoa-nut sat there against the sea on its ancient rock altar where the surf and fresh water rivulets met. Finally sunset, my heartbeat fluttered as I hurriedly fixed my hair and took the apron off of my new dress—an ivory striped cotton lawn dotted with sprays of tiny pink rosebuds. I had sacrificed style and patterned the waist slightly higher, like the old-fashioned kind with narrow sleeves that my mother and Aunt Sallie used to wear. The vertical stripes led the eye to believe that my waist was slimmer; altogether the gown was tailored to fit smoothly over a corset that I had let out an entire three inches. I estimated I had only one more remaining between me and damnation.

I NEVER TOLD Diego of our baby that night. I had joyfully rushed out to meet him in my blue cloak that I knew would melt me, unseen, past the town in the cobalt light. The night was warm. An early moon appeared in the East over clouds that shape-shifted visibly, spilling over the ancient volcanic mountaintops from which I had flown with the Bird-catchers. A papaya-flesh streak glowed to my left as I made my way north up the long beach past large, dark green sea turtles nesting in the twilight-blue sand.

Then I saw the profile of his face searching for me, his strong, wide shoulders and lean body silhouetted, dark as the reef, against the fading orange west. The sunset flamed inside me as my heart leapt towards his and I decided I would tell him of the secret we had made.

"My beautiful dove," he said, low and soft, when our lips finally drew apart. "I have longed for you. We have been up the slopes capturing more wild bullocks." Between our embraced bodies rustled the sound of paper. I looked down as he opened his coat.

He pulled out a dark ivory envelope addressed to him and he

unfolded the paper inside. Lacy swirls of brown ink in the light of his cigarillo made me jealous even before I read it.

I took his cigarillo from him and held it up to the letter, slowly translating the words that echoed piercingly against the pounding in my chest. Her name was Manuela, and she had been waiting for him. She was being pressed to marry but held out hope for Diego's return, for her father wished her to wed an older man who owned one of the largest ranchos near Monterey. *Please, if you still love me, return as you had promised*, she wrote.

I stepped back, glad for the darkness that hid my stricken face as only the waves murmuring on the reef broke our silence. *They will murder him if he stays long enough and you are found out*, gushed one. *If the babe resembles Diego, you will all three be in grave danger*, warned the next. *He has a good life with Manuela waiting for him in Monterey*, whispered one more.

"Diego, you are in danger here," I told him.

"Sail away with me then to California. I have reason to return to Monterey."

I answered him with a long, desperate kiss. He gave it back with the intensity of his offering: the rest of his life.

I turned away and looked up at Jupiter and Mars glowing brighter in the western sky. It was a difficult journey sailing east against the currents, and leaving too soon would not give the baby a chance to survive if born early—we both could meet my mother's fate. I feared being in the middle of the deep ocean or in a strange land when my time came. If I stayed, surely Emmaline would help and protect me and I would have time to decide my course.

But I could tell Diego none of this without changing everything between us and making him choose between freedom and danger. Just a few words from my mouth could kill him.

He quietly held me as we watched the Big Dipper appear towards the north end of the darkened island, hanging low enough as if it might dip up the black sea. I stared at it, imagining my mother in her final days, living in my same condition, safe in my father's tender care. She must have watched her belly swell, looking forward to bearing me

—not knowing that her life would end before she could even hold me.

Diego turned me to face him, eager for my answer. He tried to smooth my wrinkled brow with a tender kiss, his hands pulling me towards him as if to draw out my answer.

"I will always love you, no matter how far away," I finally said, watching his hopeful face fall, stunned. His eyes pleaded for some glimmer of mercy. "My dearest Diego," I said, "let us treasure our remaining days together. I must release you."

CHAPTER 32

$\mathcal{P}$ua knew, of course. I think she had been the first. When I began to wear a different corset, when I had stopped wearing the dresses with long rows of buttons, and especially the day that she first noticed me wearing the new rosebud cotton lawn with the Empire waist.

Pua's intelligent, inquisitive nature made her aware of most everything. Native girls learned of natural things at a young age, so free were they from a culture of secrecy and embarrassment. One day she had breezed in with a calabash of melons and eggs, then stopped and looked at me, knowing.

"So the Mission sent a barrel of olden-style dresses again?"

I didn't answer.

"Your dress is new, but you made it look like the ones Mrs. Goodwin and Thatcher always wear—the waistline is sewn as high as can be. You'll soon be a mother, won't you Mrs. Kittie?"

Then came the day that Mary and Charity found out. I was scraping cold gravy and chewed up, spat out gristle of beefsteak that was stuck to a plate. I had washed twenty dishes and there were at least twenty more as my stomach writhed with nausea. It had been another sermon disguised as a dinner: 42 guests including chiefs, chiefesses, captains, first mates and harpooners, merchants, traders, and visiting missionaries. The next plate was smeared yellow by the runny yolk of an egg and I looked away with a pleading breath, as deep a draught as I could manage. My corset felt tighter than ever; I had been too afraid to let out more than another half inch. I looked at the tall stacks of plates, dreading what the next one would reveal, and called weakly to Charity.

"I have cut on my finger on a knife," I lied. "Let us trade—I will dry."

Charity paused and looked me up and down. "Catherine, you are quite pale, are you sick? I will do both. You must sit down." Before I could protest, she swept behind me and untied my apron. My throat suddenly went dry and my ears roared as Charity paused, her eyes examining my apronless waist. Slowly, her look of concern changed into a smile. Her eyebrows raised, deepening the lines on her forehead like seams sewn in thin velvet. Horror pinched my cheeks as I realized what she had just guessed. I sank down into a chair and bent over, vomiting into a water pail.

"Mary, Mary! I believe that we have tidings of great joy!" Charity called as she pressed a damp dish towel to my forehead and mouth. A moment later, Mary Goodwin was there, holding me up by my shoulders.

"Bless your heart," Mary said, causing a wave of sickness to return and I bent over the pail again.

"A blessing, a joyous blessing," echoed Charity. "We had worried over what degree of success your marriage had achieved," she confided. "The bond of matrimony is forever, but children cast chains of iron." My stomach turned, and I vomited once more.

"Does your Mr. Webster know?" Mary asked in an excited voice, as if she meant to hurry right over to tell him the news. Engulfed in misery, I sank my forehead down into my palms, wishing desperately to escape my life.

"You poor dear," Charity fussed kindly, bringing a cool damp cloth to the back of my neck. "It was the same way for me."

"My husband will be so happy to congratulate yours," Mary smiled, and if there had been anything left inside me I would have lost that too.

"Dear—sisters—" I coughed though a raw acid throat. "I have not told my husband. I—I want to wait until I know it will last."

They understood, all too well, as any woman bearing the physical strain of missionary life would. They nodded and pled me to be careful and go rest. I rushed away, leaving the noisy scene of voices and harshly clinking plates and silverware. I turned past the hedge of pink hibiscus flowers that shook their sympathizing heads at me in the light breeze and I began to cry and did not stop crying until long after I lay down in my bed hugging a bunched up quilt with Aloha perched faithfully upon my hip.

CHAPTER 33

Article Twenty-Six: A Letter from Emmaline

November 10th, 1834

Kittie,

Perhaps your letter was mistakenly delivered to another island, or somehow lost, because I had to hear the joyous news from Charity first—has the Lord blessed you with the child for which we have prayed and hoped for so long? You know how sweet but overly inquisitive of personal matters Sister Charity is, and she wrote to me asking if I knew you are with child, as of course I, being your closest friend, would want to know. How could you not have written me at the first indication? May I tell Stuart the good news? Or perhaps Herman will want to proudly tell him. Put a letter in the next packet and tell me!

Emmaline

CHAPTER 34

THE FIRST WEEK OF NOVEMBER, 1834

Article Twenty-Seven:
A Hatbox Containing a Straw Stovepipe Bonnet, Damaged by Brown
Cinder Marks

Hardly a precious day passed without a green cocoa-nut set upon the lava rock. How many kisses left? How many eighths of an inch let from my corset would mark our end? It took a woman to detect my condition, but soon all would know. I watched Herman closely for any sign of suspicion, but he continued his fascination with printing and preaching and gave no attention to my presence unless he sought a hot coffee or a clean shirt.

. . .

DDIEGO and I met in broad daylight one afternoon at a remote cliff-enclosed bay where the paniolos had rounded up cattle. In the afternoons the sickness completely left me, replaced by a torrential, bittersweet craving for Diego.

I studied his face in the sunshine, past my straw stovepipe bonnet with the wide jade green ribbons as he untied the bow; darkness had always robbed me of the details of his face, and in the sunlight I could sadly try to memorize it all to keep for the day when it would fade and I would have no painting to remember his features clearly. His face was smooth and square-jawed, his forehead wide and clean, his hair thick and dark, his body stalwart.

We desperately kissed. I pulled him down hard onto the stretch of pale yellow sand where arms of black lava embraced us, protecting us from the rest of the large bay where the cattle huddled faraway in the shade at the tree line. We lay under the sun with the mighty ocean at our feet, the island at our backs, the earth turning just for us; we were its axis. Little did we know that a solitary figure was making its way in our direction along the lonely trail.

TTHE PATH LEADING to the secluded beach was narrow, insulated by a precipice that dropped down to the sea on the makai, or ocean side. A steep fortress of rising cliffs bordered the mauka, or inland side, and in places it was bordered by a stone wall and wooden gate the natives had built years ago to keep out wild bullocks. It was an ideal passageway to drive horses and cattle up towards the bay where they could be collected, for there was nowhere along the rugged path that they could escape.

Too soon, Diego kissed me goodbye, was up in his saddle, and our hands let go. With a sad smile I watched him ride away down the trail, wondering if it was the last time as my body hummed like a note that hangs softly in the air long after the finger leaves the string. I was to wait a quarter hour and then follow down the trail until it would let me go inland into a forest where my horse was tied. But I grew impatient and left before Diego had vanished around the coastline, out of sight.

I followed until the last glimpse of him disappeared. I squinted. A piece of black lava suddenly moved in the waves of heat. I blinked, but it moved again. The dark figure came from narrow rock steps that led up the cliff from the beach and from its vantage point could have noticed Diego coming down along the trail from the secluded bay. Set against the impossibly blue sea, something black flowed around it—a frock coat? Was it Herman? It drew closer. It was a skirt billowing in the breeze, and she was heading in my direction.

I had already left the bay and would be seen if I ran back. I slipped behind a small cluster of lava, knowing that it would hide me for only so long. The stone radiated heat like an oven and soon sweat rose upon my face.

Here came the figure carrying a basket, striding doggedly over the rough path, a grim soldier under command of the Almighty. She stopped to look from side to side, down the path where Diego had ridden and then peered ahead towards me. Her hand reached up to adjust her spectacles, a familiar motion. It was Mary Goodwin. I tried to stand as motionless as the lava.

"You wish to hide," said a soft voice suddenly behind me. I was afraid to move enough to turn around to see who it belonged to.

"I can help you," she said. "Wait until I go speak with her, and then creep backwards into that crevice. It leads to an open cave. Look for the *koali ʻawa*, and it will lead you out."

A few moments later I peeked cautiously around the rock to see the back of a tall young native woman walking down the winding footpath towards Mary. They stopped together in conversation. The young woman wore a cardinal red flower lei and she circled so that Mary's black wool back turned to me. I crouched, turned, and found the slim lava passageway where one slab of rock overlapped another. The crevice wound its way into a high open-air chamber with a floor of sand, a ceiling of clear blue sky, and a thick bower of koali ʻawa. Beneath the green trailing vines bearing fading blue morning glories was hidden a primitive staircase leading up and out into the verdant forest.

I FOUND my horse patiently waiting, and I rode along a clear freshwater stream that edged the little village before it curved to fall into the sea below. I searched for the woman who had delivered me but all I saw was a glimpse of Mary far away through the trees entering the village through the cliff trail gate, turning to shut it in a strict, diligent motion, and patting the linen atop her basket, ready to deliver a charitable deed.

A few more paces safely out of Mary Goodwin's sight, something made me turn around and look back. There, stepping out towards me from a hedge of flowering yellow hibiscus, my savior in the red flower lei came, her hand raised in farewell. She moved with a woman's grace as she stood there in her missionary blouse and ti leaf skirt, her hair unbound past her full breasts to her waist. I waved back, and in that instant we both turned our heads away, I caught sight of a familiar indigo mark on the side of her cheek—the very one that had anguished me for so long. She was the mother of a child that Herman had long denied me. I was thankful to God that he had.

As if I could flee all the pain that I had borne as the wife of Reverend Herman Webster, I kicked my horse into a run. As I galloped home an uneasy feeling began to pound inside my heart. It grew stronger the closer I got. Something there was very wrong.

I smelled something different in the air. Smoke. It was the scent of koa wood burning. Around the next turn I met the dreadful sight of a dark column roiling up from the beach not far from Moku'ula.

CHAPTER 35

It took both Herman and Goodwin to lift Princess Leilani's surfing board onto the bonfire. Flames greedily licked up the kukui-nut oil surface devouring the lizard design with black smoke, stoking the tinder of boards beneath it until it all burst into an inferno like a ship on fire.

Herman stood before it with triumph in his eyes. "Hear me, one and all! Be Satan's guest if thou so chooseth; step into these flames and thou wilt have but a tiny idea of what lies beyond Hell's front parlor," he told the silent gathering throng. "Proceed with your games of Whist and Snap-Dragon and Able-Whackets! Drink your bottles of rum! Romp upon the waves, but behold—before ye lies the consequence!"

I dismounted and dropped the reins as Herman's voice changed into an eerily compassionate tone.

"My native children, I have come in love to tell you good news. Centuries of your kind have gone to perdition. You stand at the dawn of a new age of salvation. Surrender your will to God and you will be granted an eternity in Heaven."

The nose of Leilani's board stuck out at the edge of the bonfire and a line of flames crept along it like a serpent towards the last to go.

Suddenly she was standing there in her blue velvet dress, rigid with grief, as close as the heat would let her. I had not seen Princess Leilani since the evening on the Captain's ship and I had never seen her speechless. Everyone waited in the crackling silence to hear what she might finally say.

Herman strode slowly towards her, long-sought triumph on his face. For the young king had grown old enough to rule now and was often over on O'ahu, the friendly Queen of the Yellow Feathers had since passed, and Leilani was no longer a fairy piece in his game of chess. She was converted. She was contained. She was under control. They had won.

"Your idols are burning. Bow down before God now," he said, pointing to the sand at his feet.

She was staring down solemnly. She was staring at her heart.

She jerked her head up, eyes wide with fury. It was a moment that forevermore will be seared into my memory—Leilani and those flames, facing each other fearlessly as if that fire was her spirit rising up, made visible.

Slowly, she raised both hands up to her neck, grasped the prim collar of the cotton pelerine that covered her low neckline and ripped it off. She untied the wide silk sash at her waist, wrung it in her hands and looked as if she would choke Herman with it before she threw it into the fire. She slid her fingers between the buttons of the smooth blue velvet bodice and tore apart the precious fabric that I had carefully sewn cut from Diego's cloak. She snapped the little stitches made by my needle and thread and soon the white silk petticoat sleeves and underskirt that I had sacrificed was reduced to shreds. I looked from the ripped cloth in the sand to her burning surf-board and felt destroyed.

The fire devoured the rest of her dress until only a fine cotton chemise remained barely covering her long, golden brown limbs. Somehow she looked more regal without all her Western clothes. All eyes followed her as she slowly began to walk away.

She stopped at me. I was crying, my wounded heart wringing out every bit of sympathy and sorrow it had ever owned. She said two words.

"Remember Hina."

I searched for words and a handkerchief, and when I pulled the white cotton away from my eyes she was gone.

SOME SAY that she never left that day. An angry wind began to blow through the cleft between the mountains that guarded Moku'ula. It was the Kaua'ula wind, the wind of legends, told of for hundreds of years by aged voices that had once witnessed it. Little whitecaps appeared across the surface of the lake, and cocoa-nut trees bent their bodies to the ground in supplication. A high chief, a champion of missionaries, was crossing the Mokuhinia waters to the church when his boat was violently capsized. From all around, people came running towards the steeple and took cover inside the sanctuary walls, huddled between the pews as the wind howled in the eaves. Little chunks of coral plaster fell down onto the organ keyboard playing a demented melody. Then, with a groan and a roar, the roof cracked and began to lift. With a blast of light it flew off, disintegrating into the sky.

It was not until the great wind blew the flames of Herman's little Hell into the sea that it gradually calmed down, leaving great embers burning in the sand.

Mary Goodwin served me tea from her treasured English set. "I lost most of the teacups on the voyage here from Boston… so long ago," she said sadly, and I wondered if she was unhappy because of broken cups or because of all the years she had spent so far from home.

"Are we expecting others?" I asked, avoiding her eyes as I looked at the delicate bone china with pink roses on translucent white porcelain.

She poured two cups and then sat down facing me. The dining room was silent, save for a faint faraway sound of voices repeating the alphabet that floated from the school hale in through the open window.

She stared at me over the rim of her cup before answering. "Catherine, how are you feeling? Your husband has not yet announced the good news to us."

"I have yet to tell him," I said, blowing across the surface of the searing hot tea.

"Surely he will know that it is his," she said icily.

I did not answer.

"Have a slice of pie," Mary offered, her treasured silver pie spade holding it towards me, waiting for me to raise my plate. I hesitated, looking at the little brown specs of baked vermin in the crust. A crumb fell to the table as the slice of pie waited in mid-air.

Its heaviness weighed down my plate, and I set it down with a soft thud on the tablecloth. For many moments the only sound at the table was her spoon ringing in her teacup as she stirred, and then she finally spoke.

"That Catholic vaquero has been here quite some time, hasn't he?" she said, watching my face intently. "Our native boys must be well trained by now. I saw him just the other day riding down the trail from the cattle beach. And thought I saw a figure in a pink dress following him out. You must know that his days here are over."

I stirred in milk with a pewter spoon, feeling as if I might be sucked right down into the whirlpool spinning in my teacup. Trying to gather my thoughts, I put the rim to my face and deeply inhaled the steam, smelling what was once green leaves growing in the mist on a faraway Chinese hillside, fated to wither in the Celestial sun, then packed for weeks in the dark hold of a British Indiaman tea clipper, brought back to life into the teacup before me.

"As our mission here relies on a solid foundation of marital harmony, it is imperative that your husband receives the news of your condition with joy," she went on. "Surely it would not come as a surprise to him?"

I forced myself to swallow my first sip and then set the thin china teacup back into its saucer. "Of course not," I murmured, knowing full well that it would.

"As Godly women, it is our duty to devote ourselves to our husbands and make our marriage unshakable, bearing quietly any pain or hardship they may cause us," she said with a voice made grim by years of acceptance.

"But a man's love of God is reflected in the way he loves his wife."

Her voice rose. "You will copulate with him so that he will suspect nothing. If your babe does not resemble your husband it will be said that it came 'early'. We will consider it unripe, and require Doctor Thatcher to have it taken care of."

I jumped up, my hand hit the edge of the saucer and sent the teacup delicately clattering and splashing across the table.

Mary reached for her napkin and began to furiously wipe it up. "Sit down and listen to me! Think about all the money given to the church, all our printed pamphlets proudly describing the mission to all the people in America—all the very lives sacrificed to win these islands! We will not be taken down by your shameful wickedness!"

"I began with pure intentions, Mary. In many ways I was still a girl when Herman once wooed me so deceptively. Am I a sinner now to have fallen for him so long ago?"

"There are sins of the innocent. Your beauty was once a quality that put you at the top of their list, but in the end it was your undoing. Satan has used you. You have failed."

"Judge me then, Mary, despise me, hate me, but you cannot shame me. Loving Diego was sacred—sharing a bed with Herman was a sin."

"One half-caste spawn of the Devil will not destroy our cause!" She stopped wiping the table and crumpled the hot damp cloth in her fist, leaned in upon it and lowered her voice, sharp as the edge of a scalpel. "Its removal would be a small price to pay so that others may have eternal life. God would will it to be erased."

I leapt away so quickly that my chair fell backwards to the floor. Hand on the doorknob, I glanced back at her. She was desperately trying to fix a wooden dowel that had come loose from her cherished tall New England ladder back chair.

"Look what else you have ruined!" she cried, all composure lost as the tea soaked its way across the tablecloth behind her and began dripping down onto the floor.

*I*t was just after candle-lighting the next evening when I sat alone at my dining table across from a large basket of flowers that had been plucked greedily by the great Kaua'ula wind and thrown violently to the ground. The tender scent from the heap of fresh petals rose up towards my lifeless cheeks, as if it were a lover gently trying to lift its cherished one out of a troubled mood.

I paused, a half-strung lei in my hands, as I heard the metal tap and leather slap of Herman's footsteps growing louder. He had nailed flat iron plates to his leather heels to make his shoes last longer, but the sole at the front of his right shoe was beginning to come off. Tap. Slap. Tap, and then he was there in the room.

"This is a vain use of time," he said. Perhaps never before had pretty blossoms endured such looks of hatred and scorn. "Souls are being lost for eternity, whilst thou labor over adornments that will wilt in a day? I suppose thou hast been painting your frivolous pictures of them as well."

I gave him a weary, stale look of disdain as I pulled another flower onto the string. I picked up another blossom and looked at it with a sigh, envying its happy innocence.

"Thou may better employ yourself by packing your trunks,"

Herman continued against the silence. He took the stem of one unfortunate flower between his fingers, looking as if he wished to kill it.

"Are we finally sailing home?" I asked.

He laughed in his stiff way and gave the flower a withering look before letting it fall and crushing it with his narrow black shoe. "We are moving to the vacant cottage inside the Mission compound, at Charity Thatcher's suggestion," he said as the leather flap slid over the petals and he stepped on it again, this time with a twist of his iron heel. "There are visiting pastors over from Honolulu who need a place to stay; they can be here, and we can be there where thou can spend thy time on more Godly work and less strenuous pursuits such as riding up and down the coast. Mrs. Thatcher told me that ye do not feel well of late, and suggested that you may be exhausting yourself; she said it would be best for you to be under her watch. It is very generous of her, and we will not refuse her kindness."

Stunned, I thought of the double row of high lava brick walls around the mission buildings and realized that any wall raised to keep something out is also a wall that can keep someone in. I would never have another chance to escape to see Diego again. I took another flower and pressed it to my lips before adding it to the garland as he continued on.

"I, as well, would like to know that my wife is safely locked up inside our Mission walls. The sailors are growing more and more defiant to missionary principles. As bad as savages they are, and should know better being civilized men, but alas, we have a multitude of lawless spirits among these sea-rovers collected in our port. I will go out soon and preach to them and will not be home tonight."

"And what kind of duties have you and the Goodwins in mind for me?" I asked. "The Princess has left, and with her the sole reason for my being here as dressmaker; perhaps it is time for me to voyage back to New Bedford. I can sail before you do, leaving you here to finish your work."

A short laugh scraped its way out of Herman's throat. "You will stay with me and make sensible clothes such as shirts, and you can teach the girls at the school how to sew simple, modest gowns."

There was a soft knock on the open door as Pua stepped in. She looked me straight in the eyes with a look of a message in hers, then she quietly sat down to help me string flowers.

"Cornelius has gone over to O'ahu and I need help at the Hale Pa'i in the evenings," Herman said. "Thou mayest do his job and put the type sorts back in order. Pua, help Mrs. Webster pack her trunk." He paused and looked at her hesitantly. "I thank ye for all thy assistance. The time has come to let thee find another employment."

"But Reverend Webster, it is not work. I—" Pua started.

"My wife will need your services no longer. The Mission women and the seminary girls are all accustomed to helping each other."

"Herman, I have a say in this," I said.

Pua's mouth stayed open, hurt welling up in her young eyes. "But when will I see you, Mrs. Catherine?"

"God bless thee, dear maiden," Herman dismissed her, "We will see thee in church. May thou seek His will in all things."

Herman placed his hand around the back of my neck, digging his fingertips hard around into the soft hollow at my collarbone and I shrank away. "I will leave tomorrow on an expedition with Goodwin," he said, "He says there will be dangerous game to kill."

He went to the tall cabinet in his study and opened its glass doors. White painted shelves held sermon reference books and native curiosities that he sometimes sent back to New England to boast of his dangerous, exciting, and purposeful life. Precious, sacred, or sentimental to their owners, to him they were trophies, souvenirs, scalps. He pushed aside a koa bowl taken from a chief's table and a pair of *'uli'uli* rattle gourds with feather tops.

Herman reached up to the very top shelf, pushed aside a carved wooden idol with human hair, and then pulled out his Pepperbox revolver.

"Goodwin said that I will be told of our prey once we are deep in the tropical forest. Perhaps this is a test that will have him at last regard me as his equal."

"Reverend Webster, I object to this," I told him. "I will not move to the mission grounds."

"Then I will bind thee and carry thee if I must. Thou art my wife. Flee to the natives, and we will punish them severely. Flee to a ship, and they will be refused water and foodstuffs before their captain, being sympathetic to another man searching for his mentally distraught wife, will surrender you."

I could not think of a reply, hating the fear and helplessness that he was slowly infecting me with. The chance to fly away with Diego burned inside my heart.

Herman smiled, smug in his little triumph. "I will send some men to fetch thy trunk in the morning. I leave now to go preach to those rum-soaked souls disturbing the peace, and I will rejoin you at our new cottage after the hunting excursion."

As soon as he was gone, Pua told me the reason for her visit. Thaddeus had been told to have three horses saddled up and tied waiting at the Mission gate in the morning: one for Reverend Goodwin, one for Reverend Webster, and one for the vaquero Diego.

"There has never been a hunting party made up of two preachers and a paniolo with no extra horses to carry supplies and dead animals, Mrs. Kittie."

I went out into the yard. Floating up from the darkening shoreline came the sound of a single cannonball and a raucous drinking song. With both hands gripped on an axe, I lifted it high and felled what lay wedged between two stones on the ground. I went down to our rock at the edge of the sea and placed upon it what was once a large green cocoa-nut, now cut in two.

The sun slowly went down and finally the sound of silver spurs chimed in the darkness outside my window.

"Don't worry, your husband is away down in Lahiana," came Diego's whisper. He leapt over the window sill as easy as if it were the back of a horse and stood squarely before me.

"I wanted to see your face again before I leave tomorrow on an expedición. Did you break it in two? You cannot mean we are done?"

"We have been found out; I do not think Herman yet knows, but you passed Mary Goodwin on the cliff trail the day we last met. She must have seen us both, and whispered her suspicion in her husband's ear. I know of this expedition; Herman was told to bring a revolver, yet he doesn't hunt."

Diego pulled my waist close to his. "You say that there will be only three horses saddled up at the Mission, and only one gun? I must arrange a pack horse, extra reatas, and…" His voice trailed off thinking of the work a horseman needs to do to prepare for such a trip.

"Do not go with them, Diego, but flee the island as quickly as you can. Find the next ship headed out." My voice faltered. "They mean to kill you. It is time for us to say goodbye."

"How can you say this, dulce amore?"

"Is it love? You said the same to your Manuela."

"I did not understand love then."

"I think I understand it now better than ever. Go and live the life that's waiting for you."

"I want you in that life. I have word that my ship on the Big Island has loaded horses. I can have our horses ready and we can quickly sail."

I pushed him away and took my mother's hymnal from my nightstand. "There is not enough time—and I fear making a long voyage. My health has not been good of late. When you fail to appear at the stables they will immediately search the island for you." I pressed the little book into his palm.

"But this is your treasure," he said, indecision across his face.

"May it protect you," I said, and I kissed him hard.

I turned my back on him, opened a tinder box, and lit the lantern wick. The whale oil flared up into a bright glow. I did not want him to see my tears, so I stayed there, staring into the light, smelling the fumes of life, of a whale that once swam free. When I finally turned around, Diego was gone.

. . .

I WAS up at the Hale Pa'i early the next afternoon cleaning up inky type sorts when I spied the sharp white sails against the dark gray-blue island of Moloka'i.

The ship began tacking up the Pailolo channel, sails trimmed tightly against the wind. Her colors—little flags flying bright and brave—told me that sure enough it was the *San Carlos*, Captain Vasquez, of Monterey.

I ran outside and up the rise where the young mango trees were growing. There, the land, the sea, the islands, the sky lay stretched before me. Panting, the strong morning breeze behind my skirts and bonnet ribbons flying I squinted, type sorts still in my fist.

The ship had come unexpectedly in the night and stood in the pewter waters of Lahaina roads at dawn. They must have begun boarding early, swimming the horses out and raising them up to the decks by ropes, straps and pulleys. I looked down the hill at the mission nestled in the trees by the shore. How long had Goodwin and Herman waited at the mission gate, checking their timepieces, waiting for Diego to arrive with their mounts, ready with their overnight valises, two rolls of bedding, and one Pepperbox revolver?

My clenched hands stung. I tore my eyes away and opened my palms to see ink and blood coating the sharp-edged metal type sorts. Sick to my stomach, I looked back out at the *San Carlos*.

She would be heavy with salt and saddles carefully protected against the dampness of a voyage. In her hold at the fore would be the stallions, the mares aft, reluctant to eat, shifting restlessly. He would be down with them, reassuring them, or perhaps up at the rail wishing for one last sight of me.

He was safe.

So there sailed my heart, farther and farther away until her sails were a tiny pale moth. She leaned hard as she met with the trade winds, passed the northernmost point, and then disappeared forever.

CHAPTER 38

THE THIRD WEEK OF NOVEMBER, 1834

Up from the shimmering Lahaina Roads floated the faint sound of a fiddle and melodeon. Wisps of melody danced across the silver water from the deck of a close-anchored ship and up to me. Just offshore stood hundreds of ships at anchor: American, French, Russian, Spanish, British.

I moved through each day like a crude, hollow, wooden imitation of my former self; a puppet in tangled strings, lost in thought, remembering every minute Diego and I had spent together, regretting that I had not been brave enough to leave with him that sudden night.

I felt a tiny nudge beneath my corset. Lying with Herman might fool him and protect me from his rage but unless my baby was fair and blue-eyed the Goodwins would find a way to make me senseless with opium and helpless to protest the horrible act that they planned to carry out.

I searched the harbor anxiously for any savior; even for the *Fair Wind* perhaps back amongst them. I could make the short sail to Oahu and have Emmaline's help and mercy. When I was able to make the voyage home Aunt Sallie would welcome me with love, no matter what my circumstances, even if my father and community would not; my heart ached at the thought of all her sacrifices for me and the failure that I had made with them.

What had I to sell?—I had not the money to even buy a passage home.

Thin strips of cloth still wrapped my hands. Inside were the little badges of despair on my palms, etched by cuts and ink like tiny tattoos as I had clutched the type sorts the day my Diego had sailed away. My spirit ached, my eyes were swollen, but my hands hurt far less than my heart.

Days and years of my independent thought falling on the wasteland of Herman's heart had almost evaporated part of my spirit; that is how one becomes helpless and hopeless. Despair is not something like an unbecoming hat to be simply taken off. Each day with Herman was like a little stitch—tenuous, powerless, but now I had almost sewn myself in.

Suddenly, like hundreds of cold sewing needles pricking my skin, I sensed his presence behind me as the feeling crept from my arms up the back of my scalp and across the crown of my head. I smelled the strong pungent odor of his body shrouded in black wool. I looked frantically out at the ships. Heavy pewter clouds moved in to cloak the setting sun and whispered raindrops.

"Finish up now, our work is nearly done for the evening." Herman said. "'Tis nigh two minutes to six o'clock. I suspect there is a little bird who has been gazing out the window, longing for thy return. It knows that at any moment it will see her mistress through the glass, and waits faithfully for her to come home and feed her."

Herman had been uncharacteristically nice to me ever since I lived like a little dancer in a music box. He knew where he could find me any time of day: enclosed in the mission compound, or with him up at the Hale Pa'i in the late afternoon. There my job was the one nobody else wanted, and one I was best at. The moveable type press used letters each placed by hand, upside-down, into a wooden composing stick making what would be one line of words assembled together into a piece called a forme. This was then mounted on the press, rolled with ink and pressed into pages of paper. When the day's work was done, an impossible disorder of tiny iron glyphs lay scattered and piled across a work table waiting be put back in the little wooden compartments in the type case, each the unique domain of an alphabet letter or punctuation mark.

I tore my eyes from the ships and islands and turned around. Behind Herman's detestable face hung the palest moon, almost full, translucent in the fading daylight. I avoided his eyes and stared at it as Leilani's words returned to me: *Remember Hina. She watches over all women, ready to offer strength when they are in darkness.* Suddenly, nothing seemed more tangible to me. If legends are born from the spirits of people, and if Hina represented the brave love and the spirit of all womankind that holds power to help one another, then in that moment I began to believe that she was almost real enough to touch.

Herman offered his arm to usher me back inside as he continued on in a chillingly companionable way. "What a life we have chosen, haven't we, dear Catherine? More difficult than most. It will be cool enough to build a fire tonight, and thou can sit by it while I will make soup for our supper. We will have the thin corn pancakes with it, the new kind introduced by the vaqueros."

I kept my voice as calm as could be. "Charity brought me those corn tortillas, she has learned to make them."

"Of course," Herman said, a dark sound creeping into his voice. "I am not always a stranger to what is in our cupboard. The Vaquero hath left his mark here, is all I intended to say."

I struggled for a deep breath. Guilt and fear were playing with me. Why would Goodwin tell him now that Diego was gone, now that they expected I would lie intimately with Herman? He had a temper. A murderous missionary would be one more liability, yet a missionary deserted of his wife would be no missionary at all.

Herman bent over his desk by the front door. Through it flowed air that dried the freshly printed newspapers that would be ready to be folded and distributed in the morning.

I sat down at the little mountain of iron letters staring at the confusion of tiny glyphs, that, like my life, once made sense. Everything that I thought I was, or had, was gone. Where was the force of life within me—the hope, the freedom, the pride, the power? Mana, Leilani had called it.

I gripped the edge of the table and sat up straight as I let out a breath and listened to the sound of it: *Ha*. I was alive. I was breathing. It was a thread of hope. That is enough.

A whisper of peace drifted by me as I sorted the metal type pieces until they were all put away except some left carelessly remaining in composing sticks. I emptied one onto the table and slid the two "t"'s together with my finger, and then two "i"'s together before dropping them in their respective compartments. There remained a capital "K" and a lower case "e". Peculiar—they were the letters in my name. I struggled to think of any other word that shared them.

I pulled the other composing sticks towards me. The next held four metal glyphs, spread apart, left behind as the rest had been cleaned out. I-t-'-s.

Two letters and a comma still lay loaded in the next stick. M-e-,.

What was left in the last composing stick made my heart race. P-u-a.

"Kittie, it's me, Pua."

I softly let out a breath, spreading my fingers wide on the flat tabletop. Pua had indeed found her new employment just as Herman had urged her: she must be one of the morning girls that swept the floors and emptied the waste cans at the printing house—right where she knew I worked in the evenings alphabetizing the type. I put the rest of the metal sorts back home each to their little boxes and Pua's message was safely gone.

"It is six twenty-nine," Herman announced from across the large workshop.

I hurriedly found a scrap of paper and a pen, dipped it in the inkwell and wrote hello, Pua. I emptied one waste basket into another and then put my message in the bottom of the empty can by the table just as Herman pushed his arms into the sleeves of his coat.

We walked down the hill and past the pretty white-painted home he had built for me that had once seemed like it might be a box big enough to hold all of my dreams. When the mission gates closed behind me and I stepped into our little lime-plastered cottage Aloha uttered a glad cry. She eagerly fluttered up to my outstretched hand and pecked a gentle kiss on the side of my smile.

CHAPTER 39

$\mathcal{R}$ed ginger leaves rustled lazily against the side of the blue-shuttered building that housed Mary and Charity's Christian Female Seminary. The girls sat in the shade bent over their sewing, whip-stitching yards of seams inside their new dresses.

"Simple, and becoming," Mary Goodwin pronounced, pleased with her pet project. "The cotton calico is a bit too loud, but we cannot be too choosy with donations. I deem these dresses to be a great success."

They were the plainest dresses ever designed, in a loose sense of the word: a gathered tent, draped from neck to ankles, thus hiding any feminine curve or form that moved beneath it. I could hardly bear being involved with Mary's drab, lifeless endeavor, and fought to at least put a deep ruffled flounce along the bottom from knee to heel.

"Mary, our Kittie is right," Charity had told her. "A large ruffle will allow the movement of industrious feet." She was thoughtful enough to look through another's eyes—sensitive to my feelings of being once the esteemed dressmaker, now employed as a simple seamstress under the command of an unqualified superior.

All day long, my thoughts had kept returning to Pua up at the printing house. Did she see my note in the waste bin? Would she leave another message? Could she tell me more about Diego's last hours before he sailed?

When the last dress was finished, Charity took the girls away to bake bread and the porch was soon quiet save for the gentle brush of ginger leaves along the walls. Glad to make my own exit, I dropped my pincushion into my basket, shut the lid, and was walking towards the gate past the chicken yard when a curious sound from the henhouse stopped me. Clucking softly in a voice certainly never heard outside the company of her feathered pets, I recognized Mary's voice.

She popped her head out and spotted me. "Tell me, dear Catherine," Mary called to me across her brood of brown hens, "How are you and your husband faring?"

I paused to choose the right words as she turned the feed pail upside down and carefully scraped it, making sure that every crumb went equally to each bird. She cast dirty water out of a large shallow bowl, and after cleaning it with the swish of a rag my eyes caught the inside of the basin and scraped my heart. Carefully pieced together were broken pink roses and butterfly wings: hundreds of small pieces of her delicate porcelain cups and saucers that had not survived the voyage across the ocean or across her years, carefully saved, too precious to throw away, painstakingly set like misfit puzzle pieces in a plaster mosaic.

Mary disappeared back inside the henhouse to look for eggs. From within the wooden roost her voice murmured caringly as she talked to her hens. "Bless your heart," I heard her say. "Move along now, sweet girl." Then, in another voice: "You know, Sister Catherine, and I say this in the most motherly way, Herman is quite a handsome man —God has blessed you. Have you..."

I did not want her conversation, especially on that topic, and had taken up my skirt to walk away when I tilted my head to hear a queer kind of muffled baby talk sounding within the henhouse. She must have found the eggs she had hoped for.

Glad for the opportunity to slip away, I made two steps forward when her head poked out of the small, low doorway, the tone of her voice changing from muffled echo to clear in the open air. "Your nest has been empty far too long," she was saying, and I was perplexed; was she still speaking to a chicken?

"Have you welcomed him at night? Has he cleaved unto you as his wife, have you two become one flesh? We rid your cottage of the old bed of mats, and put a comfortable mattress in its place."

"So thoughtful of you, Mary, but you must excuse me—I feel sick," I said.

"Of course you do," she said so coldly that I knew she was not talking to her hens.

CHAPTER 40

I eagerly returned to the Hale Pa'i that evening, and as I walked in I spied several wooden composing sticks left on the table set apart from the mound of metal type sorts. Herman stood close nearby, putting oil in the press joints with the help of a couple boys from the school. I sat down to sort, putting capital letters in the upper case drawer and the others in the lower case beneath it.

Herman put the oil can down next to the composing sticks that I hoped would contain another message from Pua, perhaps a last scrap of news about Diego before he had sailed. Herman leaned his palm on the table, touching one of the composing sticks with the side of his hand. It tipped towards the edge, in danger of scattering down on the floor. My hand leaped towards the sticks and I pulled them safely over to me.

The first one had five letters, spread far apart so that a casual glance would not group them as a word. I slid them together.

H-e-l-l-o.

The sticks were arranged in order; the second one held the letters

P-a-c-k.

The next: y-o-u-r.

The last: t-r-u-n-k.

CHAPTER 41

At the morning breakfast table Mary was in uncommonly bright spirits, pouring me coffee and placing a fresh slice of cantaloupe on my plate as she hummed a hymn. Reverend Goodwin joined in with her, his jagged smile brightly flashing.

"I believe I will have another one of your biscuits, dear wife. Have you had one, Catherine? None make them better than my Mrs. Goodwin," he smiled. I didn't answer him. I always went out of my way to disregard him.

A breathless boy flew in the door. "Sure enough Reverend Sir! 'Tis the very ship, and she is on a broad reach down the channel now!"

Mary began to cry and Charity embraced her. "O, 'tis a joyous day," Mary said.

She took a napkin and dried the tears that had made their way down to reach her hard set mouth. "It has finally come to pass, praise our Savior," she beamed. "The ship from New Bedford has made our islands, bearing our daughter Tabitha home!"

We all exclaimed at the joyful news, and it momentarily swept me out of my anxious circumstances.

"A letter preceded her," Mary said. "Now that we know our dear daughter has safely made the voyage, we are not afraid to share the news."

"Our Tabitha turns seventeen soon," Goodwin said proudly, "and she is returning with the exceptional Reverend Davis, her betrothed, a godly young man, newly ordained to be a missionary in these Sandwich Islands!"

Chair legs scraped against the floor as all rose up from the table and the children scattered like fish in clear water before a ship's bow. Herman neatly re-tied the scarf at his throat, donned his tall stovepipe hat, checked that it was straight, and left with the Goodwins down to the shore. Charity and her girls started in on the dishes, and I went to start in on packing my pine dome trunk.

I found two boys to help me pull it out from a small storage room and as I looked inside I realized that it had waited for me, mostly packed—a hidden part of me had always been ready to fly. Almost all of my favorite keepsakes and dresses were already folded and tucked neatly. Pua knew I was an unhappy prisoner, and I wondered feverishly what her message could mean as I folded and sorted. What else might I fit into my trunk? My ivory comb. Those hair ribbons? Which dresses must I leave out?

I finished putting my most precious things in between the folds of dresses and before long I was closing the humpback top and turning the key.

CHAPTER 42

It was very hot for five o'clock in the afternoon. I walked with Herman up the long steep path from the Mission Houses to the Hale Pa'i, hoping for a breeze that never came, trying to keep up with him to hide any hint of my condition. We were silent, and I was out of breath from not just the heat nor the hill but from the effort of being alone with him. A walk for two people can be an awkwardly intimate thing.

Herman cleared his throat. "Ah, yes. I have news to tell." He made several more steps before continuing. "Cornelius is returning any day, and we will have to find a new task for thee. Thou dost no longer need to help with the printing chores."

The flaming air became ice. "Then I will have no escape from the Mission at all," I said.

"Escape?" Herman said, eyeing me. "I should think that the Mission and Church is a place to escape to, not from, unless thou hast a particular reason. Come along, thou art falling behind."

"No reason at all."

"Our little Miss Tabitha looks well after her long voyage. In her place is a virtuous young woman. It was a sound decision to send her away from native influences."

"I hardly recognized her at first; her wardrobe is stylishly fresh from New York."

"Her betrothed, Reverend Davis, looks the same. I have never seen a dark cravat and such a small-waisted frock coat. It must be what men now wear at the pulpit in New Bedford."

"She brought me the most beautiful gloves."

"I have been meaning to commend thee for thy sensible dresses of late, yet I regret that thou hast lost thy girlish figure," Herman said, looking down and up at my rosebud cotton lawn with the Empire waist, the only dress I could fit into until I had time to sew another. "Thy once fashionably small waist was a small vanity, yet I do not want my wife to resemble a matron who has borne children until it is time for you to do so." Then his voice became eerily tender. "Perhaps it is time. Shall we shall set our mind on procreation?"

"No."

He prickled. "Then take up thy corset-training again, for a comely wife is a blessing, and thou art not."

We reached the printing house, and I rushed past him towards the tin drinking cup and sank it into the pail of cool water. I forgot my discomfort when I reached the type table: there were seven composing sticks left there in a haphazard row.

M-i-d-n-i-g-h-t.

My temples were throbbing, and my throat was still dry.

O-u-t-s-i-d-e.

There was a loud knock at the door. "Dear wife, answer it," Herman said, consumed with setting up the printing press.

I tossed the metal letters into the sorts pile and those two words existed no more. Not wanting to draw his ire, I slowly rose—but the front door creaked, and in strode Cornelius.

"Brother! A delight to see thee again," he greeted Herman. "I have missed our good work, and praise the Lord for bringing me back here to gladly serve Him."

"Welcome, Cornelius, thou hast been missed," Herman said jovially. "Here I have had to put my wife to work at your job!"

"Well then, I shall get right back to it," Cornelius said, rolling up his sleeves and walking towards me.

I had just put together: t-h-e-w-a-l-l T-a-b-i-t-h-a.

In my panic I must have arranged it wrong. Sweat rose above my corset cover, I longed to unfasten the damp pelerine that trapped heat at my chest. Then, my mind clicked and I saw that I had missed a space:

t-h-e

w-a-l-l. The wall. The Mission wall?

"Did you procure the sheet of copper?" Herman asked, and to my relief Cornelius turned away.

"Yes, I finally met with success! We can now engrave it with our Map of Souls!"

"Well done, Cornelius! Soon the churches in America shall see this achievement that the Lord hath made with our humble hearts and hands."

"Look here, I also brought several colors of ink." Their voices faded as they strode excitedly into the adjoining supply room.

Relieved, I went back to the composing sticks.

k-n-o-w-s w-h-e-r-e.

I touched the letters with my fingertips, puzzling, and then I had it:

T-a-b-i-t-h-a

k-n-o-w-s

w-h-e-r-e.

A wind from the ocean suddenly gusted through the room, in from the lanai moving eastward through the tall open windows that framed the deep green mountains basking in the last sunlight of the day. Paper wings of newspaper pages took flight and stray pieces of hair at my temples moved up and off of my face. The sun was setting, and a fine veil of mist floated down from the clouds above the mountains, catching the light and coloring the air outside with gold.

Something unearthly was happening. I looked down and touched my necklace. Rising up within me was a glow so bright my little golden sun seemed like a candle disappearing in bright sunlight. I was part of the air, the earth, the moment. It was alive around and inside me, like the feeling of catching a wave. It was my mana, and my *na'au*, as Leilani had taught me—the Spirit moving through me. I breathed deeply. *Ha.*

There were three composing sticks remaining, and I somehow knew they would change my life.

My heart stopped beating at the first: D-i-e-g-o

My fingers shook so much as I slid the next composing stick towards me I almost knocked the letters out.

i-s s-t-i-l-l

And the last said:

h-e-r-e.

CHAPTER 43

"Thou shalt improve my appearance, even if it takes all night," Herman said to me with a menacing look. "By morning I must have a new waistcoat and a smart new frock coat like Reverend Davis."

I rummaged through my old collection of fabrics and managed to find a bolt of smooth boiled black wool, enough black silk to line it, and after scrambling through the bottom of my button box I produced a handful of mis-matched wooden buttons.

Impatient, he kept looking up from his Bible to see how my work was coming along. "He only just finished seminary," he said.

"Who?" I asked.

"Goodwin's future son-in-law. He was ordained just six short months ago and Goodwin wants him to stay here and help lead our church."

"Your days of being the Reverend's favorite are over."

"May God punish thee for your tongue, likely the least of thy sins," he said. "I need thee, or I would take that upon myself. Perhaps I yet shall."

The whale-oil lamp was burning low by the time I had the pieces of the coat basted together. "Please fill the lamp so I can thread my needle, Herman," I asked. My eyes stung, and my hands were weary. The clock on Herman's table chimed eleven thirty. Tabitha was to meet me in the churchyard soon.

When I did a quick fitting he became agreeable, pleased with the way the coat was conforming to his body. Suddenly, a pin pricked him like a tiny sword, and he became vicious again. "I regret to have taken thee for a wife," he said. "Where is thy hand-mirror? I should like to see how I look."

I had packed it. I went into the bedroom and after looking over my shoulder I pulled my valise out from its hiding place under the bed. Outside the window, Tabitha's dark shape moved along the wall. I rushed the mirror back to Herman's hand and in it I caught a savage look in its reflection—chilling, haunting in the candlelight. How does one make a specter leave a house?

"Herman, I am tired," I said. "Let me rest and I can finish this up early in the morning. Perhaps you can study your sermon over at the church like so many other nights."

He took up his study Bible with all its little scraps of paper place-holders and walked towards the door. I exhaled with relief and kept my head bent over my work, waiting to hear the door open. It did not.

I finally looked up to see him sitting still in a chair.

"Perhaps I will stay should thou need to do another fitting," he said. "I will conduct a sermon tomorrow just after our new junior minister has his try, and mine will naturally be superlative." He began reciting his sermon under his breath, stopping, rephrasing, practicing.

"Job 1:16," he mumbled, "yes, that is better: *The fire of God is fallen from heaven, and hath burned up the sheep, and the servants, and consumed them... Upon the wicked he shall rain snares, fire and brimstone, and a horrible tempest: this shall be the portion of their cup.*"

He stopped and turned to me. "Hear me, wife. How glad the others will be to hear my plan to purify that village to the north that lies along the cliff trail—the one that will not submit to church and civilization. It sits along the banks of one of the best streams on this side of the island. God wishes us to burn the unrepentant natives out, and then we can claim their fresh water source and channel it towards productive use as the Mission Board has charged us. I envision the farming of crops such as sugarcane, which grows easily and wild here. Thus the natives will be forced to depend on the Mission for their water and food. Let Davis try to conceive of a greater accomplishment."

"Are you truly so lacking in compassion that you would set fire to a village?" I asked, incredulous. "To endanger women and children? Or perhaps that is exactly it—you really yearn to destroy the reminders of your sins."

He looked at me with inhuman eyes. Panic seized me, and I loathed the way his spirit had long sought to seep into my thoughts and confidence. I struggled to find my mana. Herman sat back down and silence roared between us.

I re-threaded a needle as the clock chimed three-quarters past the hour. I looked out the window, trying to see Tabitha, hoping she still waited. My fingers shook, sending my box of pins spilling all across the floor.

"Silence, Mrs. Webster!" he said, exasperated. "How can I work? Thou hast scattered my line of thought!"

There was my answer. As soon as he became engrossed in his work again, I slowly slid my hand along the table towards my scissors and then pushed them off in a clatter onto the floor.

"God is great!" Herman shouted in exasperation. "He hath spoken unto me this very moment in prayer as I have lifted up my plea. For my eyes have just seen Luke, chapter six, verse twelve: '... *he went out into a mountain to pray, and continued all night in prayer to God.*' This is what I shall do. Thou shalt sew here all night if need be, and I will go find the quiet that I need to hear His voice. I will return early to wash and dress and you will have my coat ready."

When the door slammed shut and his footsteps faded away, I said my own prayer, a prayer of thanks.

I walked alongside the lava wall looking for Tabitha until she found me.

"Come," she said, taking my hand and we walked carefully in the shadows sharply edged by the light of a full moon.

A soft clucking sound came from my pocket and I put a hand gently over the form of Aloha. "You are leaving your cage forever, and so am I," I had told her as I cupped her in my hands moments before I had flown. To my relief, she had let me slide her into my deep dress pocket as if it were a little nest.

"I used to escape this way as a girl to meet with Thaddeus," Tabitha whispered once we were away from the sleeping buildings. "How is Thaddeus? I have not seen him."

"Steal away with me, and you will."

"I do not wish to," she said so low I could barely understand her. "I am in love with Reverend Davis, of course. Thaddeus was a girlhood fancy. Oh, I missed him at first so terribly that I nearly threw myself over the side of the ship and gave myself to the sharks. How silly one is, believing there is such a thing called 'true love.'"

We reached a far end of the Mission yard where tombstones rose up from the red earth.

"When I married Herman, true love was something I had conjured up in my heart and wishes; he stepped inside of those wishes and they became a cloak that hid who he truly was."

"I have chosen my true love's destiny," she said. "One that will give me a happy and purposeful life. When our minds are righteous, our hearts are not to be trusted in the matter. Reverend Davis is my destiny. My love for Thaddeus changed as I changed."

"Then maybe whatever is true love reflects who we truly have become," I whispered. "Whether love pulls us by the mind or by the heart, I would not be led by one without the other."

Tabitha stopped at a large square grave marker with tiered sides standing next to the lava-stone wall. "Now, give me your arm and I will help you up here," she told me.

She let me lean on her and she pushed as I scrambled to stand up on the top of the high gravestone. My winged heart promised to fly me away to Diego, and thus her next instructions did not sound difficult at all.

"There are hand and footholds that protrude from the wall beneath the vines," Tabitha told me. "See that large branch there, growing over towards us? It lends its arm to usher you up into the old tree, and then it is an easy climb down the trunk on the other side—that will be the first wall crossed. To conquer the second one, walk left between the walls for one hundred and twenty paces. You will come to a wooden gate." She reached up to hand me my little valise and then placed a cool iron piece in my hand. "Take this old key, it will open it. And do not worry about your trunk; the merchant will read your note and keep it safe until you send for it."

"Can the seamen who carried it down to him be trusted to keep a secret?" I asked.

"I know them well from the voyage over. Once they delivered it to your merchant you can be sure that they drank themselves into a good night's sleep and lie passed out by now on the beach. And they are not the kind to step foot near the Mission again, God save their souls."

"Tabitha," I said, "Are you sure you don't want to come along to see Thaddeus?"

"He was another heart ago. Some things break and cannot be put back together. Are you really sure you wish to leave your husband?"

"He stopped being a husband long ago. I will be bound to him no longer." I turned my head to look back at the Mission houses for the very last time.

We embraced tightly. "You were always kind to me," she said. "May God forgive me for helping you, and may He bless you."

Tabitha disappeared into the darkness. At that moment, the moon lit up the great arched branch of the tree like a moonbow—like the path the Goddess Hina took to leave her cruel husband. I was in her legend now, and she in mine, as real as anything I had ever felt.

I tugged the plain silver wedding ring from my finger and threw it down into the graveyard. There with the moonlight in my face and the sounds and smell of the island night pounding through my heart I pulled myself up into the rescuing arms of the gracious old breadfruit tree and climbed its path up towards the moon.

CHAPTER 44

Article Twenty-Eight: The Spyglass

*P*ua was waiting for me outside the gate and with a rush she put down her little tin lantern and hugged me with both arms. I bent down and smiled into the top of her head, grateful, wondering. She took a bower of lei from her neck and stood up on tip-toe to place them around mine. "I brought you wedding flowers," she said. "Diego has been planning your escape—he waits for you now. Come with me."

Long before that night a wall inside my heart had come tumbling down. "Pua," I said as we hurried along, "In the other village, the remote one in the next ahupua'a to the north—do you know the tattoo-faced woman with the gray-eyed child? You must warn her they all must stand watch and be ready to flee—Herman wishes to burn her village down."

Her look of alarm showed even in the darkness as we drew beside a thick wide hedge high as a tree where ancient hibiscus grew. The village hale stood sentry like dark giant letter 'A's making pointed shadows tattooed onto the ground by the moonlight. Then Thaddeus stepped out from the wall of sleeping blossoms.

"I knew Tabitha would help you," he said excitedly, looking hopefully behind and around me. "Tell me, did she—" he said, losing words as he realized that her form was not to materialize from the darkness.

"I asked her to come with me. I am sorry, Thaddeus."

He turned away from us, his head bent low, stricken. Then he remembered himself, looked up, and softly whistled.

There was the muted sound of a horse blowing through its nostrils. "Diego," Thaddeus called out quietly.

A silver spur chimed softly, I felt his presence in the shadows, and then he was there before me. For a long instant we stood frozen, as if the sight of each other was enough—and then he caught me as I leapt into his arms. He lifted me up as if I weighed a feather and spun me around so that he could see my face in the pale light. He cradled my head with both hands, bent down and tenderly touched his lips to mine. My heart gratefully beat against his once more.

It was a kiss that lasted but a moment but the heavenly feeling stayed as he took my hand and led me to where several horses stood waiting. Thaddeus was tying my valise up behind a saddle.

I turned to embrace Pua. "Thank you, dear Pua," I said.

She was crying softly. "I will never see you again, will I? Thaddeus said that his dear teacher Betsey Stockton never returned."

"I am going far, far away, but one never knows. We can write letters. I will never forget you. Be well, Pua. Find yourself a wonderful future."

"The Thatchers have been good to me, and the doctor has asked me to assist him. He is proud that I already know my letters, Latin, and arithmetic. I think I will be a doctor when I grow up."

I was letting her go when she embraced me again as hard as she could with her slim young arms. I returned it, knowing she would live half a world away from me for the rest of my days.

Diego helped me up on the horse, its swaying, living being beneath me, eager to go. I pulled Aloha carefully out of my pocket and she sprang to life the way she did every morning when I took the cloth off of her cage; flapping her wings and rising up against the stars she then floated down to perch on the back of my saddle.

Thaddeus went over to his horse. A second one was tied to his, standing quietly wearing an empty saddle. A flower lei hung expectantly over the horn and flowers and ferns were carefully braided into its mane.

He dug in his saddlebag, then placed something in Diego's hand. "Thank you for teaching me the vaquero ways," he said, and then we were ready to go.

With farewells fading behind us, Diego and I turned up the King's Highway, reached the silken ribbon of moonlight road and galloped away.

The hooves clattered along the rocky north shore, an open windy cape by day where we would have had no cover, but wrapped in night we had the freedom of darkness. By dawn we reached the northeastern side where the island became verdant again. Finding a protected nest between trees and high grasses, Diego tied the horses, gathered ferns and covered them with a blanket to make a soft bed and a pillow for my head. He lay down beside me, took me in his arms and, exhausted, we fell fast asleep to the sound of the waves.

I AWOKE to see him sitting up, looking out over the churning sea spread out beneath us in the late afternoon light. He turned to stare at me with wonder on his handsome face cast golden brown in the sun's rich glow.

"We will stay along the coast to watch for ships, and will know if we are being followed," he said. "They will not take the treacherous path on land along these cliffs."

He dug from his pocket and pulled out my little hymnal. "I took it because I knew I would see you again," he said. "I wanted to keep something of yours while I made our plan to take you away."

The world felt wide open, new, glorious, frightening—I had just placed my heart, my life, my trust in this man. All words vanished in the vertigo of being next to him as we both stared at the sea, as if looking into each other's eyes was as bright as looking at the sun.

"Look at what Thaddeus gave me," he finally said and handed me a brass and baleen-wrapped spyglass. I took the spyglass and scanned down beyond the cliffs where the great white waves crashed up to their rim. I gave it back to him and smiled; seeing mine, his smile broke wide open and we both gazed boldly at the miracle of each other.

The sun set the clouds afire with persimmon flames. We sank down into each other's arms as the sun began to set and the colors turned brighter, brilliant, deeper.

I WAS STILL bare beneath my cloak when he ran his hand up my thigh, across my stomach, and stopped. He had lingered there earlier as we were passionately reuniting our hands with each other's bodies and now he tenderly pressed his palms above my womb, sending a gentle warmth deep down inside me. He stayed there, waiting on me. I took a breath to steady myself as I looked into his wide eyes.

"Yes. Of course it is ours," I whispered.

The joy and pride in his face surprised me, for I had not thought of my condition to be other than a fearsome, shameful plight. He was speechless for a few moments, but his expression in the sun's wake told me everything: love, delight, pride, protectiveness, tears.

"My *paloma*, I will protect you and our child," he promised fiercely. "My dove, I will love you more each day, I will never desert you; I crossed an ocean to find you and I would do it again. Nothing will ever separate us. We will have a sweet, long life together. Do you trust me?"

He reached for my left hand, brought it to his lips, and slowly, purposely, kissed my bare ring finger.

"I do," I whispered.

· · ·

We stayed in the same embrace until the first star appeared. We rose and prepared to start out again. By dawn we reached the hill above the north of the isthmus where the shallow harbor lay, not far from Abigail and Henry's mission. There Diego had arranged a ship to take us away to Oahu where we would find passage in any direction we wanted.

There were newly-built warehouses and cottages, and glowing from their windows lanterns were coming to life, one by one. Trees had been cut down to build the growing town and we walked our horses through the thin forest. As we rode I could almost feel the forest's plight, as if its soul was fading away.

And then we heard a shattered song, sharp like crickets, a sparse cry for something lost.

We pulled up our reins. All around us, near and far, came a fractured symphony. We had once witnessed the wonder together when it was alive and powerful and as joyous as the sunrise.

"The land shells. Kāhuli," I spoke softly, words wrung from my swelling throat. "The voice of the forest. It has changed."

We fell silent. Diego brought his horse up close beside mine and took my hand.

I waited for the sound to swell, rich and full and light like once before, but it didn't. A sore, constricted feeling began creeping up my throat beneath my collarbone.

As if in sympathy, I began to cough. "It's nothing," I said, trying to erase the instant concern on Diego's face. I did not want to break the moment, the reverence, my mourning.

"We must take care of you. You slept outside on the ground and are used to a good bed," he worried. I began a fit of coughing and the baby began to move.

"Does not every mother-to-be use laudanum?" he asked. "We must have some—it will stop your cough. The mission nearby would have it?"

I felt uneasy. That was not our plan. "They surely will, if it could be spared—it is a coveted supply there," I said, thinking of poor Abigail. How I longed to see her one last time. "But Diego, I do not want it, and the risk of our being recognized is too great—and what if we miss our ship?"

We rode on, listening to the hoarse, fading song of the shells. The great volcano Haleakalā that had created the entire eastern body of the island began to appear, silhouetted by the dawn's first light that had reached its far side.

I was glad that Diego had quit his idea until I caught sight of the Adamson Mission house through the trees and realized that he had led us not to the harbor but straight there.

"Let us keep our flight," I protested. "My absence has surely been found out—our ship waits for us."

Diego did not listen, and pulling up our horses he dismounted. "That is the medical building," he argued. "I will steal in and find what we need."

I pushed away my irritation and uneasiness. It would be fine. "No—let me go, if we must. My friend Abigail lives here and I might explain if caught. She can keep a secret. That is her window there, the one with the lantern on."

I crept towards the sill with unnamed dread, but my mind spurred me on. It would take just a minute or so, then we would surely go find the ship that carried our deliverance, freedom, safety. My second chance at life. Everything that meant everything.

Then through the deep, cool still air that hangs at the end of night, pregnant with the land about to wake, came the hypnotic sound of someone humming a lullaby. I looked in the window to see Abigail holding her baby swaddled in a blanket with a long, trailing white skirt of an infant gown falling through its edges, billowing, floating, like a ghost.

"Abigail," I whispered. Slowly, she turned to me. "Abbie, do not tell anyone that I am here—I will not be in Lahaina when you stop over—I wanted to say goodbye."

"Kittie?" she said sweetly, amazed and touched to hear my voice; I could hear the loneliness in it. I drew closer and suddenly a look of fear seized her expression. "No!" Panicked, she spun away from me.

"Henry? Henry!" She cried as if I were a demon. She called down the hallway, "Henry! Kittie is trying to take my baby away again!"

"Shhhh! No, Abigail—" I tried, but she began humming the lullaby again, letting her baby's arm dangle as if it were a rag doll. Footsteps hurriedly approached from down the hallway.

I stepped back away from the lantern's reach, but the light outside had been growing and we no longer had total darkness. Diego was right behind me, gently pulling me towards the horses as we both stared at the illuminated room as if it were a stage. Henry entered and gently tried to take the baby out of Abigail's arms. Pain and grief were carved across his face. "Abigail, let go. We must not take it from the coffin again. We will bury her today."

Abigail ignored him, cooing into the silent little bundle. "There, there," she said, and began the horrible lullaby once more. Henry approached her carefully, walking closer towards the window as I backed away slowly, numb with grief for my friend. Did she need me? Did I have any help to give?

Diego's hand was protectively on my waist, urging me to move away more quickly. There was a sharp call from a waking bird, and then another and another. A dog began barking, sounding louder and angrier as it drew near. By the time I looked back to see Henry moving questioningly towards the windowsill I was digging my fingers deep and desperately into my galloping horse's mane in anguish for the choice I had made to desert my friend Abigail and the horror of her situation. Perhaps I had no power to save her, and what lay in balance was the life of my child, Diego's, mine. The life of my own spirit that Herman had sought so hard to kill.

Feeling the horse's shoulder muscles churning beneath me, we swished through the trees towards the harbor until the mission and the last tie to my old life was soon far behind us. The sun appeared from behind the big volcano touching the West Maui mountains to our left.

We would be at the beach in full daylight.

CHAPTER 46

$\mathcal{I}$ turned the barrels of the spyglass at the ships and found
her, the ship that waited for us, all men up in the rigging
readying to sail. Diego stepped out from our cover in the cluster of
trees that grew on the edge of the sandy beach and he flew his red
scarf above him. After a breathless wait, her boat finally came rowing
in to get us.

Our horses would have to be set free. Diego sadly placed his hands
on his horse's neck, then began loosening the saddle cinch.

He paused, turned his head and narrowed his eyes to look far away
down the beach. I hesitantly turned the spyglass in the same direction,
and my fear came true—in the circular picture dancing before my
eyes Reverends Goodwin and Davis came into focus standing by a
pyramid of offloaded barrels. To my dismay, Henry Adamson
approached, waving and heading towards them. Then with a sick thud
Herman's tall black figure appeared in my shaking lens, his coattails
flapping in the first breeze of the morning.

"It's them," I called to Diego. My fingers trembled too much to use
the spyglass, so I set it down as I motioned for Aloha to fly to my
shoulder.

The ragged surf was making a landing difficult, and the small boat sent out from our ship stayed suspended on the outside swells. Maybe the next wave, or the next would be the right one to speed it in towards us. Diego sadly put his favorite saddle on the ground, set the horses free, and we both ran towards the water's edge as Aloha's feet tightly clutched my shoulder.

We were standing in plain sight as the rowboat floated up and down, letting a large swell passed beneath it. With oars dug deep and backwards it was clear that the boat was going to wait for the long set of waves pass until it could take a smaller wave in. Meanwhile, in the distance, horses were being brought to the mission men's blurry forms.

Could Herman see us? Did he have a spyglass? I reached for ours and remembered that I had left it behind on a large log of driftwood.

I dashed back for it as quickly as my feeble body could. Back in hand, I was returning out of the trees when I froze mid-stride, afraid to move another inch. My nose was pinched by a sharp and bitter stench and my brain stammered, trying to tell me I had just seen a wild bullock standing by the spyglass. I slowly looked back, hoping I had imagined it. But there he was.

His legs were matted with mud and dried foliage, and his head was up, eyes glinting straight towards me. There was a scar across the top of his nose. He was old and had won many battles. Then he lowered his cruel horns and from the dark cavern of his lungs came a deep, monstrous whoosh of air.

A bullock will explode towards anything that runs away from him. He trotted towards me and then stopped and pawed the sand.

I took a tiny step, afraid to call out, but Diego instinctively turned to look for me. Quicker than a thought, his hand went to the coiled lasso that hung on his belt and he cast it high and far. The noose circled perfectly through the air and landed like a lei around the neck of the bull. In horror, I realized that there was no horse to counter the weight of the animal as it charged away, Diego flying and skidding past me across the sand.

But he knew what he was doing. As soon as he reached the trees he leaped through the air to the side of a strong cocoa-nut trunk, ran the rope around it and wove it around another beside it. The force from the bull pulled Diego against the trunk with a thud as the trees shook, but he rolled his shoulders around and made another circle able to keep the burning rope from slipping away. It gave him just enough time to circle the trunk again, and then once more, giving him a chance to tie a strong knot.

Our boat still floated in the choppy water just beyond the surf as people came running down the beach to see the man who on his own two feet had roped a charging wild bullock. His skill had been plain to see—as expert as a vaquero, his form excellent.

Unmistakable.

The men in black abruptly turned in our direction.

CHAPTER 47

Article Twenty-Nine: My Azure Blue Cape

*D*iego whistled, and the horses appeared trotting towards him, their master, the one who fed them and treated them well. Upon their slippery backs we galloped down the trail from which we had come. I ducked low against my horse's neck, my hands buried in his mane for balance, Aloha's claws deep in my hair. Where on the island did we have left to run?

With every jarring stride beneath me I breathed down as deep as I could, as if the answer might be inside me. The branches whipped my face, moist green leaves chattered against my horse's legs and the sound of hoofs clapping against stones were like voices urging us on. And then I heard a voice like Pua's, and I remembered something.

After Leilani had left Lahaina, Pua told me that the princess had returned to the heiau where she had grown up as a child. Its location was kept hidden, but I knew that it was built as a sacred temple dedicated to he'e nalu, so we would go east along the coast where the great waves were. We crossed the isthmus and before long we were well into the tropic forest that clung to the steep slopes of the massive Haleakalā.

The going was as difficult as it was beautiful as we went deeper into the forest, far away and safely lost to anyone in pursuit. We passed waterfalls, long white veils spilling down into thick green mantles of living, breathing forest. We crossed down into deep gulches where streams ran over slippery rocks out to meet the sea, and up steep hills, every turn revealing flowers and plants I had never seen.

We were as free as the sun and stars that rose and set in a rhythm like an ancient song. Mud splashed up to my hems and my fatigue melted away under the contentment Diego had left inside my body. I didn't fear the thin trail that wound along above the churning sea, because I felt immortally alive with the man I had chosen. Aloha circled high and free above us, calling to all the island birds before always descending to land lightly back down on the horse's back behind me.

I took off my corset. The air was a silken cloak, the sunlight caressed my bare arms and lit up my amber necklace, throwing a thousand tiny golden suns dancing across my chest.

I shined with the might of one thousand suns.

Enlightenment. Freedom. We were Adam and Eve, tearing through Eden.

WE CAMPED that evening at a flat, green clearing on a cliff with a precarious view of the jagged coastline where deep blue waves crashed up in mast-high white plumes of spray and mist. Not far away, a thin waterfall spilled off a cliff down into a small bay below.

Diego made a fire, and we watched its yellow light grow on each other's faces. "Could you be happy with a simple horseman?" he asked as we leaned back on soft blankets to look at the twilight sea and the stars that appeared shyly, one by one. His fingertips absentmindedly lingered along my arm as he continued.

"I must go visit my family's home in Monterey. My father was a Spaniard, but my mother was Chumash. They died young, and I was left with the rancho that he built. Its size is second only to that of—Manuela's —father." He said her name quickly, as if even the mention of her did not belong in our new world. "We were betrothed since we were young to join both large ranchos given under Mexican rule and when I became a man I was still not ready to begin a life I had not chosen. All were angry except my brother when I signed on for the voyage to these islands." He touched my hair tenderly, smiled, and cupped the side of my face.

"Can we create a life for a vaquero and a shipwrecked missionary?" I asked softly. "I long to see my Aunt Sallie; she will welcome us, but I am afraid my father will not help us—especially not when he sees the three of us. And I cannot offer you a large rancho like Manuela can."

He shook his head, and his rich voice played with a slight laugh. "You are much more," he said as he took me in his arms.

We lay there, happily staring at the sky as the fire crackled and one of the horses contentedly blew through his nostrils.

"You will have no worries. I can take care of you and our little one," Diego said, getting up to stoke the fire, pacing thoughtfully around it as he began to tell me a story.

"I hold a secret that has never been told. My father was once in command of a gold mine in the California hills where the Spanish forced native Chumash to dig. He fell for my mother, a Chumash from the Dolphin islands. This love changed him into a different man: he set the slaves free and also took some gold for himself. As he made the adobe bricks to build his hacienda he hid it in the mud forms, and when dry he used those bricks to set the foundation. There the gold would be kept safely until I grew into a man. He told me all this as he was dying.

"Now I must go back to the hacienda; my younger brother will try to take it while I am gone. He will fight for it—he always loved Manuela, always jealous of me, and wants the rancho to help win her."

I was glad that another man loved Manuela.

"My father told me this on his deathbed: 'You are my eldest. Do not spend your time in pursuit of idle pleasures and fandangos like your brother, and you will have my fortune. Find the kind of love I had with your mother. If you do not love Manuela, promise me you will find a woman who would take you without the gold—then take it and my blessing.'"

Diego kneeled down and rested his head carefully in my lap, placing his hands upon my heart. "Precioso, I am worthy of it now."

I pulled him closer so that the length of his body covered me. We lay there moving together on the soft blankets, other words silently spoken telling each other everything that had long been kept inside, lonely and waiting in our hearts.

I awoke to a muted dawn to see Diego putting oilcloth over us to protect us from rain. It fell harder until our blankets were wet and cold. I burrowed beneath them to find the warmest place, stifling my cough. Past the smell of damp wool drifted the comforting scent of a campfire that Diego was stoking in an indentation in a rock ledge. By and by the rain lifted and the sea spread before us, gray and dull with smudges of rain far out on the horizon.

Diego shielded his spyglass with a hand, peering up the coast, not speaking. I moved slowly around our camp, held under a helpless feeling, heavy as the dark flannel-gray clouds. Only Leilani might know how to help us escape the island.

My body was leaden, my lower back ached, mosquitos vexed me. With no chores left, I took refuge from the misty air and curled back up beneath the oilcloth, my blue cape comforting me like a blanket while Diego kept watch to see if we were being followed.

By noon I sat up, startled awake by sunlight beaming through parted clouds setting everything around dripping in shining, brilliant colors. With our blankets and stockings drying by the fire and our hearts lighter, I began to admire the flowers that grew around our little camp like a lei. I picked and pressed my favorites between the pages of my hymnal.

Diego checked the horses and had begun to break camp when he stopped to take up his spyglass again and held it, frozen.

Struggling through the choppy water along the coast a ship came into view. Its sails were wet and tight, whitecaps splashing over the railing, and her signal flags told us she was the one we had tried to board! A rainbow grew in the misty sunshine above the mast, surely a good omen.

Diego shot his gun twice, waving at the ship as I put out the fire. Aloha waited on the rump of a horse preening her damp feathers. Soon we were up and away down to the small rocky beach as the ship cut closer to us through fields of whitecaps. It tacked against the wind towards the shore and I thought I heard the faint rumple of a dropping anchor.

Diego waved his arms and fired two more bullets into the sky. I could hardly breathe. I clutched my round stomach protectively.

The ship slowly kept moving, dragging anchor or perhaps heading closer towards shore to get us. It grew smaller. It became a tiny speck and then disappeared around the curve of the island. It had passed us by.

WE TOOK up the trail going east, chasing the ship. It led us along high sea bluffs and down into steep gulches where waterfalls emptied into ice blue waves. Some crossings were so muddy and treacherous that we almost turned back, but Diego always found a path where our horses could carry us onward.

Unexpectedly, the trail abruptly stopped at the base of a verdant cliff that rose straight up like a wall. The horses were glad to stop, their heads low, catching their breath. Diego dismounted, handed me his reins and his boots scraped through the thick flowering plants and grasses as he tried to find the trail. Then he stopped. Pulling away a veil of vines, he called to me.

"Kittie, come see this."

I brought our horses forward to see lichen-covered blocks of stone expertly stacked, higher than a house. "It looks like the wall of a castle," I said, little goosebumps rising down my weakened arms, my head dizzy from the strain of our wild flight.

"It goes on," Diego said, striding alongside it, hands feeling it through bowers of glossy, green *maile* vines.

I followed Diego along as he searched for some kind of stairway, door, or corner. "It is as massive as the side of a ship," I said, feeling small and awestruck as one does beside a large great ocean-going vessel.

"Two ships," Diego figured. He suddenly stopped, giving me a sign to be quiet. My horse flinched, shot his head up high and then began dancing in place, ears darting from front to back. We were not alone.

"*Kū!*" shouted a deep voice—commanding us to halt—and sweeping towards us through the forest came a small army of native warriors. In that eternal second my mind clung to flashes of still images: yellow, black, and red feathers. A tattooed fist. An arm muscled with the weight of a heavy koa wood spear, a weapon with sharp, white shark teeth laced in a row all along its edges. I saw my hands clenching the wide saddle horn for balance, like a lifeline. The saddle swayed beneath me. Diego's face looking at mine in alarm. My white fingertips. And then the ground punched me, making all those pictures go black.

The fear is not in the fainting, but in the waking. An earthquake gives you moments to let you feel the foundations of your world shake and crack, but passing from a dark dream back to life there is only the sound of your breath to guide you as you wonder who you are, where you are, and what just happened. I began to see again: feet, sideways. Bare heels, thick ankles marked with indigo. A boot, and I wanted to cry with relief because it might be Diego's. He was holding my hand, but a woman held my head.

I must still be dreaming, I thought, for I looked up into her face and recognized Princess Leilani.

CHAPTER 48

$\mathcal{S}$he looked into my eyes just as she once had—with affection, not fury. We did not need pins and needles and dresses to be friends, she had once told me, but dresses are sometimes outworn, changed. She had changed.

Gone was the fight to find peace with who she was; she now embodied it. Gone was the determined effort to be strong; she was strong, strong the way one is when they have taken off everything that makes them weak.

She helped me sit up, and I squinted at a rocking sea and spinning clouds. We were high atop a lava fortress that had an omniscient view of the coastline below. Miles of ocean swells that came from a million fathoms and leagues across the Pacific knelt before us, finally lifting, peaking, crashing and churning before us. I sat upon a thick, soft pile of kapa mats and someone gently placed a cup of water to my lips. In a semi-circle beside and behind us towered carved wooden gods and surfing boards. A line of warriors, mighty heads bowed, motionless and obedient, stood several paces away, making me recall our capture. The captain of the warriors held a sharp tooth-edged club with an arm so muscled it was perhaps more deadly than his weapon.

Then Princess Leilani stood up, her abundant body heavy, yet superbly nimble. She looked taller than before, her bearing more powerful, as if her spirit were emanating out from her in all directions. She wore a skirt and cape of pounded mulberry cloth dyed with an intricate pattern. About her throat was a necklace thick with tiny braids of hair from which a large carved whale's tooth hung, resting just below her collarbone.

"My friend Kittie," she smiled. "Our last parting was a sad thing to carry within me."

Diego was there beside me, squeezing my hand as she spoke to us. The mammoth stone shrine beneath us was both castle and altar that faced the sea. Diego and I were privileged to be welcomed there, for this was a heiau—a temple—to the God of the Surf.

"Welcome to the Heiau of my ancestors," she continued. "It is both monument and a source of power, mana, like Moku'ula; here where the fresh water of land meets that of the sea a Divine power comes to life. The name we call this surf break is *Kapua'i*, 'the flow of water.'"

"Your Majesty, is there a river here?" Diego asked, puzzled.

Leilani paused, weighing which words she would choose to release. "There is a great stream of fresh water here," she said. "It flows beneath us.

"Your Diego has told me the story of your plight; my runners tell me that you are being followed. I will try to help you." She made a gesture with her arm and soon an old man bowed before her. I recognized him as the kahu, or priest who always chanted the long unfailing prayer for her protection whenever she was out riding the waves. She said something to him, and he nodded and smiled. He made his way over to a large stone placed like a statue on the edge of the platform and struck it, making a bell sound. Then he took his leave, disappearing down a moss-covered stairway.

"The *'ōhā* stone will call for the ocean surface to smooth and the surf to stand up," Leilani told me. "For now, let us sit down and talk like we did once upon those warm, happy Lahaina afternoons when you sewed. You look tired, and you have a cough; you must eat."

A feast was brought before us of steamed pork, melons, poi, lobster, chicken, and fish seasoned with seaweed and salt. We dined from wooden calabashes with heavy silver forks and bare fingers. Thick Celestial silk pillows cushioned us from stark blocks of coral-reef beneath us. European-bound books were casually set upon the sharkskin head of an ancient drum. Leilani's world would always be a story written with words from both familiar and faraway places, and not always easy to understand.

The great heiau was aligned to the coast in a way that gave a dramatic view of the breaking waves not much more than 100 yards away. Similar to an amphitheater, a seating area was built into the stone with a grand view of the breaking surf. As Diego and I looked from our bird's-eye view the next set came in, larger than the last. Dark blue lines of swells, like a row of tucks sewn in indigo cloth were appearing farther out past the surf line.

From the edge of the cliff below us rose the voice of the elder priest. His chant mingled in rhythm and melody with the sound of the waves.

Ku mai! Ku mai!
Ka nalu nui mai kahiki mai
Alo poi pu! Ku mai ka pohuehue
Hu! Kaikoo loa
Arise! Stand up ye great surfs
from where sky meets horizon
The powerful, curling waves
Arise with the beach morning-glory
Well up, long raging surf

Down along the rocky coastline I spied a long line of people. They raised their arms and then threw them down to beat the surface of the water with beach morning-glory vines. The effect of the ritual, the rhythm of movement, the sound of the chanting and the waves made a reverent hush fall all around us.

Leilani smiled as she surveyed the scene. "The missionaries will never find you here," she said matter-of-factly. "Great waves will keep a search boat from making a landing. And our island will surround, protect and hide us, like a cloak." Then she looked at me with lips pressed firm and straight. "I want to make sure you escape that barbaric man—he committed yet another heinous act since the day he burned our surfboards. He seems to be obsessed with hellfire. Just days ago he orchestrated the burning of a village. Fortunately, they had been warned, and no one was hurt."

Suddenly, she gave a short, pleased laugh. "And there is your miracle," she said, pointing to a ship making its way up along the coast in our direction. "It is one of our royal ships, the Prince Regent. It will take you to Honolulu."

Swift with authority, she raised her hand and a lithe young man appeared. "Signal the Regent to anchor there just beyond the waves."

The sun was falling behind the mountains to our left, and down in the surf the rising wave foam was turning lavender. Diego sat tall, taking it in, watching the horses far down below where a little speck of bright green could be seen perching on the back of my horse.

Protected by the impenetrable forest and the stone fortress about us, my breaths fell deeper and slower as I conversed with Leilani.

"Will you ever return to Moku'ula?" I asked her.

"When the time is right. When my surfboard was burned, I fled here to make sure that this place will never be destroyed. I will not let outsiders take anything else from my people. Did you know that on one island a Christian church is being built directly on top of a toppled heiau?"

My thoughts were in scraps, and I could not assemble a reply to that. I looked down at glimpses of the gray stone floor peeking from the bright green grass that was growing over it and I counted the mosquito bites on my arms.

"Another new foreigner invading our islands," Leilani continued, gesturing her ruby lead crystal goblet towards my itchy red welts. She raised the glass to her lips and took a long sip before speaking. "You're a missionary. Believing must be so simple for you."

"Nothing has been simple here. Everything I once believed in has come undone," I said. "I once thought I could mend almost anything with needle and thread."

"I have come to think that to learn of a different God is merely learning another culture," she said.

Our conversation paused. The waves crashed down below and the calls of the wild birds chanted from miles of forest around us as my eyes took in the massive stone heiau. "How will you hide all of this?" I asked.

"By letting the island do it. It is claiming it already. The earth and growing life are Hina's powers; especially when the moon is full you can feel and almost hear the forest growing under her protective light. Soon we will be embraced by the island, lost to any seeker who does not come in goodwill."

"Will Moku'ula be lost someday?" I asked. "You have left it, the Queen of the Yellow Feathers has passed, and the young king prefers O'ahu."

"Lahaina has and will always stand on the front line where cannonballs and spears clash like waves against a shore. The adventurers and foreign ships have made themselves at home, yet our people there are strong because they are forced to choose what they will hold on to. The spirit of Moku'ula can never be lost; even if it were buried, its spirit would rise up like the long-forgotten sacred fresh water springs that bubble up in the surf there at its shore."

The clouds were gathering to make a magnificent sunset. Suddenly something caught Leilani's eye and she turned and looked over her shoulder. A large flock of birds was lifting up from the trees, their many feathered throats squawking in a chorus of alarm. Leilani's wide, smooth brow wrinkled.

"I was told they were coming by ship. They must have somehow made it through the forest by tracking you," she said. "The birds that rest at sunset have been disturbed; something is traveling towards us through the trees. They are coming this way."

CHAPTER 49

*E*verything happened quickly as Leilani gave orders. Across the dark green grass below, our horses were set loose and they galloped away. Aloha circled high above, looking for me. I held up my arm to her and she began to descend.

Diego and I looked at each other, questions mirrored in our eyes. Boarding the ship was impossible; the large surf was pounding in and there was not much beach below the steep cliffs, just a shiny black reef bearing the brunt of the Pacific Ocean. Our horses were gone. Aloha shook her feathers and settled down by my neck just in time to join me as Leilani bid us to follow her down into the torch-lit bowels of the heiau.

The stone staircase descended until it opened up into an immense cave. It had been formed centuries ago by molten lava when its crust had cooled into stone, and the rest of the living, red lava had drained away into the ocean like a snake shedding its skin. Like a cathedral of the sea, it was filled with the light of countless kukui-nut torches. Shafts of fading sunlight fell down through natural rocky windows high up from the heiau structure above and fell below to light up a quiver of ancient surfing boards.

A large rectangular freshwater pool lay in the center of the chamber. Its water overflowed past the burning torches into channels that ran in the direction of the ocean. A surfing board lay drying next to the pool, rinsed of salt, patterned just like Leilani's water lizard tattoos; it was one of hers.

"Come along," she said. Her warriors stayed behind as we crossed a natural stone bridge that led us over a freshwater stream and across to the far end of the great chamber. Through an arch in the lava we continued on into a tunnel. Diego put my cloak around my shoulders as we hurried to keep up with her.

We passed an opening in the cave where Aloha suddenly left my shoulder and flew away through a fringe of ferns towards the periwinkle sky.

"Aloha! Come back!" I cried, then coughed, the sound echoing before and behind us. She darted back to me and clucked reassurances in my ear as we kept walking onward.

And then from outside the vines and ferns we heard the small, distant sound of a voice.

"Ho there! A cave here, Goodwin! Davis!"

Leilani froze and turned, eyes wide and her face bitter, her jaw muscles tightening.

The tunnel was wide and straight and tall enough to drive a carriage through. The light from our torches jumped up along the dark cave walls as Leilani led us in a run. Suddenly, with a movement of her hand, she pulled us against the jagged side bringing us to an abrupt stop, listening. I heard it too, and my heart slammed.

Tap. Slap. Tap, went the iron plate of his shoe on the hard lava stone floor.

Then the sound of a match came scratching along the lava walls. I smelled burning whale-oil and twice the light reached out for us.

"Dost thou detect the smell of sulphur, Goodwin? We must have surely reached the outskirts of Hell," he shouted over his shoulder. "Hath mine ears heard the sound of a voice? For it belongs to my wife, who hath surely descended there! Come along men, I detect the stench of sin this way!"

He sounded frighteningly close as his voice pounced along the rock walls towards me. "Satan's mistress must be nigh. Hear my voice, wanton whore, for you have nowhere to run."

I struggled to squelch another cough, burying my face into my blue cape until my lungs screamed for air. To my horror, Herman's silhouette crept towards us along the rugged wall cast by their shining lanterns, and like a wild animal, his eyes reflected the light. I finally burst into a cough my cloak could not smother.

"This way, men," he called, "we have found our prey—the half-beast and savage princess are with her! Follow me!"

Then I heard the sound of terror as a bullet from a pepperbox revolver ricocheted towards us, stinging from side to side along the rock tunnel.

Faster we went, but the lantern light still leapt at us from behind. Diego grabbed a knife from his boot; he knew well how to use it.

"There is no need," Leilani told him."We will have to go another way, and leave them to wander the labyrinth until they become dry bones."

She led us towards an outcropping of rock. It was not large enough to hide us, but we followed her desperately and just when I thought I would press into Leilani she became empty space. I squeezed into the narrow place to find a passageway that zig-zagged tightly until it opened up into another tunnel. We took turns through a narrow opening that was sweating salt water and we reached a dripping chamber. Drop by drop, fallen for centuries, the water had formed tall white ghosts. Finally, the light and voices faded behind us. We paused to listen. It was dead quiet, save for the distant sound of pounding waves.

We wound around the salt ghosts, our torch-shadows making faces on them that seemed to turn and watch us as we passed. I suddenly gasped as I found myself looking at not a row of salt statues, but a line of white skulls that sat on a ledge like gatekeepers, staring at us with hollow eyes. Leilani was taking us through an ancient burial cave.

A seafaring canoe supported tall feather standards crossed against its mast. We passed an ancient surf-board made of wiliwili wood, perhaps 24 feet long, draped with strings of shells, nearly touching the roof of the tall chamber. Leilani stopped and knelt down before bundles of kapa-cloth that held the bones of her ancestors. She lowered her head and then placed her flower lei down before a carved figure with gleaming shell eyes. I shivered, and Diego put his arm around me as we waited respectfully.

I leaned into the crook of his arm and listened. We were deep in the bowels of the island, entombed in black lava darker than night. Not far away, giant waves reverberated low and monstrous. Aloha's little body pressed against the high collar of my thick blue cape. I shuddered, and Diego gently pressed my lower back with his firm hand. Somewhere ahead of us a great wave moaned with a deep, low frequency in the depths of the lava-rock, and then spouted somewhere up through the cliff like the blowhole of a whale.

As if being given an answer or a blessing, Leilani rose regally and we moved on. The cave became small, low and narrow and wound along before it opened up and we suddenly found ourselves in an orange blast of sunset light. We were at the opening of the cave as large as a whale's mouth that gaped over the churning, deep waters away from shore where the swells appeared and grew into smooth hills. The salty breath of waves filled the air and there, silhouetted in the golden mist, sat a large double-hulled outrigger canoe waiting on the wet lava-rock floor.

Out beyond across the water the *Prince Regent* sat waiting for us perhaps a mile down the coast where the waves missed a far cliff and melted back into deeper waters.

I looked out through the cave mouth at the massive surf coming in. These were sacred waves, and could be caught only by outrigger or by leaping off of one onto a surf-board—*lele wa'a*, Pua had called it—and ridden—must be ridden, for life depended on it.

"Get in," Leilani commanded Diego and I. "I will launch it."

I pulled up my skirt and climbed in, feeling uneasy siting there without her aboard.

"Remember what I taught you," she said. "There will be a wave that is meant for you and you will know it. Find your place, catch as much wind as you need to skim before it, and as the swell rises up behind you steer her true."

My blood froze. "You're not coming with us?"

"Farewell, Kittie. I must stay. You can do it." She held out the steering paddle to me and as I placed my palms and fingers around it she didn't let go. I felt her energy, her life force, connecting to mine.

Behind me was a dark cave and Herman, ahead were monster waves—the only way to reach the *Prince Regent.*

"Go and create your future, as I will mine," she said. "And then let us keep looking forward." She let go.

I took my place at the back of the canoe, a riptide of fear sweeping through me. I tried to take a deep breath, and another.

"We will wait for the right moment," Leilani said. "Tell Diego how to shape the sail. You have no other paddlers, so you must catch a wave to get to the ship."

Holding the rail of the great canoe, she leaned up on tiptoe and pressed her forehead to mine.

"I am sorry," I said. "I tried. I tried to bring some good."

After a long breath, she pushed me at arm's length, looked me in the eyes, and said quietly, "You did."

Leilani gazed out at the lines of swells coming in, patiently examining them, waiting. "I'm sorry I destroyed your blue velvet dress Kittie—but dresses have of way of becoming a part of us, our spirit, and in that moment of destruction I loathed it. With the mightiest little stitches you gathered love given to you—a vaquero's cloak, a New England petticoat, and with a needle made from the bone of the 'Iwa seabird you brought our worlds together."

I suddenly saw my memory of Aunt Sallie's spools of thread—love, in rainbow colors. And then we both uttered the word Aloha.

Her eyes caressed the darkening silhouette of her island with its palpable hum of thick, growing green life that spread out over the land, claiming the heiau. The light from the pale rising moon—the strength of Hina—was singing with the breathing earth and shined in her hair and glowed on her face. With eyes wider and brighter than I had ever seen, she suddenly looked back at the sea.

"Now," she commanded suddenly.

She quickly shoved the outrigger across the salty lava rock and we slid silently into the deep velvet water beneath a phosphorescent sky.

So many times I had gladly watched Leilani guide and correct our course. Now, terrifyingly, it would be me alone. The outrigger was twice as big as the one I had sailed with her in the friendly surf at Lahaina.

I dug the paddle into the water as hard as I could and Diego grabbed the ropes like reins and pulled the sails in to capture the wind. Aloha nested somewhere deep in my skirts beneath my azure blue cape.

The little lights sparkled far out on the *Prince Regent* and I desperately paddled hard for it. Then our canoe began to lift up as if we were riding astride a giant whale, and the pulsing cadence in my ears fell into a throbbing rhythm like a chant. This was the wave.

The sound of the hull drummed louder against the surface of the water as we picked up speed. Something eerie about it arrested me for one eternal heartbeat. From across the twilight water I sensed a ghostly presence coming towards me like Hawai'ian spirits half-slipping through a fracture in time; powerful, ancient people, the bottom of their sea crafts one with what was beneath me, beating and cutting through the water.

I was no longer alone, as if that spirit was joining, becoming me; it pushed away my fear of the waves that could overturn and crush us. We must slide the wave that approached us. I dug my oar deep, then pulled with all my might. Diego pulled the sail in tighter.

Then, like a Ka'upu bird, we started sliding down the steep wall that was beginning to break behind us, giving us wings. A thrill rushed through me as a force came up through the deep water to connect with our outrigger, bringing it to life, and embodying my spirit.

Our swiftness was stunning as we slid along, flying, free. I watched its shape move before us and I steered diagonally along it in the dusk by feeling, hearing the loudly churning waterfall in our wake.

To our left passed the heiau with its massive shoulders, glowing with torchlights. I spotted the faraway silhouette on the high reef of the elder kahu invoking the God of the sea to protect us as he chanted in his unwavering voice.

We gradually slowed until our craft drifted into calmer waters beside the Prince Regent. Breathless, dizzy with relief and exhilaration, I looked back over my shoulder at the surf. I owned a new energy inside of me. My mana.

The crew called down to us and Diego caught their rope ladder. He helped me up to the rail after a Hawai'ian came down to take the canoe home.

There would be no going back. Everything was about to change. And it did.

PART IV

CHAPTER 1

DECEMBER 3rd, 1834
Honolulu

The anchor chain rumbled throughout the ship as it was cast into the waters of Honolulu. Diego held me at the railing where I had stayed most of the journey, violently sea-sick. I looked fondly at Diamond Hill, and if I could I would have embraced it, so glad was I to see land.

"I agree," Diego told me as I bent over into an uncontrollable fit of coughing. "An ocean voyage is too much for you… and the baby." He spoke softly, his lips near my forehead, his warm breath in my eyelashes.

I thirsted to feel land again and a motionless bed with nice, soft pillows. We could feel the anchor flukes dig into the harbor floor as the ship creaked, stopping us to moor just between two other ships in a field of hundreds.

"I will reach Emmie—she can find us a safe place to hide."

The Captain approached and brusquely pulled us into the galley. "I am charged to protect you, and we have trouble," he said. "Did you see that chase boat approaching? They are searching all ships arriving from Maui, with warrant for the arrest of a Diego Cruz and his companion."

My stomach turned with despair and the baby moved within me like a butterfly as I realized that our flight was not yet over. The Mission's reach was spread across the islands like tentacles. Diego sighed, pained, and pressed his forehead to mine as the Captain left us there in private.

"You will be safer here without me," he said after a long thoughtful silence as each of us breathed deeply each other's pained exhales. "Have your friend find you a good doctor. I will go on to Monterey and visit my family's hacienda to collect what is mine. In eleven month's time you will both be able to make a voyage, and we will have the means and freedom to live wherever we please. Take the spyglass. See those two cocoa-nut palms on the bluff by Diamond Hill? Let me find you there, at three in the afternoon, ten months from now."

I held him tighter, not wanting him to leave me. He stroked my hair. "My beautiful dove," he whispered. "I hate to leave you, especially now."

"I will be fine. Do not risk your life for me again—if you stay here we will have no future at all."

The Captain knocked as he entered again. "They are coming up along the larboard side."

"Can you hide my wife?" Diego asked. "Do you vow upon your life to keep her safe?"

The Captain looked down at my cloaked figure. "Of course. I am commanded by Queen Leilani to do anything in my power to help. But what of you?"

"I will go to Alta California. Do you know who sets for her?"

"You are in luck: the *Huntress*, starboard there, is pulling up anchor for San Francisco. I will see to it that Madam Catherine stays under Royal protection and care at Waikīkī for as long as she chooses."

It all happened so quickly. Diego held my face in his hands and pressed his lips hard against mine. I kissed him back with all my heart. And then he leapt astride the ship's rail, ready to dive, but paused once to look back at me, and in the next moment he was gone.

CHAPTER 2

Article Thirty: A Letter, Hand-Delivered From Honolulu to Waikīkī

December 23rd, 1834

Dearest Kittie,

I hardly know what to say—I would never have imagined you to take Satan's hand and follow him down this path. Of course you realize that your mournful circumstances have put Stuart and myself in danger of losing everything we've worked for—our home, our standing—render all of our sacrifices for naught, and jeopardize the success of our Lord's work here in the Sandwich Isles?

I will try to help you, old friend, but need time to consider just how. You tell me you wish to find a doctor, but I fear we cannot risk your presence here. The children are crying, and I must go. I am six months with child now—how far along are you? Do you think we might enter our confinement together?

Emmaline

The Captain of the *Prince Regent* had arranged a small grass hale for me to stay in that stood on the edge of the Royal cocoa-nut grove at Waikīkī. It was nestled against a deep white sandy beach upon which pretty waves broke perfectly, and it was said that when the swells of Kalehuawehe were large they could be ridden for more than a mile.

There beside that warm shore in the gentle breezes my cough lessened.

I replied to Emmaline, and eternal days passed without hearing back from her. Without Leilani I was at the mercy of the young King in Waikīkī who did not respond to my request for an audience. He was not a devotee of Christianity, so the missionaries on O'ahu courted him as persistently as the waves that broke upon the shore. Every day but Sunday they would walk the path that wound right past my hale to call on the King, hoping to find a way for him to need them.

Gradually I became restless there. I loved the call of the waves and the rich scent of flowers, but the risk of being seen was too great. It was no life staying hidden inside a hot grass cottage, peeking out my door cautiously every time I wanted to get air. One morning I stole out to a merchant's store in Honolulu town to buy fabric, needle, scissors and thread. I would fill my time sewing more clothes; all I had was the rose-sprigged cotton dress I had escaped in, now washed until it was weary.

Honolulu had quadrupled in size since the last time I was there and the mission houses no longer stood out as singular beacons of New England civilization. I took the side streets and narrow alleys that ran behind coral houses, wood storefronts, palm groves, old grass hale—some abandoned, but some still homes—homes that in the past would have been disposed of and made new of young and green fronds, but these were gray and aged, weakly sheltering hardship and struggle, sickness and death. A feeling of compassion and horror brushed across my skin, lingering in the back of my mind, bothering me like a loose thread.

There was a moment's pause as I stood near the mission houses and Emmie's proud wooden two-story home. Next to it was the printing house, and between that and the church stood the grandest new monument to the authority and permanence of missionaries in the isles: a two-story building made of coral walls sculpted to look like New England bricks and frosted with a facade of white lime.

I continued on and found a large merchant store. Its size and contents were vast, rich, overwhelming. I found my way to the fabrics, and every other bolt inspired me with happy visions of dresses I might sew; dresses that would become cherished little stories as I wore them with Diego in our new life.

I was looking at my choices of cotton calico when I noticed a well-dressed woman looking at satins from Canton. She was as exquisite as a china doll, with a porcelain face, strikingly beautiful almond eyes, and a rosebud mouth.

"Such beautiful silk!" she said to me.

"Yes, it is. The satin is very thick, and luxuriously woven."

"And look at this brocade," she said. The silk was shuttle-woven into a raised pattern of lush cherry blossoms in pale pink set against a slightly darker shade of rose.

"What a charming pattern of birds in this brocade," I said, examining the parrot green, yellow, azure, and silver thread. "They look like my own bird flying in a sky of pale blue silk, past clouds with silver linings."

"That cotton is poor, but this one from America is very fine quality," she said, gliding it between her thumb and fingers. "It would make an elegant day dress."

"I agree. I can almost see every gown that each fold wishes to be," I said.

The beautiful woman sighed. "I only wish I could find a good dressmaker. Do you know of one?"

I glanced down, suddenly aware of my faded, mended dress with the unfashionably high waist that had seen me through my escape across the island of Maui. Only I could see in it the beautiful memories it held of my unfettered days with Diego, a dress that rode across the island, had flown up and over mountaintops, was cast down by a sea pool then buttoned back up again by the only man I would ever truly love. It had been a matronly barrier between Herman and I saving me from his hands; its skirts had cradled me as I woke up on the hard stone floor of the ancient and perhaps largest heiau in all of Oceania. It was a dress that had lived more lifetimes between washings than any dress in New Bedford.

I took a deep breath. "I am one. I was once a dressmaker to a Princess."

Her eyes widened and she looked at me from bonnet to hem. "But can you sew something like this?" she asked, reaching for the latest La Mode from Paris and opening it up before my eyes. I assured her I could.

"If you can, I want you exclusively—I will have a great deal of work for you and will pay generously. I can see your condition and you will not want for good care. I can give you an attic room with good light; my house is a very large one, and newly built. It is just north of the harbor, painted white, and has a hedge of yellow hibiscus all along the front porch. Would you come call on me today at two o'clock?"

THAT AFTERNOON I became the esteemed dressmaker of Miss Helen's house of entertainment for men. Her connections ran underground throughout all of Honolulu, so I had the latest news while being well-hidden right under the Mission's nose, in a place they would never look.

I took all the sleep I wanted, and dined on bountiful food late every morning with the young women who lived there. They laughed and gossiped good-naturedly, still in their dressing gowns, and I found myself immediately at ease; I was alone and with child after all, also what formal society would consider a disreputable circumstance. I was not one to pass judgment; if sin meant separation from Divine Love, then my few times with Herman would qualify as such.

Miss Helen urged me to take leisurely breaks, and often. The grand house was quiet and still in the mornings and through my open window came only the sounds of birds and the occasional rumble of wagons bringing deliveries. I strolled in the large, shady private garden that was deserted in the early afternoon sun, and I made flower lei from what I'd collected there.

My expansive working table sat between two large dormer windows that looked out over Honolulu harbor. The room was light and clean; folds of beautiful fabric were stacked neatly next to a glass-door cabinet that held spools of ribbons and lace trim. It was a bright, colorful studio—charming and easy to work in. Aunt Sallie would be so pleased if she could only see it.

Mornings in my attic room were very quiet, and the room was flooded with sunlight. In the late afternoons as the light shifted the sound of music and laughter would come up through the floor as I worked.

In the evenings as night fell over the harbor and little golden lights twinkled from their ships, my worktable was illuminated by two large whale oil lanterns on either side and another hanging from the ceiling above. Surrounded by exquisite textiles and trims I worked happily, feeling like a dressmaker to butterflies and ethereal clouds. At night I dreamt peacefully of island flowers made of colorful silks, birds with feathers of satin and velvet, and pale green moths with muslin wings.

My every other thought was of Diego, our precious baby inside me, and of our life together just waiting to start. My days were both happy and bittersweet with so much longing in my heart.

CHAPTER 3

SPRING ~ to ~ FALL, 1835

Article Thirty-One: A Newborn Baby's Gown

And

Article Thirty-Two: The Last Letter From Mrs. Emmaline Ives

On the more difficult days I would bury my face in an ivory newborn's gown hoping to smell some sweet memory of my babe who had briefly breathed inside it. I still saw her tiny, precious lips and the eyebrows of Diego.

Emmie had arranged for a doctor from the other side of the island to visit during our time of trial, for she was miraculously as far along as I. He promised to keep our labor confidential, and as it was not unusual in confinement and birthing she had her whole wing of the house sealed in privacy from back door to second-story bedroom. The good doctor and his assistant had helped us, and as women whose bodies are in sympathy and proximity strangely do, we both had a baby in our arms before the fateful night was through. I remembered every wondrous inch of her in the soft lantern light as my fingertips and eyes caressed her, memorizing each dimple and all ten fingers and toes. I recalled holding her to my chest as I cried great tears of relief for our safe passage from Death's hand. With longing as strong as the pains that had seized me I wished Diego was there by my side.

But by sunrise I was left holding nothing but the empty gown. Miss Helen said that when she had arrived at the back door before daylight I was clutching it furiously in my delirium. She told me that my baby had lain safely in a little bed next to Emmie's, and the doctor had strictly ordered that the infant stay for a full week in his care to ensure her survival. Helen had told them she would consent to leave her there under only his watch on the condition that she would return to claim my babe after six midnights. Six turned to seven, to eight, to weeks as Miss Helen, a woman of ill-repute, was repeatedly turned away from the mission by a guard of large and imposing young men conscripted by Stuart, his soldiers for the Lord.

"I am not one to be easily thwarted and I can manage most any man," Helen softly argued later, "but your so-called friend has ordered me banned. I expected her, as a religious woman, to keep her promise. As you were in no condition to nurse, it was best, Kittie, to bide my time. If only you had chosen to bear the child here, with our good doctor."

I told Miss Helen then that I would be the one to claim my baby from Emmaline Ives as soon as my strength returned. It was something I had to do myself—I needed to look into Emmie's eyes and somehow find our friendship still there.

At Miss Helen's I was given special care by all the women. The doctor of Miss Helen's house told me I had lost a great deal of blood, that it had been critical—I had almost met my mother's fate. He insisted that if I strained myself too soon my baby could yet be motherless.

Every day I stared longingly from my bed at the tiny ivory gown hung up in the corner of the room on a tightly strung ship's rope. I anxiously counted each day until I would become strong again, when Emmie would surrender my babe back into my arms. And Diego would soon come for us, and I would be back again in his.

May 4th, 1835

Kittie,

The Almighty works in miraculous ways. It was such a blessing that we bore ours on the same night and I could take your babe unto my own as its sister. The news that Stuart is the proud father of twins has been met with much rejoicing by the congregation. The Church's reputation remains unstained, and you must admit that your child is better off here, free to begin her life without shame and hardship.

I saw you knocking down at my door again early this morning. Please do not keep showing up to claim her and risk being seen or I will have no choice but to share your shameful plight with my husband who will then surely banish you and lie in wait for your vaquero's return. I will not surrender this innocent babe to live in a whorehouse. You will be happy to know that I have named her after your aunt, and you may have your little Sallie again if you leave that unspeakable place where you reside and find a respectable husband who can give you a new name and help you permanently disappear from these islands.

May I suggest the Captain Swift who brought us here so long ago? Surely our old Fair Wind *will call on Honolulu again. He was always quite taken with you. A man like that would have no trouble with your unfortunate reputation and could take you away far across the ocean, never to return. If the babe begins to show the features of that vaquero then I will surely give her to you, and, God-willing, as you go through life it will appear that your child is in fact Captain Swift's, borne from a native mother.*

I was told that Revs. Herman, Goodwin and Davis had finally returned from a trek deep in the island's wilderness, half-starved, after being lost in a lava cave for days—they had been searching for you, fearing you had wandered off and been lost, only to discover your body dead by the horns of a wild bullock. Only death can set one free from marriage—and I suppose their account of your death will have to do.

Your little one resembles mine—dainty, long dark eyelashes, and I think her newborn hair will stay dark like hers. I am growing quite fond of her, so you can rest in the fact that she has the best of loving care.

Emmaline

Gradually, other little dresses found their place hanging from the ship's rope, each made with stitches of rage, despair, and disbelief that she had presented my child to the world as her own. Each dress marked each time I had gone to Emmaline's hoping to bring my baby back in it. Every empty dress brought on another desperate mood as I feared she was beginning to love my baby as her own. I could only bear the separation knowing that Diego would soon return, and together nothing could stand in our way.

CHAPTER 4

MID-SEPTEMBER, 1835

Nine months and fifteen days since Diego and I had said farewell I put on a new gown copied from a Parisian fashion plate, so intricate that I required help not just with the corset but with the long rows of mother-of-pearl buttons down the back. It was the palest shade of yellow, edged in places with frothy white bows and ruffles. The shoulders sloped low down into sleeves as round as paper lanterns. The hat was a light straw with butter yellow ribbons. I carefully arranged my hair just so and patted drops of orange blossom essence on my neck.

At three o'clock I stood on the bluff between the cocoa-palms at Le'ahi, or Diamond Hill, my bonnet and skirt ribbons like long mast-head pennants streaming aft as I searched for ships coming 'round towards Honolulu harbor. I adjusted the spyglass, looking for one flying a California flag. What joy burst from my heart when I saw one waving! I waited there all that afternoon until dark, and then all the next day.

Three weeks later, another ship came around with California in its flags, and I smiled with relief. Of course, an ocean voyage could not be timed exactly to the hands of a clock. I was part of the islands now, and the living force was my timekeeper; it was in my breath with an ancient rhythm as perfectly timed as a set of waves, a flower from bud to bloom, the time it took the sun to arc across the sky.

Halfway through November, I began my watch each day with a nervous heart. I had found a rock to sit on and began to memorize its surface until my doubts settled into each crack and hole. Had Manuela and her father enticed Diego to stay? There, an ocean away, had he forgotten his love for me? Or had he met with misfortune?

On December 3rd, the one-year anniversary of our farewell on the decks of the *Prince Regent*, only one East Indiaman sailed in. Surely Diego would return by the end of the year.

I KEPT HAUNTING EMMALINE, waiting in a thick hedge of hibiscus near her window on Sundays when the houses were empty and the new church building was full. Sure enough, one day I finally saw her through the window glass so I knocked persistently on her door.

It finally opened, a fist width. "My boy has a nasty cough, or I would be in church," she explained as she peered down at my nice dress. Somewhere behind her eyes had to be the old Emmie that loved to admire smart gowns. She still wore her hair parted down the middle, but the straight edges that framed her face were threaded with tiny strands of gray. "Kittie, I told you to stay away."

"Diego will surely come for us soon. Explain the disappearance of your 'twin' any way you like, but I demand that you give her back to me now. She is already eight months old." I pushed against the door but she had set the safety latch.

"Catherine," she said, "as a friend I will be blunt with you. You were a novelty to him, a beautiful woman to be conquered—a boast— someone outside of his own society. What kind of missionary were you to not remember Matthew chapter seven verse six: *give not that which is holy unto the dogs?*"

I was speechless, so she went on. "That vaquero has abandoned you. If you and an illegitimate child were to be discovered in Honolulu—thereby rendering our account of your death a lie—your existence will surely cause Herman and my Stuart to hunt you down. There are few places to run and hide on an island."

I slammed my hand on the half-open door, making her flinch.

"Kittie, I want to help you. Find your Captain Swift, and I promise I will surrender the girl to you." With that, she pulled the door shut and slid the bolt.

A baby began crying upstairs as I turned and fled home, holding my throbbing hand against my raging, humiliated heart. She was wrong. It would not be long until Diego returned, maybe even tomorrow, and together we would take our baby back.

CHAPTER 5

Article Thirty-Three: The Book of What Once Lived

At Miss Helen's I had a waiting list for my skills. Competition grew as each young woman sought the next new dress, striving to look better than the rest. All around my room hung from rafters or fitted onto dress forms my new creations gathered like ladies waiting to be asked for a dance. There was a fine pale gray cotton with buttons of black pearls, a canary yellow dotted Swiss with shiny black satin bows, an ivory calico printed with lavender sprigs and trimmed with soft velvet bows the color and texture of lavender blossoms, silk organza corselets of robin's egg blue, and embroidered petticoats. I had to admit that my studio looked as fine and as full as Aunt Sallie's shop right before a new season.

The Girls, as Miss Helen called them, were a mix of Hawai'ian, Celestial, French, Spanish, African, and Caucasian blood, and together they were as becoming as a bouquet of many flowers. They had ready laughs and witty remarks, and despite my worry over Diego's great delay I had a new habit of smiling—a welcome change from my hard days as a missionary wife.

"Kittie, after you measure me, come escape with us to the Flower Palace this afternoon," said a tall ebony-haired girl in an exquisite white French dressing gown who bore an ornate tattoo like scrimshaw upon her ivory chest. "Opium is the same as doctor's laudanum—it's all from the poppy flower, and flowers are a gift from Heaven."

How I longed to fall into opium's embrace and forget the loss of my babe and Diego—but it was for their sake that I wanted to be very much alive, even if it hurt, so I chose pain over a world where nothing hurts because nothing is real and where what is precious fades away, the most painful thing of all.

"Kittie is always saving her money like a wise old owl," said another with a breathtaking face who wore a cream-colored chemise that contrasted starkly with her dark body, rich as teakwood. "But if I had a child, I might do the same."

"I am smart enough to avoid that disaster," countered the ebony-haired girl, "but I save most of my money just the same. When I tire of this life I will have the means to begin again in another country where no-one will know of my past; I will marry a wealthy man who will be won by my skills in the bedroom. Come along, girls, let us cast aside the worry of tomorrow, and enjoy the freedom of today."

They left me to go change into their elaborate costumes. The girls never stepped foot outside without wearing dresses fit for a fashion engraving; not a word needed to be said, but their advertising was quite effective.

ON DAYS when the new issue of The World of Fashion and Continental Feuilletons arrived at Honolulu Merchant & Trade we would all gather around to devour the beautiful colored fashion plates, and I was delighted whenever a ship came in bearing the beautiful fabrics that Miss Helen had ordered.

My artwork weakly distracted me from the time that kept on

passing without Diego's return. I took the sentimentally pressed flowers from my days with Diego and laid them all out on my work-table along with my sketches of birds and land shells. I had purchased a set of watercolors and began working on my illustrations in earnest, dreaming of them being sold someday to be made into chromolithographic plates to be bound in a book.

Over the past year my drawings had taken form as expertly as my new gowns, and often I would bring home more sketches from my walk to Diamond Hill. I finished watercoloring my best pen and inks and in time there were enough to be made into a book. On the manuscript cover I penned:

My Days With The Birds Of The Sandwich Isles
~ Curiosities of Fauna And Flora, 1830 - 1835
by Catherine Helmsley

With great pride I looked at what I had collected together, all those hours of my life, all those living things that were long gone but had once lived and moved in the sunlight and air on an olden day when the birds ruled Moku'ula.

CHAPTER 6

The year of 1836 was my year of the doldrums. By December 3rd, the second anniversary of when we had parted, the thread of hope in me finally ran out leaving my heart like an empty wooden spool. I had faithfully kept up my lonely watch between the cocoa-nut palms until I had no more reasons left to tell myself why Diego hadn't returned. It was a remote spot, where no-one might notice a woman standing alone on a windswept bluff with a bird on her shoulder, always looking out to sea.

I walked home from Diamond Hill one hot afternoon struggling against the heartless wind in my skirts. It pulled me this way and that, and the stronger it blew the faster I walked. Hat ribbons whipped my face as my jaw set tight. *The wind is Spirit,* Pua had once told me. Remembering this, I cried out into the furious tradewinds, breathed in the fearless air, and became it.

I had met the same fate as Aunt Sallie.

I ran up the steep flights of stairs to my room, slammed the door, and tore off the butter-yellow dress faded colorless by the strong Hawai'ian sun. Faded, like old dreams made by a proud, determined newlywed who once wore such fine dresses and ambition. I dropped it into my basket of scraps to be cut up for rags.

My mana blazed bright as fire. I would find a plan, another way, another life with my head held high, another day where I would reign over my circumstances.

I pulled out bolt after bolt of the finest fabric and cast them on my worktable in the sunlight. I tore ribbons from their spools and splashed them across the fabrics, seeing what might belong with what. There was a madwoman in the mirror, swirling in corset and petticoat, strands of hair still flying wild from the wind, designs unfolding invisibly before glazed eyes. For I was looking at my future to see what I could create.

My eyes scanned the room, taking in all the souvenirs of my life. The empty little dresses hung, moving in the air from the open window. Fresh fabric waited to be made into something beautiful. A new dress pattern, a small fire burning companionably in the corner stove. Aloha perched on the back of a chair, tea waiting for me on a tray brought up from downstairs with a leather envelope tucked under the edge of the saucer, hopefully a letter from Aunt Sallie.

The wind sighed around the eaves as I worked and before the sun went down there were muslin pattern pieces pinned to neatly cut fabric pieces striped with silken jade blue, an empty teapot, and my heart still full of a howling wind.

There was nothing but damp tea leaves lying unfolded in the bottom of the teapot when I took up the leather folio that had lain beneath my napkin. It was made like the cover of my miniature hymnbook. An image of it held in Diego's wide palms flashed in my mind like light caught on the edge of a dagger, and I gasped aloud sending Aloha flapping across the room.

I held the folded leather gingerly and then opened it. It contained paper money. Nothing else, save a small note tucked in front, merely a few words hastily penned by Diego's hand: 'To care for you and the baby'.

After two long years since we last parted with kisses and promises, just a letter from him?—that was his only message? Merely money, to provide for the woman and love-child he had cast away?

It was a cruel goodbye. By now he was either dead or, if in the arms of Manuela, he was dead to me.

Incensed, I walked to drop the leather packet into the stove but decided to keep the money, for my child's sake someday. I rushed towards my sea chest and angrily buried it as far down as I could beneath dresses and memories.

My love Diego Cruz
At First Sight: 1832
Died in my heart: The year of 1836

It was time to lay him to rest. For my heart was now a trunk, locked up tight.

And then I let the lid fall with a thunk and shoved the key into the lock.

PART V

CHAPTER 1

OCTOBER 2, 1839

DAWN ~ THE FAIR WIND IS READY TO SAIL

Article Thirty-Four, The Last Thing Remaining At The Bottom Of
The Trunk:
A Letter That Had Wandered Its Way From Ship to Ship to Ship to Me

It lay flat against the bottom of the trunk—thin, brown, rectangular cowhide blending like a chameleon against the cedar floor. I brought it up to my lantern with its whale oil dark and low; the morning stars were rising, the night of exhuming my past nearly over.

The leather was worn and stained, having voyaged like a lost ship for more than a year and a half before it had finally found its way to land on my tea tray that windy day in 1836. Sometimes the mind is just like a wooden chest—one can stuff something in its depths, locked and forgotten, so it will not be remembered, yet deep inside a faraway part of you knows it is still there.

I hesitantly opened the leather folio again, dreading that it would hurt as much as when I had first opened it almost three years ago with a pounding, passionate heart. I might need the money for the voyage. I took it out to count it and sighed. It still made me want to cry.

The last bank note was thicker than the rest. It was the same size, but folded in thirds. My breath stopped. It was not money.

I let the bills flutter down to the floor as I slowly unfolded it, closed my eyes, and then, when I was as ready as I would ever be, opened them to read it.

February 1st, 1835

My Dove Preciado,

I never knew an ocean to be desolate or how empty a starry sky could be. A song about you cannot be completed until you hear it. Nothing will be whole until we are together again.

We stopped to trade in San Diego, and I found Thaddeus's father. He has married a Kumeyaay woman and lives on the beach curing the cowhides that come in from the great ranchos, making them flat and stiff, ready to be stacked tightly into merchant ships. The horses there have only one pace—a dead run—so in the weeks we were there I trained several to surrender to their rider a smooth, collected walk and a steady, gentle trot. Immediately the wealthy and prominent man of San Diego Juan Bandini bought them with the banknotes that you hold in your hand.

Our ship is under sail again, tacking her way back up the coast where now seventy leagues northwest lies—at long last—my old home of Monterey. I received news that my brother recently married Manuela, and so I pray I will arrive in time to claim my father's adobe home.

Santa Barbara's mountainous coast lies to our right and its islands to our left. A ship now struggles to approach us on rough seas, but when she manages to come alongside to trade news I will give them this letter.

How do you find my English? I have spent long days aboard ship studying it—I gained permission to read books from the Captain's library, and I have been conversing with those on ship who have mastered the finer points of the language. Last night I was invited to eat at the officer's table.

I have endeavored to write you a song. Until the day I will serenade you, please consider my wish: the next time you go to bathe in a sea-pool, stare out at the horizon and listen the voice of the sea singing this to you. I will picture this scene to help me through whatever lies ahead.

As I pause to dip my pen, I look up at the sky—dark, menacing storm clouds are gathering but they will not sink a ship that carries such a buoyant heart as mine.

I've been building a dream
Ere we last parted
Out here upon an ocean of wishes, uncharted
O! How I have cried tears of anguish
At the way we departed

And my ship rolls onward, onward now
towards a distant shore
Onward ho! Close to the wind
I sail to you, amor
And in my chest lies fathoms down a heart the deepest blue
'Till I'm close
'Till I'm there
'Till I'm home to you

Every league and rolling swell, every breath of wind
Your distant shore makes me not pine
For my heart is pinned
An old adobe waits, my dear
And there within the clay
Lies golden treasure waiting

Hidden from the light of day

And now that love has found this man
His heart shines like a gold doubloon
And I will build another house
With love in every room
No longer just vaquero
Are the words I pray
But a worthy man of consequence
For love has found a way

And my ship rolls onward, onward now
towards a distant shore
Onward ho! Close to the wind
I sail to you, amor
And in my chest lies fathoms down a heart the deepest blue
'Till I'm close
'Till I'm there
'Till I'm home to you

Catherine, please do not forget me. If this letter should ever be held by your hands that feel loneliness instead of hope, know that only God has the power to separate us. While we are apart, keep your heart from turning on days of doubt and pain. Fight to keep it open. Never doubt our love, for as long I am alive I will love you and no other, heartbeat by heartbeat.

These banknotes will care for you until I return. Until I step once again upon that fair isle with gold in my pockets and a bright shining heart,

My heart is pinned to yours, my love.

Diego Alejandro Fernando Vicente Cruz

I pressed the letter to my heart and looked up. A single white muslin dress hung from a low rafter. My sorted and folded belongings sat on the bed, wrapped neatly in oilcloth, ready to be put back into my trunk for the voyage. Aloha had her head tucked under her wing, her down blanket of feathers puffed about her. Sailors sounded below —knocks and boots and voices echoing up the flights of stairs. And then I heard Miss Helen's voice just outside my door.

"The *Fair Wind* is at the ready and her men are here to fetch you, Kittie. May I help you? Kittie, are you awake?"

I held Diego's letter up once more to the sputtering light of the lamp, unable to answer her.

"Kittie? Are you well?" The door latch released and her candlestick brought light in with her just as my lamp coughed its last breath.

"I didn't sleep last night," I said, carefully folding the letter and putting it inside my pocket next to my little hymnal.

"That is no surprise on a night before a sailing, and a wedding voyage at that," she said. "Why, you haven't finished closing up your trunk. Let me help you."

Soon my trunk was in order, dome closed and locked, and taken away down to the ship.

Helen latched the door and turned to me. "Now for your dress. What a perfect choice for today—such pretty layers of white Swiss muslin, and what a long row of glass buttons all down the back."

I squeezed my waist with both hands as Miss Helen pulled my corset laces tight. Through the wavy window panes, little lights were floating and glowing like fireflies from the ships making ready to cast away at dawn.

"I have found out more news of your old husband's arrival yesterday," came her voice behind me. "He is here to curry favor with the King, who finds those who know the intricacies of both Hawai'ian and English language very useful. Men who can advise on customs, the missionary mind, translation, printing, and map engravings."

Miss Helen, by virtue of her social connections that spread underground like the roots of a banana tree had more detailed information —and much sooner—than any newspaper. "When your old husband's indiscretions with native women were found out by the missionaries, he was forced to give up his title of Reverend," she said.

"That must have nearly extinguished Herman," I said breathlessly as Helen pulled the corset even tighter. "You know, he had always felt possessive of these islands, not unlike a child who holds a toy tightly and tells the others that he had it first."

"Every man stakes his territory, whether a small home bound by a white picket fence, or an entire kingdom," Helen said as she started up the long row of glass buttons. "If he could not have Hawai'i by being at God's right hand, I would not be surprised to see him trying to lay claim to it standing at the side of a King."

"Like a missionary, a high-ranking official does not benefit from scandal," I said. "He would still wish to remove any traces of me—a stray wife with a baby that is not his. It would make it difficult for him to remarry into the land, the title, the power that is the dowry of a native woman with royal blood."

"It is providential that you and your child will sail safely away today," she agreed. "Captain Swift will give you a good life; he is a Christian man, and wealthy. Emmaline will surely meet you at the dock with your daughter?"

"She promised."

"It is early yet, but you are rather somber for a bride."

"I overheard two old sailors telling yarns at the opium house yesterday about a shipwrecked man found off the California coast. His ship had come from Honolulu, bound for Monterey. A vaquero."

She paused between buttons. "Kittie dear—a man who deserts you is a man unworthy of a second thought. Those stories are like pearls, begun from perhaps the tiniest sandy grain of truth; and that is all it takes for us to begin to believe again in something that we wish for."

"But what if he was injured terribly? What if he has been delayed or killed by his treacherous brother? What if he overcomes great odds only to return and find me gone? I will never know the answer, and I fear it will plague me for the rest of my life."

"If you do find him, you may find only heartbreak—a man does not stay away from the comfort of a woman for long," Helen said, finally reaching the buttons at my neck. "Swift is a good-looking man. Your melancholy lifted ever since he came back to Honolulu last summer when you finally put to rest your hope for that vaquero. You told me that your Aunt embroidered the thought of her lost suitor until none other could compare, did she not?"

There were no more words spoken until Miss Helen finished the last button. I turned around to look at her, surprised to find a face I'd never seen. Gone was the lighthearted amusement; her lips were lifeless, her eyes bare and direct.

"You are fortunate to be offered so much," she said heavily. "There are many women who dream of such a second chance. You have a new life in the offing—seize it now! Before Herman extinguishes it, before your babe is any older and would refuse to leave her 'mother'!"

Her choice of words splashed away the daydreams of the night. I was dressed, and a sailor impatiently called up from the bottom of the stairs, waiting to escort me down to the *Fair Wind*.

"Come along, Aloha," I said, and her head popped out from under her wing. She fluffed her feathers, left her perch on the high back chair and fluttered to me. "I am ready, dear Helen—thank you for all your kindness—I will never forget you."

CHAPTER 2

I found my pine trunk still waiting on the dock to be loaded. I paced beside it, scanning the shadowy forms carrying lanterns that moved along the wharf. As time passed, questions boiled up from my screaming heart—*Emmaline, you gave me your word! Did you not get my message? Are you on your way?*

Sounds crescendoed all around me as the night began to slip away. Barrels rolled, men shouted, and up in the ropes, masts, and yardarms hung sailors singing the song they sing when making ready with the sails. Then I spied him up in the light from his ship's lanterns: Captain Jonathan Swift, there on the quarterdeck barking orders to his First Mate, wearing the well-dressed conquerors' air of a man on his wedding day. There was still something about his commanding presence that had attracted me from the first day we set out of New Bedford and I had been too much of a dedicated newlywed to admit it. Did what had once flirted in the heart of Mrs. Herman Webster still live? The Sandwich Isles had changed her. I was no longer that girl-woman who lived in that olden day.

He took off his hat and ran his thick fingers through his hair. His weathered profile was cut harsher, his jaw wider from clenching his teeth. He briefly glanced at me and then turned away. I had hoped for more—it was our wedding day, after all. *He is occupied, in charge of a ship about to set out*, I reminded myself. But I was captain of my heart, one about to commit to a voyage that would last for the rest of my days.

I wished for a sign that this ship, this marriage, was well and fit, ready to be trusted to cross the great oceans of life. An uneasy feeling crept into the edges of my imagination, the kind a seafarer might push away from his thoughts before an ill-fated sailing. What had the men on the doomed ships *Essex* and the *Two Brothers* felt in the bottom of their hearts the day they first unleashed their sails to the wind?

"Ready to hoist yer trunk if you please, Mrs. Swift," a sailor said with polite deference, because I was soon to belong to a Captain.

Emmaline was still nowhere to be seen. "No," I said, standing between him and my pine domed chest as Aloha pecked in his direction. "My trunk and I are not yet ready to board. Tell the Captain to wait."

He raised his eyebrows, wincing in anticipation of the firestorm the Captain would unleash if the launch of the *Fair Wind* was delayed. I looked back up again to the upper deck to study the man that would soon slip a ring on my finger. He might captain a marriage safely through the years, but was not one to rush down and carry me across the gang-board in his arms—yet his *Fair Wind* would carry me to New Bedford where my child and I would have a comfortable life with a heavy purse and a grand home, nestled in the society of family and friends. A fine future was in the forecast. It made sense. Would that fade forevermore the burning question of whatever became of a man named Diego and the love that we once shared?

"I'll grant ye a few minutes more 'fore I do," the seaman said as he left the trunk with me there on the dock amid the bustle of the ships making ready to set out.

I stood on tip-toe, scanning the wharf wildly for Emmaline. On the off side of the *Fair Wind* floated an East Indiaman, heading out for Canton like us. To the near side, raising a Hudson Bay Company flag, was a British bark heavy with salt, bound the opposite direction for the Pacific Northwest. It would trade the Hawai'ian salt for furs and salmon, then make its way down the Alta California coast to round the Horn east for the Atlantic, Nantucket, possibly New Bedford.

In the dim light I feared it would be difficult for Emmaline to recognize me, and I her. Then at last came a dark figure, with no lantern, hurrying along the wharf. I leaned against my trunk, palms resting on the arched lid, my thoughts repeating like a chant: *God, let it be Emmaline. Please let that be her.*

The shadowy figure carried a large bundle beneath a dark cloak and I let out a great sigh of relief when Emmaline drew before me.

"Our old *Fair Wind*," Emmaline said, gazing up and nodding in approval through thin lips set in a face ghostly with determination. "Very well." She paused as her eyes fell on me. "Kittie, you have changed so."

"We both have."

Emmaline set her bundle down and stepped back. Out from a curtain of cloak my tiny girl appeared on wobbly little legs, and then she fell on her well-padded bottom. I knelt down to embrace her, but to my horror her little blue bonnet turned away as she reached for Emmaline, calling out a word strong enough to stab through my corset—"Mother!"

"Hush child!" Emmaline commanded her, as with a mother's instinct she flew down to pick her up. "You know children must be seen and not heard."

Our faces were suddenly close. "Take her now, and go," Emmaline whispered. For a thin moment I saw it—a crumb of leftover friendship. She had risked much to meet me here, especially with the child. Sallie stretched her little arms up to her.

"Kittie, her dark features are lately growing more prominent by the day," she went on, our nearness allowing us to talk freely. "We cannot have evidence of your adultery, and you know I cannot have people think it was I who sinned with another man. Surely you understand—I was forced to explain it all to Stuart, and I am afraid that he confided this to his old friend Herman."

"I saw Herman on the street yesterday," I told her. "He seeks to kill her; and is why on this dawn we must fly with the *Fair Wind*. And

Emmie, Abigail is still here! I found her at the Flower Palace. Our friend needs help, for she has completely succumbed to sorrow and tragedy."

"Sister Abigail was always weak and homesick, never truly committed to our cause," she sighed sadly.

"But you'll help save her, won't you? Take her in, wean her from her cruel master, reunite her with Henry and her boys."

"I cannot be seen stepping foot in that den of opium," she said doubtfully. "I will pray about it." She picked up Sallie and we rose to our feet.

In the next moment as the dawn shifted a shade lighter my little child looked up at me, and as the brim of her bonnet tilted back I gasped—it was clearly Diego's face and his dark eyebrows and honey-colored skin, coupled with my blue eyes and fair hair, looking nothing like Emmie and Stuart with their inky dark hair and paper-pale complexions.

Stunned at the sight of her, I felt the lock on my trunk blowing apart, every memory set free once again. The way he'd drawn close to me beside a horse's mane and smiled. How my little hymnal gained a fine new leather cover and began to sing another story—the song of us. The stained-glass waterfall. A paper lantern moon. The magical song of the land shells. The night we rode away in the moonlight. How he had stayed on Maui to risk his life for mine.

"I will treasure the memory of the Kittie I once knew," Emmaline was saying.

"Yes, I have changed, Emmie, you have changed, the islands have changed. I will go back to New Bedford and it will have changed. My aunt Sallie will have gray hair, my brothers will have all married, my father taken a new wife."

Shaking her head, Emmaline set Sallie down on her unsteady legs, and drew her long black skirt away as she stepped back. "Goodbye Catherine. May God bless your heart."

"Thank you Emmie, I will miss you—" I said as she darted quickly away before anyone could recognize her, back to the life that she had built. She never turned around to wave.

Sallie looked so small and lost as she watched Emmie walk away. She hugged a doll against her heart, leaned back, stared doubtfully at me, and pulled her tiny hand away as I reached for it. Slowly, she turned the doll's face towards me, as if its cotton heart held the decision whether she should shriek for Emmaline.

If I did not proceed gently she might cry out. I smiled, opening my arms to her for a forever moment as a wave swished beneath the dock and the dawn's light brought another shade of color to a gray world. I stared at her eyebrows that were wrinkling the way Diego's had when a storm was brewing inside of him. I fell in love with her proud chin, her strong Spanish nose. I desperately wished to see her smile.

Another wave passed beneath us, softly crashing on the pilings below as she leaned close to her doll's china face and whispered to it while I said her name with all the tenderness long buried inside me.

And then came Aloha's voice from my shoulder in a soft tone that I had never heard from her before. "Ah me sweet sugarplum. Me poppet." I looked at the bird in surprise.

Sallie's little upturned face became a beam of light as she beheld Aloha, transfixed, forgetting all else. Slowly she tore her gaze from Aloha to look at me. She studied my steadfast smile and then reached her little arms up for my neck as I tearfully lifted her and held her tight.

With a puff of feathers and the shake of wings as if to throw off the past, Aloha's feathery throat gave us orders—"Aboard, scallywags!"

Far up on the *Fair Wind* Captain Swift paced across the very deck where I was soon to be joined with him as tightly as a sailor's knot. He hurled commands and then halted at the ship's bow, arms crossed, surveying the sails from top to bottom, measuring the wind and the sea and the sky. He then spun around, noticed me, and impatiently shouted to a sailor that I should be brought aboard as if I were one last barrel to be loaded.

My eyes let him go. The breath of the wind was rising, and soon the ships would be off in all directions to faraway lands. The *Fair Wind* was ready to set west to Celestial whaling grounds, then for Canton to trade opium for tea, and then around the tip of Africa to the Atlantic.

There was her chase boat, all oars straining, cutting through the water in my direction.

The ruffles of my white muslin fluttered in the blue light like a handkerchief waving for attention. Away from the whirling scene around me and down beneath the layers of my bodice a voice pressed quietly but urgently. Before I came to the islands I had never known that it even existed. It was not the voice of others that always said that thoughts from within were sinful and foolish. It was my na'au.

I had come to convert, but Hawai'i had somehow converted me. How far we came, around the Horn, yet farther still was the journey I made from the girl who knew the way things were supposed to be. And someday when I set my foot back on that faraway coast of America it would be the first step of a stranger in a strange, new, uncharted land.

The voice was as quiet as air and as certain as a mountain. I smelled the kelp and salt air, fresh from moving in over the expanse of the open sea. I saw a seabird flying above the floating thicket of masts, past sails whispering to one another the promise of freedom as their canvas unfurled. The bird dove down towards the *Fair Wind* but landed instead on the crow's nest of the Hudson Bay ship that was also untying ropes, readying to set off to the east back across the Pacific to the northern coast of California, down to the ports of Monterey and San Diego to Chile, then southeast around the Horn.

One ship bound west, another east. One voyage charted as a captain's wife, the other but a thin thread that might lead to Diego. A life of wealth and security waited to the west—a large home with a rose garden, a respectable life. The Hudson Bay ship required me to cast everything away save my pine domed trunk and my child.

West, with Captain Swift. Eastward, and perhaps, just perhaps, Diego Alejandro Fernando Vicente Cruz—a foolish, rash, risky, journey that might just break my heart.

I took a step forward towards the *Fair Wind*. It guaranteed the most direct journey back to Aunt Sallie. She would be waiting at the wharf, her tired eyes strained from years of tiny stitches, peering out to sea at the ships sailing in. Her arms aching to finally embrace me again, to know that a piece of her heart had finally come back to her. How Aunt Sallie's face would beam at the sight of us.

With another step the tiny hymnal and Diego's letter bumped my knees, hanging heavy in the pockets of the beautiful white muslin dress she had so lovingly sewn. It had been born in Aunt Sallie's heart and traveled for months, over oceans to me. It had debuted in golden light sweeping along the *Fair Wind*'s decks one long-ago Maui evening, vainly searching the cobalt shadows for happiness. It had been buried in my old pine sea trunk and then resurrected. It had known days heavy with hurt and times gossamer with hope, but its journey was not yet over. Its destiny was to be worn in the name of love.

I had always known what Aunt Sallie had wanted for herself, but suddenly, surely, I knew what she would want for me. It was what I wanted for me.

The *Fair Wind*'s chase boat was drawing near. I looked across the busy dock to flag a mid-shipman's eye and I waved him quickly over.

"Please load my trunk—we would like to board."

I shifted my child from one hip to the other. She was heavy. So many times I had imagined holding her as a tiny babe in my arms! I was taking her back—and my life—without a moment to spare. She cooed like a dove as her little fingers reached for blue and green satin feathers. Aloha softly clucked like a little hen as I kissed Sallie's forehead, so much like Diego's.

My course was set, the hourglass empty, the time was right. "Don't be afraid, my darling girl," I said. "I am your mother. And we are off to a great adventure."

CHAPTER 3

ABOARD AND AWAY

The deck slanted steeply as the ship went speeding down each wave into liquid valleys and up again until we were perched atop the next blue shoulder of the deep. From its crest I could see a crinkled horizon, the endless mountaintops of the Pacific. Wind-shadows painted in indigo blue moved across the surface like a painter's brush.

I found the First Mate who tipped his hat to me and smiled. "I hope you are finding the stateroom to your liking," he said.

"Kindly tell me the course the Captain has consulted with his sextant and maps," I asked.

He listed distant ports that had once sounded so impossibly far away to a woman once stranded on an island of broken dreams.

"First we'll go to Lahaina Roads for more provisions by 'morrow next, and then we'll set for the open sea."

.   .   .

THE NEXT MORNING I made sure I was at the rail to catch a last look at the island that I had so desperately fled. As I held Sallie's little hand and gazed at the place where so much had happened, I discovered with surprise a sadness inside to bid it farewell.

We approached from the south at dawn as the coastline of Maui awoke before my eyes. The ship was headed straight for the great cleft in the extinct volcano shielding the sacred Kaua'ula Valley that gave its fresh water to the canals, the fishponds, and the sea. The deep green mountains huddled close to the shore wearing a thick veil of mist hiding the purple forest canyons where the Bird-catchers dwelt. The Hawai'ian flag with its British Union Jack and a stripe for each island wafted in the morning air above a new, white two-story summer palace.

Up the coast I could see the mission, and rising upslope from the shadows of dark green vegetation emerged Betsey Stockton's school, now the Lahainaluna boy's school, and the printing house.

Somewhere beneath the smoky lavender thatched roofs a young woman named Pua was rising. I saw the hospital cottage with a thin cloud of smoke rising from its chimney—Charity Thatcher would start a fire to cook breakfast for her husband who had stayed up all night saving a life. A rooster crowed; Mary Goodwin's hens were pecking in a bowl made of broken teacups.

The mainsails luffed as we slowed our approach just off the shallows. Across the calm gray water of Mokuhinia stood the sharp white steeple of Waine'e Church on its eastern shore. Tabitha was there in the church cottage, perhaps nursing a baby, while her husband Reverend Davis climbed the bell tower stairs, checking his pocket watch, waiting to ring the morning bell.

Still in blue shadows, Moku'ula lay quietly, embraced by her sacred lake, Mokuhinia. The young king had deserted it for Honolulu and it had the air of forgottenness. I spied the canoe landing where Leilani had told me the story of Hina that one moonlit night, and suddenly realized that the Kingdom at Moku'ula was an age that was passing away.

The first whispers of golden sunlight broke through the peaks of the emerald mountains and touched my necklace, making the amber rays glow as if it truly were a little sun. I pulled it harder to see it more clearly. Suddenly, the delicate chain broke, and the pendant leapt from my fingers and fell down over the side of the ship. I gasped as it sunk sparkling down onto upstretched fingers of rosy coral.

Perhaps it belonged here now, its spirit to always linger in mine, connecting us. For the rest of my life I could think of the jeweled sun glinting in the azure waters off Moku'ula as the brightly colored fish nibbled the coral that wore it. I exhaled and then breathed in the island as if to take it with me, and the little sun sung its song for both of us:

You shine with the might of one thousand suns
You cannot be broken or lost
You shine with the might of one thousand suns

The row boats that had come up alongside were beginning to push off. It was time to sail into the unknown with my spirit's voice my only compass.

It would be a fair day, with the fortune of steady wind. The captain barked to the first mate, the first mate shouted to the crew, and all the men called back in chorus as they hoisted lines from the main to the stun'sls trimming them to catch the early breeze that reached down the channel to beckon us out. I looked back once more to see light shining across the ponds of Moku'ula in the newness of day. I squeezed Sallie's hand, and she squeezed back.

Then the first mate shouted across the pale silken water. "All sails —Ho! We're underway! God be with our good ship, preserve us, make her sails taut and free—the *Majestic*, bound for Monterey!"

We passed through the turquoise shallows towards the deep blue where the sails caught the edge of the morning trades, and the ship leaned hard away.

THE END

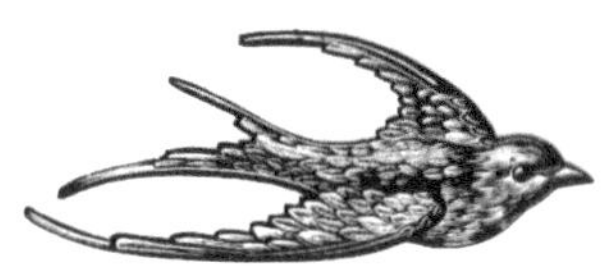

The crickets have gone to sleep. Her cup of tea is empty but for a stained circle at the bottom. A scotch glass forgotten on a wicker tabletop holds a finger of lukewarm water.

A dog stretches. She does too. She stands up and leans down to gently embrace the storyteller, and her hair catches the lantern light as it slides down from her back all around her like a sunlit cloak.

Her father returns from the barn. The horses are safely sleeping; all is well. He walks almost easily now, but one boot still patiently waits for the other as he steps up onto the porch.

He kisses his daughter's wide, smooth forehead above her heavy dark brows. "It's good to have you visit," he tells her longingly, because along with her return always came an inevitable goodbye. But tonight she leaves them only for her old girlhood bedroom, her shadow a dog behind her padding and clicking its toenails away across the dark wood floor. With one hand he takes up the lantern, and then he tenderly slips the other around the storyteller's waist.

"My dove," he whispers into her silver-gold hair before he breathes in her scent, and together they walk inside.

ACKNOWLEDGMENTS

Aloha and respect to Mary Kawena Pukui's research, which helped me do my best to bring alive again the forest, the land shells, the chants, and so much more.

I was so fortunate to have Wainani Kealoha, a guide of historic Lahaina, give me a private walking tour the summer of 2018. She led me over a baseball field and through an empty lot full of the powerful feeling of what lay beneath it. We were standing above the sacred island of Moku'ula and its lake Mokuhinia. She took me through the Courthouse museum, then walked me over to Pioneer Inn to show me an antique oil painting of the Lahaina coastline seen from a ship's deck. She walked me by the water's edge in front of the Library where the sacred Hauola birthing stone emerged and pointed out that it is part of a chain of stones resembling a *mo'o*, a shapeshifting lizard spirit of the goddess Kihawahine, guardian of the lake. Devastatingly, so much is gone now, but all that is ancient still remains. Thank you, Wainani.

Mahalo nui, John R. K. Clark, for reading with special attention towards accuracy of surfing, I am honored to have your help and the book is better for it. Thank you April Eberhardt, for all your time reading early manuscripts, and for your encouragement. I am so thrilled to have Laurie and the Ramona "Ladies of The Book" club elect to read. Mahalo, Lark Grey Dimond-Cates, I am deeply grateful for your read and comments.

Thank you Colleen Kelley Heyer for sharing information about Hawai'ian monk seals and pointing me towards an old 1959 paper by a professor who recorded that there was once a heiau on the Big

Island dedicated to surfing with a bell stone to summon the waves. Thank you, costume and textile historian Colleen Callahan, for your time and advice. I am grateful for The Costume Institute at The Metropolitan Museum of Art, Michael P. Dyer Maritime Curator New Bedford Whaling Museum, Nantucket Historical Association, Katrina Lake, Julia Porter Steele, and Anne Clermont, all part of helping my manuscript become what lives now on these pages.

Thank you to my parents whose unwavering support and Maui condo made this book possible. Laura Nisbet Peters, Maryl Bodeen, Miss Wiggles, Lilybelle, and especially Mike Waggoner, you have been with me every step of the way and you have my deepest aloha.